Praise from ... ☑ **W9-ARV-923**
Duffy Dombrowski Mystery series

ON THE ROPES

"Not since Carl Hiassen's *Tourist Season* debut has there been a novel with such superb comic timing and laugh-out-loud lines."

—Ken Bruen,
Shamus Award–winning author of *The Guards*

"An Everyman with a big heart and a wicked jab, Duffy Dombrowski may well be the new Spenser. I can't wait for Round Two."

—Marcus Sakey, author of *The Blade Itself*,
a *New York Times* Editor's Pick

"Buy this book and read it. You will be glad you did."
—David L. Hudson Jr., Fightnews.com

"Duffy's resilience and twisted sense of humor kept me coming back. His sense of irony is one of his better qualities."
—ReviewingTheEvidence.com

"Schreck is a major new talent. Loaded with suspense, charm, and heart, *On the Ropes* is one of the best debuts of this, or any, year."

—J. A. Konrath,
author of *Rusty Nail* and *Dirty Martini*

"Underdogs, colorful characters, a fighter who never quits, and a canine with more bite and heart than Jake LaMotta. A unanimous winner."

—Teddy Atlas, ESPN boxing analyst

"One hell of a debut novel."

—Jon Jordan, *Crimespree Magazine*

"*On the Ropes* is sly, funny, irreverent, and one hell of a good time. Read it or be sorry you didn't. It's just that simple."

—Laurien Berenson,
author of *Hounded to Death*

"If you've ever despised your boss or secretly wanted to save the world, *On the Ropes* is a novel you'll devour."

—Steve Farhood, Showtime Boxing

"Duffy Dombrowski—a loose-cannon social worker and a boxer—has a lot more heart than is healthy for a guy. Give him an orphaned sidekick who hasn't been housebroken (literally), jam them into the middle of a sinister murder plot, and you've got a winning combination."

—Lee Charles Kelley,
author of *Like a Dog With a Bone*

"One of my favorite writers ... Can't wait for Duffy's next adventure."

—Nancy Claus, *Westchester Magazine*

"Pure delight. The sharp-edged humor peppers you like a boxing master's jab, and the poignant undercurrent of theme delivers with the power of a left hook. Duffy Dombrowski is a major new contender in the world of private-eye fiction."

—Michael A. Black,
author of *A Killing Frost* and *A Final Judgment*

"Get ready to rumble with lovable losers, misguided misfits, and a disgustingly adorable dog."

—Michael "Let's Get Ready to Rumble" Buffer,
the Voice of Champions

"There's nothing technical about the terrific knockout that Tom Schreck delivers to readers in his latest novel, *TKO*. Tom Schreck is a contender for funniest author working in the crime genre today."

—William Kent Krueger,
Anthony Award–nominated author of *Copper River*

"*TKO* is fast-paced, authentic, and funny as hell. Tom Schreck delivers the grit and spit, blood and bruises of the fight game with rollicking good humor and real compassion for the underdogs among us. Social worker and journeyman boxer Duffy Dombrowski is a workingman's hero, and I want him in my corner!"

—Sean Chercover,
author of *Trigger City* and *Big City, Bad Blood*

ALSO BY TOM SCHRECK

On the Ropes: Round 1

FORTHCOMING BY TOM SCHRECK

Out Cold: Round 3

A DUFFY DOMBROWSKI MYSTERY

TKO

TOM
SCHRECK

ROUND 2 TWO

MIDNIGHT INK
WOODBURY, MINNESOTA
MIDNIGHT INK

FIRST EDITION
First Printing, 2008

Book design by Donna Burch
Cover design by Gavin Dayton Duffy
Cover dog image © Henryk T. Kaiser/The Stock Collection/Punchstock

Midnight Ink, an imprint of Llewellyn Publications

Library of Congress Cataloging-in-Publication Data
Schreck, Tom, 1961–
  TKO : a Duffy Dombrowski mystery / Tom Schreck.—1st ed.
    p. cm.
  ISBN 978-0-7387-1121-8
  1. Social workers—Fiction. 2. Boxers (Sports)—Fiction. I. Title.
PS3619.C462T56 2008
813'.6—dc22
                                                          2008004096

Midnight Ink
Llewellyn Publications
2143 Wooddale Drive, Dept. 978-0-7387-1121-8
Woodbury, MN 55125-2989, U.S.A.
www.midnightinkbooks.com

Printed in the United States of America

For the two Mrs. Schrecks,
Sue and Annette ... the loves of my life.

You can't beat me. I'm God!
MUHAMMAD ALI

Well, God's getting knocked on his ass tonight, then.
JOE FRAZIER

1

—

"Just because a guy slits the throats of two high-school cheerleaders, axes the back of the quarterback's head, and runs down the class president in his mom's LTD, doesn't make him a bad guy," I said.

"Duff—"

I didn't let Monique finish.

"Howard's father split before he was born, his mom was abusively schizo—shit, she used to strip him naked and make fun of his Johnson when he was in high school—and every day the football players would give him a wedgie."

"So every kid who gets a hard time in high school should be excused for homicide?" Monique said.

"No—that's not what I'm saying." I realized I had been raising my voice. "All I'm saying is given what was going on in his head, it's no wonder he flipped out. In a way, they all had it coming."

Monique gave me a look and then went back to her desk.

A long time ago, back in high school, Howard Rheinhart went away to Green Haven for murdering four of his classmates. He was bullied and abused right from first grade, and one day while he was receiving his daily wedgie from the McDonough High's all-city quarterback, Mark Woroby, two of the cheerleaders went into an impromptu cheer. That night, after the hoop game with Eagle Heights, Howard held his own homecoming. It meant releasing years of pent-up anger, and boy, did Howard ever make up for lost time.

Carl the janitor found the two cheerleaders, Danielle Thomson and Terri Snow, in their uniforms, sitting in the bleachers, still in their uniforms. "Go Team" was scripted in dried blood on the gym floor in front of the somewhat pale pep squad. Carl's been on medication ever since.

The cheerleaders had taken the time to make Howard's daily humiliation that much more dehumanizing. They literally cheered his abuse and they made it clear he didn't matter. When Howard slit their throats, he proved that he did, in fact, matter quite a bit.

Woroby, the QB, was found decapitated Monday afternoon in a field outside of town. His body was propped up against a tree, his right arm cocked back like he was throwing long, except his head was where the ball would usually be. There was no questioning the fact that Howard had a flair for sarcasm, but you didn't have to be a Freudian analyst to see what kind of statement he was making. For the first time in his life, well, technically the second, Howard was turning the tables and letting everyone know that the joke wasn't on him. Unfortunately, a lot of people didn't appreciate his sense of humor.

Class president and all-around high-school stud Jack Powers wasn't guilty of wedgersizing Howard on a daily basis. He did mockingly nominate him for "most likely to succeed" and was leading a campaign to have Howard win as a joke until the student advisor,

Mrs. Kyle, put a stop to it. Howard flattened Powers, gunning the eight-cylinder LTD from two blocks away and never slowing down.

It was Howard's way of saying that he would not be mocked, that he was an individual too, and that he demanded to be treated like one. He went from total victim position to total dominance in a matter of days. Sure, he went overboard; sure, he might have been better off with a little assertiveness training; and sure, one might say that his actions were a bit out of proportion. But did anyone stop to think what that guy must of felt like day after day, getting abused at home and at school and just about everywhere he turned?

They arrested Howard in Canastota at a Thruway rest stop, listening to Frampton sing "Do You Feel Like We Do." It's a pretty fair bet that no one did quite feel like Howard Rheinhart back in high school. It was probably a pretty good bet that now that he had been released from prison, no one quite felt like him today either. He did his pretty lenient thirty-year sentence and was let out on time served. Here he was, back in Crawford, living in a parole halfway house and assigned to my caseload at Jewish Unified Services. The geniuses at the parole board discharged Howard with the provision that he get intense psychiatric care. He had his youthful offender status at the time of the murders to thank for his relatively quick release.

The problem was, Howard had no income, no savings, and no friends. That meant he was on Medicaid and that his intensive psychiatric care would involve seeing me three times a week and Dr. Jeriah Abadon, our consulting psychiatrist, once a week. I am a human services counselor with very little education and a few years experience. I'm used to handling alcoholics and addicts, teenagers who get in trouble, and guys whose jobs mandate that they get counseling or else face unemployment. I'm not renowned for my skills with deeply psychiatric multiple killers.

Howard had only been coming to see me for about a week and a half. He was never late, said very little, and acted as skittish as anyone I ever saw. I guess thirty years in prison preceded by seventeen years of wedgie-filled torment will do that to a guy. All I wanted to see the man do was learn to trust people a little bit and not go through life fearing that around the corner someone was always waiting to hoist him up by the elastic in his skivvies. Last Friday, on his fourth visit, Howard said something to me that I'll never forget. I had asked him what he wanted out of life, and he hesitated for a long time.

"I want to feel someday that the world isn't out to get me," he said and then began to cry. He cried into his hands as intensely as I've ever seen anyone cry, and then he abruptly stopped and looked up at me. His eyes were red and his cheeks were stained, but he got himself completely under control almost instantly. A long stretch in prison will teach you how to hide how you feel. I can't imagine the firestorm that brews inside of someone who can shut off emotion like that so quickly.

To me, Howard was a guy who had known a lifetime of pain and had no skills to deal with it. His mom abused him and the kids at school abused him. The killing spree was his way of standing up for himself. For me, it was a misguided, albeit extremely misguided, attempt to stand up for himself. It sounds twisted, but I respected the fact that he stood up for himself because, to me, that's what makes a man a man. Standing up for yourself can mean saying you won't allow yourself to be talked to in a certain way, it can mean defending yourself physically, or it can mean a certain inner peace that tells you that your own self-respect is worth protecting. In Howard's case, it meant some extreme acting-out, but that had more to do with how screwed-up his life had been than any innate evil that lived within him. At least that's how I saw it. He'd been to see Abadon twice, and the doctor's assessment was far less sympathetic than mine. He classified Rheinhart as "a low-functioning, antisocial, and pathologically insecure individual." It wasn't a diagnosis with a lot of hope attached to it.

It was Monday and Howard was supposed to be in at ten. It was now ten fifteen and there was no sign of him. As usual, I was way behind in my paperwork, and a good use of my time would have been to take the opportunity to get going on it. But alas, a man has to eat, and I happened to know that at ten thirty the in-service on "Art Therapy with the Vietnam Vet" was scheduled. That meant that there had to be donuts.

I pilfered one powdered and one plain just as the social workers were filing in and picking up their finger paints. I grabbed a cup of the brownish liquid that passed for the clinic's coffee and slid away from the oblivious social workers filing in. It isn't difficult to get past social workers because as a group they are usually consumed with their own issues to the point that leaving the house in the morning already sets the bar pretty high for them. The clinic's coffee tended to affect my digestive system like some sort of New Age cleansing high colonic, but I drank it anyway.

So far I'd been lucky enough to duck my boss. Claudia Michelin, a certified social worker who lived for rules and regulations, hated most folks and probably got into social work because it gave her power over weak people. The supermodel world had closed down for Claudia a while ago, as she had more chins than the Hong Kong phone book and sported a black curly perm just like Starsky used to have … or was it Hutch? Anyway, the Michelin Woman has been trying to fire me for years and came pretty close to being successful about a year ago.

I was busy dunking the second donut into the coffee and cursing at the amount of white powder that had gotten all over my shirt when the phone rang. It was my cop friend, Mike Kelley.

"Good morning, officer. Keeping the streets safe for us grateful citizens?" I said.

"Uh, Duff, you are the counselor who sees Hackin' Howard, aren't you?"

"We like to stay away from nicknames, but yes, I am."

"You see him today?"

"You know I'm not supposed to divulge confidential information like that."

"Uh-huh," Kelley said.

"I certainly wouldn't disclose to one of you heartless police officials that a client didn't keep his ten a.m. appointment."

"Hey, Duff?" Kelley sounded serious, which he always did, but a little more serious than usual.

"Yeah?"

"A girl from McDonough High was found this morning with her throat slit. Her name was Connie Carter."

"Holy shi—," I said.

"And Duff …" Kelley hesitated. "She was the captain of the cheerleaders."

2

I AGREED TO MEET Kelley after work at our usual hangout, AJ's Grill. The key to AJ's is consistency. It's consistently empty except for Kelley, the Fearsome Foursome, and AJ himself. The Schlitz, my adult beverage of choice, is consistently cold, AJ is consistently rude, and the Foursome are consistently arguing over the most inane of topics. Tonight was no different.

"I'm telling ya," Rocco said. "Mr. Ed was really a zebra."

"That's horseshit," TC countered.

"Or zebra shit," Jerry Number Two said.

"If Ed was a zebra, how did they hide his stripes?" Jerry Number One asked.

"In black and white TV, the stripes all came out the same, which is why the football players were always running into the refs," Rocco explained.

"Huh?" TC said.

"How come Wilbur wasn't always running into Ed the zebra?" Jerry Number One asked.

"Hold it." TC wanted to slow things down. "Why were the football players running into the refs? Were they watching the games on TV while they played?"

"Remember the horse in the Wizard of Oz?" Jerry Number Two chimed in. "Was he a zebra too?"

Kelley was in his seat, which was one removed from the Foursome, half turned away from them, watching the television. I decided to forgo the resolution of the Ed the zebra/horse discussion, and I sat next to Kel. AJ opened a longneck of Schlitz and slid it in front of me.

"They can't find him," Kelley said.

"Rheinhart?"

"No, Ed the fucking invisible zebra."

"A little tense tonight, huh?"

"What's to be tense about? It's not like there's a serial killer on the loose."

"I don't know, Kel, he didn't seem like he was capable of it," I said.

"C'mon, Duff, history would point in the other direction," he said.

"It's been thirty years, and the whole time in prison they didn't have any trouble with him."

"How much trouble is a 140-pound redhead going to cause at Green Haven? He probably never left his cell," Kelley said.

Kelley sipped his Coors Light and watched the TV. I say "watched the TV," but even though his eyes were pointed in that direction, Kelley faced the TV to avoid getting drawn into the Foursome's discussions. ESPN Classic was showing the Johnny Unitas story. It seemed like you could see the referees very clearly in the black and white footage.

"Look, Kel, what do I know? Talk to the shrinks," I said.

"I'm sure the detectives will. I was hoping you could give me some insight," Kelley said.

"Sorry—I don't know a whole lot about Howard. The last time I met with him, he broke down and said he wanted a life where people weren't out to get him."

"Heartwarming from a guy who murdered four people."

"Well, I'll tell you, the guy's never had a chance in life. What he did back in high school was his only way of standing up for himself."

"Wouldn't you say that he might have gone a tad overboard?"

"Of course—but this guy had nothin' his whole life in terms of a family. He had nothin' normal to base his actions on. He spent his whole life getting his ass kicked, and this was the time he said 'enough,'" I said.

"Uh-huh. That's great. You've been hanging around that clinic too much. You're starting to sound like the rest of the social workers," Kelley said.

Maybe Kelley was right, but something told me that Howard's life and motivations weren't that simple. Talking about it didn't help me figure it out, so I let it go and joined Kelley in watching the Unitas story.

Meanwhile, the Foursome had moved on. Jerry Number One was confused about Canadian Football rules.

"Why do they only get three downs?"

"Because the field is wider," Rocco said.

"What?" TC said.

"The field is so wide they don't need a fourth down," Rocco explained.

"Don't they all have an extra player?" Jerry Number One asked.

"Yeah, so?" said Rocco.

"They're Canadian, what do you expect?" said TC.

I didn't want to kick around the plight of the gridiron ballers to our north, so I got in my Eldorado and headed home. I recently had the burnt orange '76 Cadillac tuned up, and it still didn't exactly purr like a kitten—maybe like a kitten with a hairball issue. I headed out of the industrial part of town where AJ's was located to Route 9R where I lived in my somewhat-customized Airstream trailer, the Moody Blue. It's named after Elvis's last hit, at least while he was alive. I only listen to Elvis, and most of the time it's on eight-track tapes because in '76, eight-track players were what the cool Eldorados came with. I take a lot of shit for being an Elvis fan, but it's just another one of those cases where I believe I'm right and the people who don't like Elvis are wrong. Actually, it's deeper than that. If someone doesn't like Elvis, at least a little bit, I feel there's something wrong with their character or their spirit or something. Tonight, on the way home, he was singing his Dylan medley, "I Shall Be Released" and "Don't Think Twice." I never heard Dylan's versions.

I rent the Blue from Dr. Rudy, my buddy, my cutman, and an all-around good guy. Rudy has done me more than a few favors over the years and I try to pay him back, but I know I'm deeply in arrears when it comes to favors.

Al, my roommate, greeted me at the door with his customary kick to the nuts. He's a basset hound, his full Muslim name being Allah-King. He used to belong to a client of mine named Walanda who used to be in the Nation of Islam. Walanda went off to jail and I promised to take care of Al for thirty days, but then Walanda got murdered. Al never does anything he's told, he's eaten a couch, and he's never quite mastered the whole housebreaking thing. The thing is, Al saved my life a couple of times a while back and he has a patch of reddish-brown hair on top of his mostly black head from where a bullet grazed him to prove it. Like it or not, we're stuck with each other.

Al did a couple of 360s, grabbed an old running shoe, and jumped up on our new couch. The arms of the couch lost their upholstery within seventy-two hours of its delivery because when Al writes in his day planner "Ruin expensive item" and puts A-1 next to it, he makes sure the project gets done. He is committed to his time-management system.

I was wondering if I'd hear from Marcia, my latest nutcase of a girlfriend. Like many of the women I've dated over the last few years, Marcia has turned out to be crazy. She seemed okay at first, but lately she's been weirding out on me. Last Friday she started crying in the middle of a movie we were watching and we had to leave the theater.

It was a Jim Carrey movie.

She said that it was difficult for her to laugh when life was full of so much suffering. I agreed, drove her home, and got drunk at AJ's. Our sex life has been suffering a bit lately as well, and I believe the condition is known as *basset interruptus*. The other night it went something like this:

Marcia and I got back to the Blue after a night out for dinner and drinks. She wasn't too maladjusted that night, so I proceeded to lower the lights, pour some Riunite for her, and, because I was

11

going for that whole James Bond feel, I drank my Schlitz out of a fancy pilsner glass. While Elvis started crooning through "Love Letters" and "Young and Beautiful," I turned up the Duff love-tron for some steamy action.

Marcia's breathing quickened, she pulled me down on top of her and we rolled off the sofa and onto the carpeted floor. She leaned her head back and let out a sigh while she undid the buttons on her white blouse and reached for the snap on the top of her Levis. As she shimmied out of them in that sexy but awkward way that women get out of jeans while in the horizontal position, I saw Al standing about ten feet away in the threshold that led to the dining area.

I gave him a dirty look and tried to move my head in a way to point him out of the room and away from us. He just looked me up and down. Not knowing what else to do, I decided to proceed with the matter at hand and pretend Al wasn't there. I got lost in it and Marcia and I were grooving. During a certain phase of this while Marcia was executing a certain act, I made the mistake of moaning. I don't like to admit it, but I do occasionally express myself during such activity.

Well, Al didn't care for the moaning at all. I heard a growl, then successive barks, and then the rough scratching sounds of basset feet and nails. Then came the squealing from Marcia who was knocked back toward the coach with a flying shoulder block from Al the middle linebacker. I sat my naked ass up, looked at my girlfriend rolling over onto her side, and peered down at Al, who was snarling and growling on the carpet in front of me. You may find this hard to relate to, but it felt strange being naked with my naked girlfriend and having an eighty-five-pound long-snouted, short-legged hound between us.

Little things like that would kill the mood for Marcia.

The last three would-be sexual episodes have had similar outcomes, and even when I locked Al in the bathroom, he howled and slammed into the door so much it had about the same effect. Looking on the bright side of the situation, Al kept me free of sexually transmitted diseases and I had few birth-control issues.

I checked the machine and it looked like I had two calls. The first was indeed from Marcia.

"Hi Duff, I'm sorry about Friday. I've been struggling with some issues. Call me," the message said.

I hit the button for the second message.

"Duffy, this is Howard. I didn't do it."

That was it and he hung up.

3

WELL, THAT WAS JUST swell.

Hey, I wanted the best for good ol' Howard but I wasn't really up for being his middle-of-the-night confidant—especially when he was going to leave me these cryptic messages. As bad as returning Marcia's phone call could be, I wasn't sure I felt like chatting with Howard either. I didn't have a phone number for him, and he surely wasn't at the halfway house because he would've been arrested by now.

Okay—so what were my options? Call the police, which was sort of breaking the confidentiality of a client, though in this case you could argue that the community was in imminent danger. Don't call the police but tell Michelin and let her decide. Or, do nothing and open another can of Schlitz.

The Schlitz went down easy even if my rationalization for doing nothing didn't. Not telling the cops wasn't doing right by my friend Kelley, although he's a beat cop and wouldn't be in charge of an investigation. So, in effect I wasn't doing anything against Kelley. That didn't feel quite right.

Telling Michelin was out for a couple of reasons. One, she'd call in the board, fill out all the forms, and nothing would get done, and two, whenever possible, I try not to tell Michelin anything. Not telling her could get me in big trouble at work, but that wouldn't be anything new. I was always in trouble at work and I did my best not to let the Michelin Woman intimidate me.

I tend to pull for the underdog, and if anyone was ever the underdog, it was Howard. Life had been a shit sandwich for him and every day seemed like it was another bite. Something told me he didn't do. It was a notion I knew I couldn't get anyone else to believe, but sometimes you just got to go with your gut.

Speaking of underdogs and guts, Al had flopped himself off the couch and he let out a big exhale, spun around three times, and went to sleep in front of the television. Apparently he agreed about doing nothing. Though, when it came to doing nothing, Al rarely argued.

The next morning Michelin called for a special staff meeting to go over the agency's position on the recent turn of events. There was nothing Claudia liked better than an official meeting with lots of official protocol and regulations. If she could add a new form to fill out, that was like multiple orgasms for her. The Michelin Woman probably didn't get a whole lot of opportunities for real multiple orgasms, what with her being just a corn muffin shy of three hundred pounds (loosely packed on her six-foot frame), her consistent choice of man-made clothing, and the aforementioned Starsky/Hutch coif.

Claudia called the meeting to order and thanked Dr. Abadon for joining in. As a consultant, he didn't have to be part of impromptu meetings, but he joined this one because of its importance.

"I wanted to bring the treatment team together to discuss the risk management related to the series of events in the community," Michelin said.

She handed out a form about patients' rights when a crime has been committed and our duty as professionals to contact the appropriate authorities.

"If Howard Rheinhart is in contact with any of you, I need to know so I can inform the board and the police," Michelin said.

"Claudia, it sounds to me like you've already assumed he's guilty. Shouldn't we give him a little bit more of the benefit of the doubt?" I said.

"Actually, Duffy, I have every reason to believe that Rheinhart is responsible for this teenager's slaying," she said.

"I don't think he did it," I said.

"Um, I can understand your view, but in my assessment he is clearly capable of this murder."

I wasn't sure which bothered me more—the fact that she was dismissing my opinion or the fact that she was so arrogant about it.

"I just don't think he did it."

"Duffy, you're not really qualified to render this kind of diagnosis are you?" she said.

She smiled at me in such an incredibly patronizing way that it made one of the tendons in my neck twitch. I decided I better let it go before I did something I regretted.

"I think we have to be realistic. Howard Rheinhart is a disturbed individual who has a history of committing heinous crimes," Dr. Abadon said.

"You know, I met with the guy and through some real tears he told me he just wanted to live in a world where people weren't out to get him all the time," I said.

"Classic paranoia, indicative of delusions of persecution," Claudia said.

"It ain't fucking paranoia if you've been physically beat on and emotionally ridiculed every single fucking day of your life!" I said. Then I slammed my fist down on top of my powdered donut. The force sprayed powdered sugar all over the side of the Michelin Woman's head. It kind of gave her black curly hair white highlights.

"Duffy—in my office right away," she said.

You wouldn't say that the Michelin Woman was in my corner when it came to, well, anything. Now I was going to have to listen to her bullshit and probably receive some double-special secret warning for being disrespectful to her. Michelin took the seat behind her desk, reached into the top drawer and produced a series of forms. She was in her element and after neatly stacking the forms so that they were nice and even, she looked up at me.

"That was totally inappropriate," Michelin said.

I believe there is a law that social workers need to use the word "inappropriate" a minimum of eleven times a day.

"I am the executive director here and I will not tolerate that kind of disrespect."

"How about disrespecting the clients…you know, those annoying people we work with?"

"Don't be wise, Duffy, you are in enough trouble."

"C'mon, Claudia—you were being rigid. I was trying to stick up for the client."

"That is inappropriate. You need to show the appropriate respect. You are receiving a verbal warning for inappropriate language, behavior, and insubordination," Claudia said. She was down to eight "inappropriates."

"Do you really have to fill out three different written verbal warnings?"

"Yes—your behavior was inappropriate in regards to language, inappropriate in regards to behavior, and inappropriate in regards to insubordination," Claudia said.

Holy shit—a hat trick! Three "inappropriates" in a single sentence! I wonder if I could call the Social Worker Hall of Fame or something. She was down to five and it was only quarter after ten.

I signed my three written verbal warnings and came to the realization that I wasted a perfectly good half a donut by smashing it. Now there's something that was inappropriate. Grieving the loss of my donut but grateful that my little hissy fit shortened the meeting, I decided to head for my desk. Our office is small, with cubicles for Monique, the other counselor, and me, another batch of cubicles for business office staff, and a few multipurpose rooms. "Duffy's Cubicle of Love" was right next to Monique's.

Monique was talking to Trina, the office manager. They stopped chatting when I approached.

"Girls, were you talking about me?" I said.

"You outdid yourself today," Monique said. "Assaulting the director with a powdered donut," she said. Monique was wearing an orange dashiki that really highlighted her smooth black skin.

"Yeah, Duffy, you've really made a commitment to stay in trouble here, haven't you?" said Trina. Trina looked good today; she always looked good.

"You guys trying to tell me that she wasn't out of line?"

"Duff—the evidence points at Howard, doesn't it?" Monique said.

"I don't know. Howard freaked out for a period of time in his life when he was getting provoked and tormented in every facet of his life. That isn't going on now. I think—" My phone interrupted.

"Duff, has our buddy shown up today?" It was Kelley.

"Nah, no sign of him."

"There's been another one," Kelley said.

"Another what?" I feared I knew what he was talking about.

"Another murdered kid."

"Shit," I said.

"Duff." Kelley hesitated. "The kid was McDonough's QB."

4

I DID WHAT I always did when my stress climbed into the red zone—
I went to the gym. I've been fighting since I was a teenager, first as
a karate guy and then as a boxer. I had gotten my black belt as a
teenager, and one day I felt ultra-confident going in the boxing ring
against a guy with a few amateur fights. He hit me in the stomach
and I puked all over myself. As soon as I stopped tossin' my Cheerios,
I started training as a boxer and I've never looked back.

It's funny—karate gets all the hype as this quasi-spiritual thing
for deep-thinking ponderers while boxing gets portrayed as something for guys who just learned to walk upright. Yet both involve
the science of assaulting someone to unconsciousness or maiming
them into submission. Just because karate guys yell things out in
Japanese and wear pajamas with no shoes while they're learning
to kill you, it gets more of a New Age rep. The real deal is there's
something spiritual to fighting, something at our very core that
most people don't understand. I believe it's something that's inside
every person and it gets sublimated in boardrooms and bedrooms

and every place else you can think of. I also believe if people got in the ring once in a while, then they wouldn't have to be such pains in the asses with their bullshit competitiveness in life. Of course, there would probably be a gigantic dip in the sales of SUVs.

I'm what's known in the boxing trade as a professional opponent. I fight ham-and-egg guys who stink and I beat them, which gives me enough wins to make my record credible. Then, I get put in the ring with some up-and-comer whose manager wants a W for his fighter, and more often than not I get my ass kicked. The ironic thing is that the ass-kicked money is way more lucrative than beating some guy who's as big—or bigger—a nobody as I am.

I train at the Crawford Y, where the boxing gym is in the smelly old basement. The equipment is old and worn just like it should be, and you rarely see anyone dressed in spandex in the basement. The "boxercise" movement hasn't reached the basement, and even though every now and then somebody who watched a couple of exercise videos comes in and thinks he can box, he usually doesn't last long—thank God.

The best part of the fight game is that you can't fight and really think of anything else. If you do, you get smacked in the head and that has a way of interrupting irrational thought patterns. That type of meditative step was exactly what I was looking for today, and I was hoping the sweat would exorcise the Michelin Woman from my soul.

I wrapped my hands and moved around enough to break a sweat so that when Smitty motioned me into the ring, I'd be ready. Smitty worked everyone through the mitts, and you did it on his schedule—it was understood that you didn't leave him waiting. Nothing was ever said, but it got around the gym with the fighters real quick what expectations were. Smitty had been my only trainer and he believed in repetition. He would tailor your training for an upcoming fight, but before you got working on your strategy he would run you through the same fundamental drills.

You could tell a fighter trained by Smitty. One way was by conditioning—if you weren't in shape you didn't fight. That was all there was to that. The second way was we all had superb defense. Smitty used this drill to make sure that your punching hand went back to protect your head so much that I couldn't not recoil my punch because it was simply ingrained into my nervous system. I've been knocked out more than a few times, but every single one of them came when I was throwing at the same time as my opponent. It was never because I dropped my guard.

"I got a call about a short-notice fight," Smitty said after he took me through five rounds.

"Tell me about it," I said.

"Money's good. It's on the undercard of the lightweight title fight with the Irish champ, what's his name ... ?"

"Mulrooney."

"That's it. The guy you're fighting was the '04 Olympic Team heavyweight. The name's Marquason."

"Is he good?" I said.

"Real good." Smitty's expression never changed and you knew he didn't bullshit. "Hits hard, moves well. He's 12 and 0 with eleven knockouts. He's coming off an eight-month layoff because of a cut he got from a butt."

"How good's the money?"

"Fifteen grand."

"Shit—whose he got backing him?" I asked.

"You know who, with the spiky hair." Smitty rolled his eyes.

"Where's the fight?"

"The Garden."

"The theater?"

"Nope, the main arena."

"I'm in," I said.

A chance to fight in Madison Square Garden was like getting to take batting practice with the Yankees. I've fought in the small theater, the Felt Forum, a few times but that wasn't the same. This was a chance to fight in the same room, even the same ring, where Ray Robinson, Joe Louis, Rocky Marciano, Willie Pep, Joe Frazier, and Muhammad Ali fought.

The fight was only four days away, which meant I wasn't going to have a lot of time to train. I was better off warming up every day, eating right, and working on a specific strategy for the guy. The next five days would be like final-exam week in college. Smitty would drill me over and over on what the guy does, how he moves, how he sets up his punches. By the end of the week I'd want to kill Smitty, but it was what I needed.

Knowing he had a serious cut in his last fight was important. Smitty told me that the contract specified the popular Mexican style gloves for the bout. They were known as the "puncher's gloves" because they had very little padding over the knuckles. They also had a slight seam running up the side, and that seam would be an important part of my strategy. I would spend the next five days throwing my jab just to the right and dragging that seam across the bag.

I set up a schedule with Smitty and headed up the stairs to the locker room. On my way I took a peek in the auxiliary gym to check out the karate club. The guys who ran it when I was a kid didn't run it anymore; it had changed hands a bunch of times. Through the little square window I saw a class of about fifteen, mostly guys in their late teens or early twenties.

The two black belts were shouting orders in Japanese and strutting in between the lined-up formation of the students. They swaggered back and forth and tucked their thumbs inside their black belts, occasionally making eye contact with a student after eying him up and down. Their black and red *gis* were professionally pressed, and they had their names embroidered on the left sides of their uniforms.

The shorter one, Mitchell, had a thick mop of black hair, oversized biceps, and a mouth that went crooked as he barked out his orders. Harter was taller and wirier with his blond hair pulled into a Steven Seagal–inspired ponytail. Both of them had had dragons tattooed on their forearms—Mitchell's was red and Harter's was green. Hey, individuality is everything.

They were obviously pumping iron besides their karate training. Their biceps and pectorals were oversized in proportion to the rest of their bodies in that way that bodybuilders create their physiques. It always looked out of proportion to me and not the least bit functional. If you look at pictures of the bodies of Muhammad Ali, Ray Robinson, or, for that matter, Chuck Norris and Bruce Lee, you'll see physique in perfect proportion and built for function.

Mitchell had four stripes on his black belt and Harter had three, so I guessed Mitchell was one degree of douchebag above Harter. Harter, with his ultra-cool green dragon tattoo displayed under his expertly folded uniform sleeve, was going off on this one scrawny kid in the back row. The kid looked like he weighed 140 pounds soaking wet, and he had a wicked pizza face. He was on his knuckles, counting out pushups in between gasps while the black belt stood over him, smirking and letting him know he didn't have what it took to ever be a black belt.

I hated watching jerkoffs like this get their abusive shit off under the guise of martial arts discipline. It made no sense, and karate had more than its share of assholes who thrived in it because they wanted to be in charge of someone and feel powerful. It pissed me off, but that's how a lot of karate classes worked. The goal was to break students down before you built their spirit back up. The problem was that I didn't see the building of anything going on. What I did see was one zit-faced kid shaking and crying from pushups. *Not my issue*, I told myself.

I showered and hit AJ's. A lot of people shake their heads when they hear I don't forgo the Schlitzes when I'm training for a fight. Well, I cut back, lay off the Jim Beam, and I watch what I eat a little better. I'm a heavyweight and I don't have to make a certain weight, and a few beers aren't going to harm me. That's my story and I'm sticking to it.

"Hey, fellas," I said, walking toward my seat just to the left of the taps.

"Rocco's all bound up," TC said.

"Bound up?" I made the mistake of asking.

"What's he seeing, some dominatrix with a fetish for ropes?" Jerry Number Two said.

"I'm fuckin' constipated again," a very uncheerful Rocco said.

"Again … or should we say still?" Jerry Number One said.

"How about you're an asshole again and still?" Rocco retorted.

"Isn't that the problem?" Jerry Number Two asked. "That your asshole is still again and again?"

"Man, you did too many drugs…," Rocco said through a grimace.

"You should lay off the cheese," TC said. "You eat a brick of that Cracker Barrel every fuckin' day."

"Talk about shittin' a brick … or not shittin' a brick," Jerry Number Two said, somewhat rhetorically.

"You know, I read that when John Wayne died they found forty pounds of impacted fecal material in his colon," TC said.

"Fecal?" Jerry Number One asked.

"You know … shit," TC said.

"What kind of shit?" Jerry Number One asked.

"Shit shit, regular shit … you know, poo," TC said.

"No way the Duke had forty pounds of shit in him when he died." Rocco sounded annoyed. "You're full of shit," Rocco said.

"Not like the Duke," said Jerry Number Two.

"Fuck you, Jerry," Rocco said.

Kelley was in with his back turned away from the Foursome, drinking his Coors Light and watching Notre Dame run out the clock against Michigan State in 1966 on ESPN Classic.

"Never understood Parseghian's move here," he said.

"Probably impacted fecal material," I said.

"Please don't … they've been on that for two hours. It's making me sick."

"Howard called me," I said.

"What?"

"The other day, it was on the machine. All he said was he didn't do it and hung up," I said.

"And you waited to tell me this because…"

"I don't know. I believe him and I think no one else does."

"You're nuts, you know that, don't you? A serial killer disappears after two murders and you get around to telling me the next day?" Kelley said. He looked disgusted, but then again Kelley always looked disgusted. "You've got to call the precinct ASAP. They'll want to check your lines and see if they can trace it."

"That's fine, I'll take care of it. Relax," I said.

"Is there anything else you're holding back?"

"No, that's it."

"You sure, or is there something I'll find out tomorrow in between discussions of how much shit John Wayne was packing?"

"No, that's it."

"It's all over the national news now, you know. It's going to be a circus. MSNBC is going to do a live remote, and they got that asshole shrink on who used to be a forensic profiler doing commentary."

"Oh fun," I said.

I got off the topic and had a few Schlitzes before heading home. I told the fellas about the fight in the Garden and they congratulated me. On the drive home I listened to Elvis's '68 Comeback Special and gave some thought to Howard and why I felt strongly about protecting him. I didn't know much about him, he didn't know much about me, and he really only confided in me once. Elvis was singing "Where Could I Go But to the Lord" and segued into "I'm Saved" as I hit 9R. The one thing I was sure about with Howard was that he had no one else in the world who would vouch for him.

Maybe I just answered my own question.

Al kicked me in the nuts when I came to the door and he barked for five minutes straight. It wasn't clear what point he was trying to make, but clearly he felt strong about it. I fixed him a dish of lamb and rice and topped it with half a can of sardines and he calmed down. My trailer smelled like the combination of hound, hound flatulence, and canned sardines—aromatherapy.

I had two messages.

"Duffy." It was Marcia and she was sniffling. "I had a bad day. There's too much sadness in the world. Call me," she said.

She was a barrel of laughs.

I hit the button for the second message.

"Duffy, you gotta help me." It was Howard and that's all he said.

5

THE NEWSPAPER ACCOUNT OF the McDonough High quarterback slaying used the words "gruesome," "grim," and "grisly" quite a bit. For nostalgic sickos it was quite a treat because he was found propped up against the same tree that Howard's QB was, doing his Ichabod-Crane-meets-Johnny-Unitas pose. The cable news people were having a field day and ushering in a whole host of experts about serial killers. They also did profile after profile of Howard, discussed how he was missing, and went over and over his previous murders. This was getting scary weird.

I turned off the TV and called the Crawford police to let them know Howard rang me up. I was put on hold and then spoke to two different very official-sounding cops, and they both told me to not touch anything and that they'd be over right away. Within fifteen minutes, three police cars, all with their lights flashing, and a so-called unmarked car with three detectives pulled up. It was unmarked but unmistakably a cop car, with its six-foot antenna, drab blue color, and lack of hubcaps. I never understood making unmarked cars so obvious because I didn't know anybody who couldn't pick out a cop car from a mile away.

They all decided to come into the Moody Blue, which made for a tight squeeze. The Blue had been modified and customized, but it was still a trailer. I don't know if it was the extra bodies inside the metal tube I call home or the intensity they all brought with them, but the Blue was getting warm.

Al wasn't pleased with the company. As a former member of the Nation of Islam, I'm sure he had experienced his share of harassment, and he was letting the eight police representatives witness his own brand of nonviolent uncivil disobedience. He wouldn't shut up.

"I'm Detective Morris, would you mind…" The cop who appeared to be the highest-ranking guy tried to introduce himself. He was a short guy with a thick neck and a wicked five o'clock shadow.

"WOOF, WOOF, WOOF," Al said.

"Al, shut up!" I said.

"WOOF, WOOF, WOOF," Al said.

"Uh, sir…" Morris tried to start again.

"WOOF WOOF, WOOF WOOF." Al switched to a kind of staccato beat using two barks then a slight pause followed by two more. It had kind of a Rasta feel. The hair on Al's back was standing up.

"Sorry," I shouted. "The last time I had an unexpected visitor Al got hurt."

"WOOF, WOOF, WOOF, WOOF, WOOF." Al returned to the rapid-tempo single barks.

"Do you think you could possibly…"

"WOOF, WOOF, WOOF, AHOOOOOOOO." Al started to bay.

The cops all wrinkled their brows and rolled their eyes and did their best to look impatient. That seemed to piss Al off more.

"AHOOOOOOO ... WOOF, WOOF, AHOOOOOOO," Al said.

"Let me try to put him in the bathroom," I said.

I went to grab Al by the collar, but before I could get my hands on it he turned and ran. Al has a long frame, and doing a 360 for him is like an eighteen-wheeler doing a three-point turn. Just the same, he was surprisingly agile.

He started to run all crazy around the Moody Blue and just when I thought I had him, he'd run right under the coffee table. He was so low to the ground that I couldn't get at him under there, and he knew it. Al ran circles around the cops, who really didn't seem to have much appreciation for the wonderment of nature, and then ducked under the table. The last time through, he faked me left, went right, and ran for the table. It was like trying to get Walter Payton, and Al's change of direction screwed me up.

He went under the table and I ran head on into it, cracking my shin in the process. The table flipped over and I was hopping on one foot repeating the word "Fuck!" about twenty times, which Al found funny, and that got him baying again. The cops didn't find it funny and didn't bay. In fact, they just glared at me as if they were way too important to spend their time watching a dog play with his man.

"AHOOOOOOOOOO," Al said as I grabbed him.

I scooted Al by his collar and closed him off in the bathroom. This made him bark more, though it was muffled.

"Thank you, sir, we're sorry for the trouble. Would you mind giving us the details of the phone calls you've been receiving?" Morris said. The other guys stood around trying to look intense and not bored or unimportant. When Al was barking at them, they mostly looked annoyed.

I explained what I knew, which was that I had two messages and didn't know anything more than that.

"Tell us about what this guy Howard was talking about in his therapy session," the guy next to Morris said. He was tall and blond with a blond Larry Bird kind of mustache. He had a crew cut and it looked like he tried extra hard to look tough to somehow compensate for his fair complexion.

"I can't do that," I said.

"Excuse me?" Larry Bird said.

"C'mon, you know the rules."

"Sir, two teenagers have been slaughtered and you are going to interfere with an investigation?" Bird said.

"Hey look." I was starting to get pissed. "I called you guys here to do the right thing. Don't ask me to do something I can't."

Larry Bird took a step toward me and puffed out his chest.

"Fuckin' social worker ... ," Larry said.

I didn't back up, I didn't look down, I let Larry Bird feel the discomfort of moving in on someone who didn't back up. I'm sure he was accustomed to people wetting their pants when he did this, but his act just didn't have that kind of impact. He stood there for a second and then backed up like he was confused.

"All right, all right, that will probably be enough," Morris said, lightly nudging Bird with his arm. "I think we got what we need, thanks for your help. Would you mind if we check your phone lines for your recent calls?"

"Sure, no problem," I said. They all started to file out and Larry Bird gave me a menacing look. I felt less than menaced.

"So, Duff, this Polack catches his wife in bed with another guy," Sam said.

"Mornin', Sam," I said.

"So he goes and gets his revolver, kicks in the door to the bedroom, and holds the gun to his head while the two of them screw. Finally, the wife looks up at him and laughs, and you know what he says?"

I tried not to encourage Sam with a response.

"C'mon, Duff, you know what he says?"

"What, Sam?" I didn't have the energy to ignore him.

"The Polack says to his wife, 'Don't laugh—you're next!'" Sam laughed his way back to his business office cubicle.

I've been at this job for over five years, and every day Sam stops by with a Polack joke. Like a chronic pain in the testicle, I've just learned to live with it.

I had a lot on my mind. Howard was MIA and had made me his Labrador. Son of Sam believed he got all his messages from his next door neighbor's dog, and I guess that's how I felt. Not like Berkowitz but more like the dog, because here I was, getting weird messages from a guy I only knew a little bit and because of that, I was suddenly the center of attention. Sam the Lab was just being a regular old dog when suddenly his life got spun around all crazy and it wasn't even anything he did. I'm not sure what happened to him, but I'm betting he wound up on medication.

It didn't make much sense to me that Howard would use me as a confidant. I didn't feel like Howard and I had this super-tight bond. Then again, Howard probably didn't have a lot of friends.

You lop off a head or two in your youth and people never let you live it down.

I also had this fight in the Garden coming up. In my boxing career I've gotten used to being a short-notice fighter and I welcomed it. In the fight game there were always guys pulling out of fights for one reason or other. Sometimes it was injuries, sometimes it was contracts, and many times, despite what fighters will admit, it was fear. Sure, no one says, "Hey, I'm pulling out of this bout because I'm tired of shittin' my pants all week and I don't want to get punched in the head." I was nervous enough to drop a pantload and I didn't feel like getting my ass kicked by some million-dollar prospect, but for the chance to fight in the Garden—it was worth it.

I've had a difficult time concentrating lately, but with a full day of sessions I had to try to focus a bit. I say "a bit" because despite what some counselors will tell you, talking, or, more accurately, listening to someone for forty-five minutes isn't exactly rocket science. My first session of the day was with Freddie Gleason, or, as everyone called him, Suda-Fred. Suda-Fred got his name from his drug of choice—Sudafed, the over-the-counter decongestant that has a stimulant effect upon the central nervous system, especially if you took ten at a time with a quart of coffee, which was what Suda-Fred would do. I didn't need any fancy urinalysis tests to figure out if Fred had had a relapse. All I had to do was observe and listen as I greeted him in the waiting room.

"Hey Duff good to see you how's everything? How's the fight game? Man I love boxing—great game, great game, man I love boxing. How you doin'? You look good, any fights coming up? You like these sneakers? They're new. You know what, you know what? Um, uh what was I just sayin'?" Suda-Fred exhaled all at once.

"Fred, have you—," I tried to say.

"Have I what? Uh Duff, that really hurts, you think I'm back on that shit, wow that hurts Duff, man, man the Yanks win last night? Man, Duff, where's the trust? Isn't that what this is all about? Wow, heavy man. Those Yanks, man, it's warm."

Beads of sweat built up on Suda-Fred's lip between his nose and the thin mustache. He was rail thin and his face was way more wrinkled than it should've been for a thirty-eight-year-old man. His hair was pulled back in a ponytail and he wore a red velour running suit.

"Fred, uh—"

"All right, all right Duff get off my ass will ya? It's fuckin' allergy season you know. Sorry, sorry, sorry for the bad language. I took a little today because of the snotty nose deal, really Duff, it was the snot, disgustin' man, disgustin' man. I took the blue ones, you know the 418s, they got that expectors in 'em or somethin'. Helps you get that snot out of your throat, disgustin' man, disgustin' man, sorry for the language, man," Fred said.

"Coffee?" I asked.

"No I'm good, I'm good, don't need no coffee Duff."

"No, Fred. Have you had coffee?"

"C'mon, Duff, off my ass, geez, off my ass will ya? Uh, geez again with the language, sorry man, sorry. Sure, sure a little, you know that expressive kind at the Starbucks, the dark kind—is it warm?— shit I'm warm. Man, maybe it's the velour, shit. Who the Yanks got tonight? Yeah Duff, expressive."

"Espresso?" I said.

"Yeah, yeah, yeah, probably made me hot—I'm not in trouble, am I? Duff you look in shape, you gotta fight comin' up or something? I love boxing, love it, love the fight game. Shit it's hot."

Actually, you really can't get in trouble for loading up on Sudafed and "expressive"—not legal trouble anyway. Suda-Fred had a little anxiety trouble, which often led him to less than a placid existence. So for the next forty minutes or so, it was my job to find out what I could about what had brought Fred to the Sudafed. Fred's snot issues seemed to have been the trigger that brought on today's relapse, but perhaps there was a deeper emotional antecedent that together we could uncover. It was up to me, skilled clinician that I was, to deconstruct the behaviors that led up to Fred's use of the dreaded 418s.

Turns out all we could come up with was the snot, man, it was all about the snot. Fred and I spent the next forty-five minutes talking about congestion, alertness, and the Yanks—a lot about alertness.

After Suda-Fred, a session with Stanley Stillman was a welcome change of pace. Stanley was referred to the clinic by his employer's employee assistance plan for an Internet addiction. Actually, they caught Stanley surfing porn on his company computer, and when they went through his computer logs it was pretty clear that he spent about seven out of eight hours a day on the boner sites. They tried to fire him but the union prevented it, got a doctor to give him an obsessive-compulsive disorder diagnosis, and now he's getting paid time off to "recover." I guess in his position as safety officer for the power company, his "recovery" was pretty important.

Anyway, he was a welcome relief because he barely said anything at all. I think the guy's real diagnosis should have been something along the lines of "chronic traumatic embarrassment related to masturbatory activity." The guys at the power company weren't real sensitive to Stan's plight, and not too far behind his back they referred to him as "the stroke-a-matic." I wouldn't feel like talking much either.

While Stan and I put up with the awkward silences, I thought about Howard. I racked my brain trying to think about how I could find out more about him. He didn't have any family contacts and the counselors at the halfway house said he kept to himself. There was a ninety-page summary from his prison shrink that I hadn't read all the way through yet. I'd read the first twenty pages and it didn't say much of anything, so I'd skipped to the end where they had come to the conclusion that Howard was of very little danger to society, that his actions were the result of an abused adolescent mind processing extreme abusive stress, and unless those types of stressors were repeated, Howard was not a danger. They went on to say that even if Howard was placed under stress, he was unlikely to repeat the same violent activity.

Dr. Abadon read the report and he indicated that it was within the realm of possibility that Howard was in a way relapsing to his old compulsions and that if he was experiencing stress—which a release from prison to his old neighborhood would evoke—he could revert to old ways. That was a fair analysis, but I was afraid that one opinion might be enough for the police to assume Howard was the one and only suspect. With assholes like Larry "the Cop" Bird itching to do something dramatic, I was afraid Howard didn't have a chance.

Stan went on his less than merry way and I went back to check out Howard's file. Reading through assessments was like taking the time to read through the directions for a universal television remote, only not as entertaining. It just went on and on in that annoying psychobabble that had fancy names for everyday things. It talked about his shallow affect, his dysthymic mood, and the fact that he was oriented times three. In English, I think that meant that Howard looked depressed and acted depressed but knew where he was, who he was, and what day it was.

Hidden in some of this bullshit were some things that may have explained why Howard was the way he was. His mother never visited him in prison and apparently she moved to Wisconsin where she herself was arrested for kiting checks. The mother had a half-sister in Oklahoma who had eight children, though neither she nor the children ever met Howard. The father, who left before Howard was born, died of cirrhosis ten years ago. Now there's a warm bunch to pass the turkey around with on Thanksgiving.

Howard was, by most accounts, a model inmate. In his first five years incarcerated he was in Ossining, and on two occasions he was "assaulted." There wasn't a ton of information about what constituted a prison assault, but one could only wonder. After those five years he was moved to Green Haven, where he stayed until he was discharged. Twelve years before he was discharged, a guy in the cell next to him was beaten to death over some jailhouse drug dealing, and Howard had always maintained that he knew nothing about what was going on. Apparently, the drug situation was pretty bad for a while because five inmates died of drug use while in Green Haven during that period.

All very interesting, but averaged out over thirty years there really wasn't a ton of unusual stuff about inmate Rheinhart. I was just closing his file when Trina buzzed me and told me Michelin wanted to see me. Oh joy.

"Duffy, I am not pleased with this situation with Rheinhart," Claudia said.

"What do you mean?" I said.

"It's bad for the clinic. It puts us in a bad light and it makes us vulnerable."

"Bad light? Vulnerable?"

"It's bad publicity and it overshadows the work we do. It could interfere with our ability to help clients," Claudia said, running her hand palm-down through her Starsky-do, which was something she did when she was lying.

"Uh-huh. What does that have to do with me?" I said.

"You're his counselor."

"So."

"Make sure you do everything you can to assist his apprehension."

"What if he's innocent and he gets hurt?"

"Duffy—be realistic."

"I'm not always good at that," I said, and I got up. "Claudia, I better go or you'll be writing out verbal warnings for me." I turned to get out of her office.

"Make sure you do what I told you," she said.

I needed to get to the gym ... for a lot of reasons.

6

WITH JUST A FEW days before a bout there's not a ton you can work on, but it felt better to be in the gym doing something to get ready. I had been sparring on and off for the last month so I was reasonably sharp. Sparring too close to a fight can be dumb because you can get an injury that would make you pull out of the fight. When you're a fighter of my caliber, that's a big mistake because they'll just go to the boxing registry and find another guy with your weight, height, level of competition, and won/loss record. Professional opponents really have a lot in common with the bovine futures being bought and sold at the Chicago Board of Trade. If you're a boxing superstar like Oscar de la Hoya and everyone's dying to fight you and you get injured, you call the fight off and the whole boxing world will wait for you. Well, the boxing world wouldn't wait the length of a beer commercial for Duffy Dombrowski and guys like me don't see many $15,000 paydays, so I didn't want to take any chances.

I did want to get a feel for the Mexican gloves because I hadn't worn them much. They're expensive and the shows I fight on usually cut costs by using cheaper gloves. I swallowed the $250 and got a pair, figuring it was money well spent. God, they felt great, probably as good as an alligator shoe feels on someone who cares enough to buy the repulsive things. They really formed around my fists, and my hands just felt natural inside of them. I did three rounds of regular bag work and then practiced throwing the jab and just grazing the corner of the heavy bag. I saw some of the Puerto Rican fighters working this move with the Mexican gloves on the bags at Gleason's in Brooklyn one time and they had it down to an art form. I don't know about my artistic expression but I was getting a feel for letting the seam drag over the bag.

Smitty took me through some pad work, finishing with two full rounds drilling the recoil on my left cross. This was Smitty's pride and joy, and he felt like if he could train a fighter to bring his hands back after a punch, then that fighter's defense could be almost impenetrable. He was right and all his fighters did it well. If they didn't, and didn't practice, pretty soon they weren't his fighters anymore. Smitty would drop them because he felt that strongly about it.

After the last round on the pads he told me to shake down a little bit and to do some stretching. He gave me the speech of what not to eat before a fight and how to get as much sleep as possible—like the nerves I went through the week of the fight would possibly allow me to concentrate on nutrition or leave me calm enough to get any sleep. The last few days before the fight I was miserable. Irritable, cranky, and generally just pissed off, and dealing with the Michelin Woman today hadn't helped matters either.

I was undoing my wraps and heading up the stairs to the locker room when I was distracted by the yelling in the karate room. Looking through the little square window with the crosshatched lines, I saw Mitchell and Harter, the two barney-badass black belts. They were standing over the goofy kid, the one with the really bad pizza face. He was doing knuckle pushups and his arms quivered from the fatigue. The kid wasn't blessed with a whole lot of physical strength, but it was clear that he was a karate diehard. If a karate instructor wants to work the kid's ass off that was one thing. Corny and as politically incorrect as that sort of thing is, I do believe facing and overcoming adversity does build character in people. In fact, I'd argue that it's the only thing that builds character. Even in a goofy karate class where the adversity was contrived, it could still breed character.

The thing with these guys was that they seemed to be enjoying making a mockery of the kid. It wasn't about any kind of respect— it was about the opposite. I opened up the door and quietly went into the karate class and leaned against the wall.

"You are weak," Mitchell barked at the kid. "You do not have the black belt's heart."

The kid looked up from his pushups and fought back the tears. The poor kid—here these guys were abusing him and he had the loyalty to be hurt by their disapproval.

"Too weak," Harter snickered. "You can't even finish your pushups. You will never make black belt."

The kid started to cry, though he hid it by putting his head down in his pushup position. My neck started to twitch, and I noticed that my left hand was clenched. Today, something was going to keep me from minding my own business.

"Hey—that's probably enough, don't you think, fellas?" I said as I crossed my arms. I hadn't moved otherwise and stood still, holding up the wall.

The room got quiet. The rest of the students tried not to look at me while they maintained their quasi-military forward stares.

"Sir, this is a closed class. There are no visitors," Mitchell said. He glared at me like he thought I would melt in front of him.

"Good for you, but why don't you leave the kid alone," I said. I felt the vein twitch in my neck again.

"No one speaks to the sensei in this class like this. You are putting yourself in danger," he said. His partner took an exaggerated stance with his hands on his hips. He stood up straight in a posture that was impossibly rigid.

"Yeah, well, excuse me if I don't tremble," I said.

I walked across the gym floor, grabbed the kid by the back of the uniform, and lifted him to his feet.

"C'mon, pal. You're getting outta here."

The kid tried to pull away and he tried to say something to his instructors, but nothing came out. They stood with their hands on their hips.

"You're doing us a favor. He's kept the rest of the class down," Harter said.

I stopped. I put the kid down and I turned around.

The vein in my neck was doing the Twist and I had had it.

"Tell you what, tough guy, how about you come over here and make me do a pushup. Or does the fact that I'm over 140 pounds disqualify me?" I said.

"A time and a place for you, there will be," Mitchell said.

"Hey Confucius, you want to try me? C'mon!" The neck was getting intense. "You weren't all philosophical two minutes ago when you were abusing this kid," I said.

"Go now, while you still can," Harter said.

I didn't move or say anything for a while, but I looked Mitchell right in the eye.

"C'mon, kid," I said. The kid didn't want to go, and I had to pull him away. I dragged him out to the stairwell. He struggled to stand up straight, he wiped his eyes, trying to make it look like he wasn't crying, and he wouldn't look at me.

"Why did you do that?" he said. "I am a karateka. I will be a black belt one day."

"Hey kid—"

"Who are you? Why don't you mind your own business?"

He looked up at me and his face was covered with zits. The very tip of his nose had a huge whitehead on it, and it was about the size of a nickel. He had a traumatized look on his face as he held back the tears.

"Kid—you don't need to be treated like that. That's not what being a black belt is all about," I said.

"How would you know?"

"I am a black belt, have been for years." Which was true. I was a black belt as a teenager before I got into boxing.

The kid froze and looked frightened like he just farted in the Pope's presence. He came to attention and bowed.

"I am sorry, sir. I meant no disrespect."

"Kid, it—"

He interrupted me again. Something came over his face.

"You will be my new sensei. You have been sent to lead me to my black belt."

"Uh … kid … uh …" I couldn't find the words.

"Yes, it is destiny. I will put my trust in you," he said, and a calm came over him.

Oh boy. I couldn't think of what to say, but I was fully aware that I did stick my nose in this kid's life without him asking me to.

The kid gave me a big exaggerated bow.

I bowed back, which ... uh ... I guess is what you do to a karateka under your tutelage.

Oh geez.

———————

It had been a long day for about eleven different reasons, so I headed to my bastion of stress management. I needed a little insanity to balance out what the rest of the day had been, and I was still cooling down from the workout when I walked into AJ's.

"So you're saying they're what you call Native American Canadians," Rocco said.

"Yeah, have to be," TC said.

"Why not just Native Canadians?" Jerry Number Two asked.

"Isn't that what they call the Canucks from Quebec?" said Rocco.

"I don't think they care for the term 'Canuck,'" Jerry Number Two said.

"Isn't there a pro hockey team called the Canucks?" Jerry Number One asked.

"So," said TC.

"They play in Vancouver," Jerry Number Two said.

"What does that have to do with anything?" Rocco said.

"That's why they call themselves the Canucks—to piss off the Native Quebecians," Jerry Number Two said.

"So how bad could the term be if they named a hockey team after it?" Jerry Number One said. "We don't have a team in the NBA called the Alabama Spooks."

"There's the Globetrotters," TC said.

"They're not Canadian," Jerry Number Two said.

"They're Native Harlemenians," TC said.

AJ slid a bottle of Schlitz in front of me and I sat next to Kelley, who was watching the old fights on ESPN Classic. It was Basilio and Robinson again.

"What do you hear from your hackin' friend?" Kelley asked.

"Nothing," I said. "I spent some time reading his prison file today though."

"And…"

"Not much there. In his first five years he was assaulted a couple of times," I said.

"That's pretty routine."

"Then the guy in the cell next to him was beaten to death over some drug stuff. Apparently there was some bad drugs floating around Green Haven and some inmates died."

"I think I remember that," Kelley said. "Turned out the stuff they were taking was some homemade poisonous shit."

"Bad shit," I said.

"Yeah—but also pretty routine inside. Those guys are always trying to get high."

"Are you involved in the search for Howard?"

"Not really. I mean we get bulletins and shit like that, but nothing official. There's a big-deal task force," Kelley said.

"Gotcha."

"Hey—you're fighting in the Garden, huh?"

"Yeah, some hot-shit contender."

"Good luck."

"I'll need it," I said.

7

"AHOOOOOOO, AHOOOOOOO, MMMMMM, WOOF, WOOF, AHOOOOOO." It was my alarm clock.

My alarm clock has no snooze control—in fact, it has very little control. It does have long ears, short legs, and a tendency toward flatulence. This morning Al was particularly intense around the front door to the Moody Blue. Intense enough that I decided to forgo my first stop to take a leak and my second stop to get the coffee going.

"GRRRRRRR, WOOF, WOOF, WOOF," Al said. Three consecutive WOOFs usually meant something unusual was going on. Al tended to stick to the two WOOFs, a single AHOOOO, followed by two more WOOFs.

I peeked through the front-door curtains and rubbed the gook out of me eyes. It was the goofy karate kid from last night, just standing there waiting for something. I'm not a rise-and-shine kind of guy, and this was going to be a real challenge to my cognition first thing in the morning. I wasn't sure exactly what to do, but it was early and I was curious about what might've brought him to my trailer. I opened the door to see just what I had here at such a God-awful hour.

"Sir," the kid said. "Good morning." Then he bowed. He was wearing a black karate-style outfit.

"Kid, what the hell time is it?" came out of my mouth.

"Five fifteen a.m., sir."

"What are you doing here?" My pupils had constricted enough that I could clearly see him. This morning he had a new zit right in the middle of his forehead. In my morning fog, the kid looked Hindu.

"Here for training, sir."

"Training for what?" I said. "And what's with the getup?"

"Sir, this is the Karateka-Brand Nu-Breath Fabric Modern Ninja suit, sir."

I was starting to wonder what planet I was on.

"Kid, what's your name?"

"William Cramer, sir, known as Billy."

"Did I say we were going to train this morning?"

"No, sir, I am just eager to learn," he said. I couldn't stop staring at the whitehead in the middle of his forehead. It was like some sort of evil cyclops had been sent to mess up my morning equilibrium.

"You got folks, kid?"

"My mother, sir. My father passed away."

"Sorry, Billy. Mom know you're here?"

"She works an overnight shift and she doesn't get home until after I leave for school," he said.

"All right, Billy," I said. "Training will be tonight at the Y in the boxing room. Be there at seven thirty p.m."

"Yes, sir!" he said. He gave me an exaggerated bow, bounded down the steps, and started to run down the side of Route 9R.

I turned to head to the toilet, and Al was staring at me with a look that was half confusion and half amusement.

"Don't ask me," I said.

"Duff, I was just reading this book on World War II," Sam said.

"I didn't know you could read," I said.

"Did you know there was a group of Polish kamikazes?"

"Uh, geez..."

"Yep—in fact, Kamikaze Kowalski flew over a hundred success-ful missions." Sam laughed and went back to his spot.

I had just gotten in and was going through my stack of human-services mail. There were the letters from the county social services department, which would be about the reports I hadn't sent them or info on my clients that I probably should read but won't. There were two postcards announcing open houses at two other agencies to celebrate either their new executive director, which most agen-cies got every eight months or so, or to announce their new highly specialized program for left-handed Vietnam vets with carpal tun-nel syndrome and genital herpes. There were two pieces of mail announcing conferences, including the Seventh Annual Women's Symposium on Emotionally Unavailable Men and the state con-ference on Music Therapy with the Hearing Impaired.

There was also a letter with a hand-written address on it, which I opened first. It was a short pencil-written letter and the words were printed as straight as possible. It was from Howard, and it made the vein in my neck twitch a little.

Duffy,

I didn't do what they're saying I did. They want me to be blamed and they want me out of their lives. I've assured them I won't talk but they don't want to take their chances. I have to stay away.

You're the only one I trust.

Help.

H.

I would've preferred registering for the Women's Symposium; nonetheless, I had to deal with being Howard's Labrador, and that meant some professional and personal obligations. Up until now, I didn't have any firsthand knowledge that Howard was innocent, but by that rationale the guy was guilty until proven otherwise. That was the same assumption Michelin, Abadon, and the cops were making, and just because I was hesitant to follow along with their assumption, it didn't make me any better if ultimately I did the same things that they would do. Just the same, if I was wrong in my nobility, there was a chance that McDonough High could wind up being down another quarterback spot on the depth chart.

If Howard was the bad guy, which just about everyone believed, real lives were in danger. I had my gut instincts, but I also knew I had a tendency to go against the crowd just for the sake of going against the crowd. Add to that the fact that I had no respect for the Michelin Woman, I couldn't get a read on Abadon, and in general I wasn't a big fan of cops, and—I had to admit—I could've been being adversarial for the sport of it. On the other hand, I respected

Monique, Kelley, and Trina as much as anyone, and they felt that it was most likely Howard who was doing the slicing and dicing.

I called Claudia's extension, well aware that it would ruin my day. She came out briefly and then called the police. Within minutes, Detective Morris, the Larry Bird guy whose name I found out was Mullings, and two uniformed cops came to my office. Larry Bird gave me a dirty look but Morris did most of the talking.

They wanted to know when it came, who touched it, did I handle it, did I write on it—they asked just about everything except did I blow my nose in it. Then they took the letter with these fancy tweezers and dropped it in an evidence bag and asked me if they could get my fingerprints so they could tell mine from whatever prints were on the letter.

I agreed mostly because going to the police station would get me out of the office and get me to the gym sooner. They sent me to where they book real criminals, and some cop named Murtagh took my prints without any enthusiasm in about ten minutes. I was in and out of the police station in no time and fit with a perfect excuse not to return to the office. With the fight on Saturday, an extra nap would come in handy and would be time well spent. The Michelin Woman wouldn't bitch about me not coming back to the office because she'd assume I was at the station cooperating all afternoon.

I pulled up in front of the Moody Blue just in time to catch Marcia putting a letter in my mailbox. Her long, straight hair came down past her shoulders and rested on her peasant blouse. She wore army fatigues and a pair of the Birkenstocks, rounding out a look I hated. Marcia reminded people a lot of the folk singer Jewel, who recently went sort of glam with her look. I had hoped Marcia would follow suit, but she didn't.

"Hey, Duff," she said. "I left you a note."

"A note?"

"I don't know if it's something I can talk about. My therapist—"

"Your therapist?"

"Yeah, I've been seeing someone."

"Uh-huh," I said. Every chick I saw wound up seeing a therapist. Usually right before she broke up with me.

"She thinks it would be best if I wasn't in a relationship right now. I still want to be friends."

"Friends, huh?" I've been around long enough to know that when your girlfriend wanted to be your friend, she was really telling you she didn't want to have sex with you anymore. But, if she needed to talk with you to spew a bunch of therapist-induced drivel when she's lonely, she wanted to reserve the right to call you. That would make me a kind of emotional tampon she could pull out once a month when she needed it.

"Yeah, we can be friends, right?"

"Sure," I heard myself say.

"You don't sound like you mean it."

"I'm going to need a little time to process this." I've learned that if you use the word "process," women think you're being a feeling kind of guy.

"Okay, that's fair, Duff." She sniffled and there was that awkward moment when you know something's over and there isn't anything left to be said. Actually, it was a bit of a relief because she'd been weirding out on me for a while. Just the same, it still left a sickish feeling. It had been about six months, which had been about my

52

girlfriend duration for the last few years, and I've gotten a bit used to the whole breakup scene. A bit too used to it.

I was tranced out when I opened the door to the Blue and forgot about Allah-King, who kicked me right in the nuts as I opened the door. No longer in a trance, I bent over, grabbing my nuts while Al spun around in enthusiastic circles. I straightened up and Al jumped up and kicked me in the nuts a second time. They were two good shots and I felt my eyes well up just a bit. Tears ran down my cheeks.

I flopped on the couch, lying on my back to ease the pain in the nuttage, and Al jumped up with me. He awkwardly made his way up the length of my body and intermittently licked and bit my ears. It wasn't exactly what I'd call recuperative relaxation, but, to be honest, I appreciated his company. Marcia was an emotional ditz and I knew we weren't going anywhere, but I didn't really need the reminder that once again a relationship of mine crashed and burned. Rationally, I knew it wasn't a reflection on my worth. Rationally, I knew I would be fine, probably better off, and rationally, I knew it was an opportunity to meet someone better suited for me. Realistically, I was bummed.

I lay on the couch, watching afternoon cable. I took a fake nap, closing my eyes and doing my best impersonation of sleep. There was an episode of *Hawaii Five-O* on, and McGarrett just ordered Danno and Chin to get a bunch of uniforms and "seal off this rock." I wished I were McGarrett. McGarrett had the power to get uniformed police in gear and cover an entire island. Me, I just got dumped by a chick I didn't even really like that much. I couldn't see that happening to Steve McGarrett.

Eventually, I threw my gear in my duffel and headed to the gym for my last workout before the fight. I wasn't in the mood for Smitty's urgency and repetitiveness, but I knew it was needed. I was going to be about two hours early, but I could use the time to think about Marquason and work on dragging my jab against the bag. I could take my time getting dressed and do some extra stretching. Of course, that meant spending more time in the locker room at the Y, which was just a bizarre place.

You had your sixty-year-old handball players who all hated each other and argued every single day for the last forty years. There were the hoop players with their baggy shorts and headbands and hip-hop attitude. And then there were the guys who came to the Y, took a shower, and then walked around a lot in the nude.

Every time you'd go around a row of lockers, there'd be one of these guys, not talking to anyone, just walking to or from the shower. Every once in a while, one of these guys would come into the showers and you would know they just took a damn shower, but here they were again. It was funky stuff, but every Y I'd ever been in had its collection of guys who liked walking around nude a little too much.

When I got down to the gym, Smitty was talking to Billy, my new karate kid.

"Duff, this kid said something about you being his new señor?" Smitty said.

"That's *sensei*," Billy corrected.

"Yeah, that's right," I said.

Smitty rolled his eyes at me, which he did about three times a day since the day I met him.

"Well, sensei," Smitty said. "You think you'll have time for a boring old boxing workout?"

"Yeah—I think so."

I instructed my karate student to sit, watch, and quietly observe everything he saw. He went and sat in the lotus position against the wall. Smitty took me through the recoil drill, spent a half an hour on how I should move to my left to stay away from Marquason's power, and had me spin out of the corner while he threw punches at me. Then he had me shake it out with some light bag work.

I took the time to drill my drag punch, hoping Smitty wouldn't be paying close attention. That, of course, was a mistake; Smitty was always paying attention.

"What the hell is that?" Smitty said.

"Nothin' really. I saw some of the Puerto Ricans doing it at Gleason's once," I said.

"You plannin' something I should know about, son?"

"Nah."

Smitty gave me eye roll number two for the day and went to his office just behind the old speed-bag platform. I did some stretching and saw Billy out of the corner of my eye, rocking with enthusiasm. I had promised and figured it was time.

"All right, kid. In the ring."

Billy bounded through the ropes charged up in front of me and bowed.

"WASABIIIIIIIIIII!" he yelled, then snapped his fists down around his belt.

"Wasabi? What's that all about?" I said.

"It is my unique *kiai*."

"Kiai is the yell, right?" I noticed Billy had a brand-new purple zit on his left cheek that looked like a gumdrop.

"Sir, yes sir."

"Why are you yelling about Japanese horseradish?"

"Sir?"

"Wasabi is that green stuff you get with sushi, isn't it?"

"Sir?"

"Never mind."

"Yes, sir."

"All right, kid, get in your fighting stance," I said, trying to muster some vigor.

He stepped back with his left leg and with exaggerated motion hurled his arms into a formal fighting stance.

"WASABIIIIIIIII!"

That was going to take some getting used to. I noticed Smitty was out of his office, leaning in the doorway, watching the karate lesson as if he were watching the first inhabitants of Uranus to land in Crawford.

"Stepping forward, high punch," I yelled. It was a struggle to remember how karate commands went.

"Sir, I am accustomed to hearing the commands in Japanese."

"Well, you're going to have to change that."

"Yes, sir!"

And so it went. I considered having him wax my '76 Eldorado with the whole "wax on, wax off" deal, but that would mean the kid would probably be in my hair for another six hours. That, and I wasn't confident the burnt orange finish could handle a waxing. The whole car could disintegrate from shock or something.

I gave the kid a half an hour of training, such as it was. He wasn't very good, but what he lacked in power and grace he certainly made up for with excitement. When the half hour was through, I bowed him out and congratulated him on good workout.

"Sir, when will I train again?"

"I have to go away for the weekend, kid. I've got a fight."

"A fight? Western boxing?"

"Yep."

"What shall I work on in the meantime?"

"Uh, let's see. Just work your fundamentals." It was the best I could come up with. "And kid, you don't have to wear a formal karate outfit, if you don't want."

"Sir, I prefer to train in my Karateka Nu-Breath Modern Ninja uniform."

"That would be fine, I guess," I said and then dismissed my class.

8

I HATE THE DAY before a fight.

It was in New York, so we were going to head down to the city at night, go to the weigh-in, have dinner, and go to bed early. Notice I said "go to bed" and not "go to sleep" because I never slept the night before a fight. Before we could leave I still had the morning and part of the afternoon to kill, so I arranged to work some time at the clinic. I didn't have a ton of vacation time left but I could spare a half a day.

I had a ten a.m. session with Javier Sanchez, a migrant farm worker who came up to Crawford from Florida and the orange groves to work in the apple orchards. Sanchez got busted driving one of the orchard tractors on the Thruway, which was only part of the problem. The other part was that he was two and half times over the drunk-driving limit. I think the troopers got suspicious because he was in the passing lane doing eight miles per hour.

Sanchez barely spoke English and what he did say was mostly unintelligible. He really wasn't of this culture and he didn't get how the people in our country operated. He certainly didn't get this whole human-services deal at all. The idea that the police arrest you and then you have to go some place to talk about things just didn't make any sense to him. Getting locked up for a year in a smelly jail with little food and lots of bugs probably would've made sense, and in many cases might have been easier to take than the Chinese water torture of getting involved in court-ordered treatment.

To make matters worse, he hadn't paid his clinic bills because, well, he made about a buck-fifty a day and didn't understand why he was coming to the clinic in the first place. He was one of those victims of the absurd social-services laws. He didn't have an official address because he lived in a tent on an orchard and he changed orchards frequently. Without an address, a citizen can't get welfare or Medicaid. He couldn't even apply for our sliding scale because he didn't have any of the necessary paperwork like pay stubs and letters from landlords because he got paid in cash and he didn't have a social security card or a driver's license. Yet, even with all this bullshit, if Sanchez missed a couple of sessions, the Michelin Woman would make me contact his probation officer and he might go to jail.

Sanchez was half Mexican and half Filipino, and even though he was in his late fifties, he looked seventy. Lots of sun, too much work, and a steady diet of tequila will do that. All in all, he was very likable and I felt for the position he was in. As far as his treatment goals went I didn't think he was going to be getting any AA MVP awards any time soon, but then again, neither was I.

Sanchez was a half an hour late as usual because he walked three miles each way to the clinic, which he said he didn't mind. Today, he was wearing faded jeans, ratty Converse All Stars, a wife-beater, and a Chicago Bulls hat. He didn't look happy and he didn't smell good.

"Señor Duffy," he said in his thick and mumbled accent. "Sanchez no money. Sanchez no number house."

"No number house?" I said.

"No, no number house, no money, no money clinic."

"No number house?" I repeated. "Oh ... no address?"

"Sí."

"No Medicaid, no welfare because no address, right?"

"Sí." Sanchez frowned.

Sanchez had as much chance of solving this dilemma as he did getting accepted at the Crawford Country Club. This was the exact type of bureaucratic bullshit that made me want to jump out of my skin. I mean, I think welfare probably hurts as many people as it helps, but if there was ever a guy who needed some help from the government, it was Sanchez. Of course, I wasn't even sure he was a citizen, but guys like Sanchez were the only guys who would pick apples and we all love to eat those apples, at least in our McDonald's apple pies, don't we? Most people, or at least most people who call in to talk radio shows, don't get that point—oh well, they didn't get much of anything.

I thought for a second and had an idea. My ideas often got me in trouble, but I figured that was probably the case with most Robin Hood–type geniuses. I also figured that my chances of getting caught were low. That figuring was probably wrong, but what the hell. I scribbled on a sticky note and handed it to Sanchez.

"Give them this and tell them to call this man," I said. I gave him my address with the letter B after the street number, like it was an apartment building—as if an Airstream trailer could have a couple of floors or something. Sanchez smiled.

"Gracias, Señor Duff. You da man, sí!" Sanchez said.

He left happy and I called Dr. Rudy.

"Rudy here," he answered his office phone.

"Hey pal."

"Whatya want."

"Geez, what kind of mood are you in?"

"I'm fuckin' busy and the only time you call me, you need me to stick my neck out."

"That hurts."

"So what is it?"

"I got a migrant farm worker who needs an address. I told him to tell DSS that he's renting an apartment from you."

"You what?"

"C'mon, all you have to do is tell them that he rents from you when they call."

"Welfare fraud is what it's called."

"You do have a way with words."

"Fuck you."

He hung up, which I knew he would do. That was fine because I saw it as the price I had to pay for his favors. There was no doubt Rudy would come through. He always does. I'd take shit for it and maybe for a long time, but that was the surcharge I paid for his kindness.

I started to head for the coffee machine when I noticed the TV was on in the break room and all the staff were gathered around it. There was an MSNBC special report on and it was midmorning.

I walked up behind Monique.

"What the hell is going on?" I said.

"There's another one. All they're saying is that a high-school girl was murdered and sexually mutilated."

"What is 'sexually mutilated'?"

"I can only imagine," she said.

"They think it's Howard?"

"That's what they're saying."

———

What was supposed to be an easy half-day was turning into a nightmare. All I had wanted to do was get some paperwork done, see Sanchez, and then get out and focus on my fight. Now there was going to be a thing, I could sense it. Claudia loved making a thing of things, and if it gave her an opportunity to be officious and pompous, then she would milk it for all it was worth.

Turns out that she demanded that none of us leave until she gave the okay, and she reminded us over and over not to speak to the press. Then, she called in the board for a special meeting. The board at Jewish Unified Services was the biggest bunch of phony goofs you ever wanted to see. A while back, one of them actually shot me after I exposed his Internet porn industry. He was the same guy who shot Al, who happened to come to my rescue and save my life. Well, that board member won't be attending any meetings soon because he drew a twenty-five-to-life sentence and actually was doing time at Green Haven, which had me wondering if he and Howard ever crossed paths.

He owned car dealerships and I'm convinced he joined the board to network business opportunities out of the other board members, who, by my estimation, were there for the exact same reasons. There were financial guys and lawyers hoping to find new businesses, there were doctors' wives, and there were a few others who I am sure were angling for something. There was one exception.

The one exception was the chairman of the board and my unofficial Jewish grandfather, Hymie Zuckerman. Hymie started the agency to help people and he remained committed to that mission. With a chain of Crawford's most successful dry cleaners, Hymie had made a fortune by working his ass off and he wanted to help some of the people who weren't as lucky as he was. I never got the impression that Hymie felt that because he worked his ass off he deserved any more than anyone else. It was like he saw his work ethic as something he was lucky to have, like it was a tool that he had that others didn't.

He didn't have much use for Claudia, but he knew the agency needed to follow regulations and so he viewed her as a necessary evil. He gave her the respect her title warranted but he never, ever warmed up to her. He did, however, treat me like I was his adopted grandson.

I heard some noise in the lobby and I knew it was him. Hymie's entrances were never quiet.

"Where is he?" he announced, coming in with his thick old-world Jew accent. "Where's that Harp-Polack pug of mine? Where is he?"

I stood to greet him, and he reached up and pinched me on the cheek and shook my face until it felt like I was getting a blood blister. He was about five foot two and mostly bald with brown liver spots over his scalp. He had black glasses, polyester pants, white shoes, and a matching white belt. He was over eighty and his eyes were a little cloudy, but they shined when he smiled.

"Big shot, fighting in the Garden like Barney Ross," he said. He was a big fight fan from the days when Jews like Barney Ross dominated the sport.

"That's right, but no one's mistaking me for Barney, I'm afraid."

"What's this, son? Have confidence—it's your time!"

"I'll do my best," I said when Claudia appeared.

She greeted Hymie and ushered him into the boardroom to have her high-level, ultra-important meeting. I rolled my desk chair to talk with Monique.

"This sucks, having to hang around so the Michelin Woman can do her grandstanding," I said.

"Karen and I are supposed to have dinner with another couple," Monique said. "I just wish she'd give us an idea about when we could leave," she said.

"You have any guesses on why Howard has picked me to be his confidant?" I asked.

She thought for a second, gazing down at the carpet with the darkest brown eyes I'd ever seen.

"Yeah, I think I do," she looked right at me. "There's something about you, Duff. When you're for someone, you exude a sort of unconditional positive regard."

"What?"

"I'm serious. You'll joke it off, but you connect with people and when they're the hopeless type, you do it very strongly."

"Isn't it just the handsome good looks and my strikingly handsome lanternlike jaw?"

"I knew you wouldn't take the compliment," she said, and she rolled back up to her desk. She wasn't pissed or doing anything for drama. If she identified that you were about to communicate in a disingenuous way, she moved on. That was Monique.

The afternoon snailed on and I was starting to get pissed because I had to keep calling Smitty to push back our departure. I didn't really care what time we hit the city but he was all about schedules and uniformity and he'd get wacky if we varied from it. He was already getting a little perturbed on the phone.

At five thirty the boardroom door opened and they all started to file out. My desk phone rang and I went to get it to hopefully tell Smitty I'd be on my way soon.

It was Howard.

"Duffy, it's me."

"Howard, slow down and talk to me. Tell me where you are and what's going on."

"I can't stay on, Duff. I know they'll have the phones traced and I don't blame that on you at all."

"Howard, look—"

"Duffy, you need to know it wasn't me. It's them and they're afraid of what I know. It's real big and it will ruin their lives. Don't believe I did it."

"How—" He hung up.

Claudia was busy talking to the board members and Monique had gone to the lesbian's room, so no one heard my conversation. I didn't want to spend the rest of the night with Morris and Larry Bird's mustache, nor did I want to listen to Claudia go on and on about, well, anything.

I didn't say anything. I waited for Claudia to tell us we could go, and then I called Smitty and he picked me and Rudy up at the Blue.

It was fight time.

9

MADISON SQUARE FUCKIN' GARDEN.

The ring that was home to Sugar Ray Robinson, Rocky Marciano, Jack Dempsey, Joe Frazier, Ali, and my idol, Willie Pep, was soon to be home, at least for a short while, to Duffy Dombrowski.

Smitty and I got to the Garden two hours before my bout, and we went in the special entrance on Seventh Avenue for fighters and officials. They checked our IDs and directed us to the fifth-floor dressing rooms. I didn't quite get how an arena could be on a fifth floor, but that's New York for you. We went up this industrial elevator and got out in a gray loading area with huge walls filled with dollies and wire. It smelled like old garbage and faintly like urine. The shiny Garden you see on your pay-per-view and touted as the world's most famous arena has a different feel in its bowels.

We snaked around a couple of corners until we saw a sign that said "Dressing Rooms." A security guard checked our passes and showed us through a narrow corridor with a dozen rooms. I guess if you're going to have the Ice Capades every year, you're going to need a lot of rooms. As I walked through the corridor I passed the framed photos of the Knicks and Rangers and then there were framed photos of some of the performers who had played the Garden. I went past photos of the Grateful Dead, the Rolling Stones, Sinatra, and Paul McCartney.

Smitty had walked ahead and called to me.

"Here it is, Duff. Let's get wrapped," he said.

"Hang on, Smitty," I said.

I kept on down the corridor, looking for it. I couldn't believe they wouldn't have it, but then, just past Springsteen, I saw it.

Elvis at the Garden, June 12, 1972. It was a great shot of him wowing the Garden fans. It was cool to see.

Just down the hallway was a fat old security guard, and I walked down to talk with him. Smitty was getting impatient.

"Duff, what the hell are you doin'?" he said.

"Hang on, just a second, Smit," I said.

I went up to the guard.

"Excuse me, sir."

"Fighters names are on the doors to their rooms," he said, barely looking at me.

"Yeah, I know, thanks," I said. "Can I ask you a question?"

"What?"

"How long have you worked at the Garden?"

"Since '70, why?"

"Any chance you worked the night Elvis played?"

"Yeah, I did. So?"

"Did you get to talk to him?"

"We all did. He gave us watches."

"Really?"

"Yeah—I was never a fan, but I'll tell you something," he said, looking me in the eye for the first time. "You'll never hear me say anything bad about Elvis Presley."

"Do you remember which room he dressed in?"

"I'll never forget—second one to the end. It's where we got the watches," he said.

I looked down the corridor to see a pissed-off Smitty, standing in front of the second dressing room to the end.

"Sir, thank you, thank you very much," I said.

Special things happened in this place. You could tell.

Smitty wrapped my hands and went through his routine. He didn't mention anything about how this kid was the best fighter that I had ever been in with by far. He didn't mention the Garden, he just said all the things he always said and he said them in the exact same way. I don't think any of that was a coincidence.

I was the fifth bout on a ten-bout card and there was one more bout after mine before the live television started. Mulrooney was the main event and he brought in the Irish, both of the Irish-American and the recent immigrant variety. In Mulrooney, they had something to get behind, an event right here in New York that they could come out to, where they could get drunk and be Irish. Most of them would be in the upper deck, and at $75 a pop you can't rightfully call them cheap seats.

A guy in a blue blazer with a New York Athletic Commission badge on poked his head in my dressing room and said "Time." I felt that weird feeling in my throat and a flushing in my face like I do before any bout, but tonight it was a little more intense. My legs felt funny underneath me like I had rented them. It was a little more than a little more intense.

I came out first for my bout because Marquason insisted on it in the contract. It's customary for the champion to enter the ring last, and that's kind of been adopted by whoever is the favorite to win. I walked through the hallway leading to the main floor and walked through the tunnel with the small scoreboard on top of it that you see on TV at about midcourt during basketball games. I got my first look at the immensity of the arena, which was now three-quarters filled. It was, in the true sense of the word, awesome. The crowd did their best to be indifferent to my entrance.

Marquason came in to some rap song with an entourage of about eight guys. His corner was worked by two of the game's most famous cornermen, so you know that his manager thought a lot of him. The one guy was that fat old guy who looked liked Fred Flintsone's uglier brother. Marquason was decked out in brand-new gear with paid endorsements all over, and when he came through the ropes he ignored me and floated around the ring in a choreographed warm-up. I got the impression that this guy hadn't fought in a union hall or a high-school gym—at least not in a long time.

Anticipating some Irish folks there for the main event, I wore my green robe and my green, orange, and white shorts with the shamrock in the middle. The ring announcer introduced us and when he said my name a roar went up from an upper-deck section waving Irish flags. I guess they heard "Duffy" and the "Dombrowski" didn't throw them. I looked up and it was a large section of people in green.

Marquason got applause but it was more subdued, like the crowd was being introduced to some sort of boy prince. The referee called us to the center of the ring for the ceremonial instructions, and then we went back to our corners to get ready for the bell. Smitty slipped in my mouthpiece and the bell rang. I tried to focus on boxing.

I couldn't feel my legs.

Marquason didn't move—he floated. The guy looked beautiful, like he was a body made just for this. My admiration was interrupted by his first jab, which hit me just under my right eye. It felt like someone hit me with a screwdriver. The kid was fast, he had power, and his punches were sharp.

I heard the ringside announcers say something about my knees buckling, which I wasn't aware of. I was aware of the loud "oooh" that came from the crowd. It was what came after that really startled me.

"DUFFY, DUFFY."

"DUFFY, DUFFY."

The Irish were in the house and they were pulling for their boy. I got chills and I began to feel my legs and enter that state of mind where I'm just boxing.

The chills didn't last long because Marquason stabbed me with his screwdriver again, only this time he followed it with a right and I found myself on the seat of my pants. It hurt but I was all right, and I sprang back up just in time to hear the bell ring. Well, I made it through one round, albeit by getting totally dominated and knocked down.

I sat on the stool that Rudy slid through the ropes and sipped the water Smitty offered. Smitty spoke to me in his usual steady and measured pace, but I wasn't focused. My head was ringing and my heart was beating fast.

"DUFFY, DUFFY."

"DUFFY, DUFFY."

It was getting louder.

I was up off the stool at the sound of the bell for the second. Marquason started to screw around and treat me like a prop. It was as if I were a piece of equipment for him to use to get his win, and even more than that, I was something to embarrass and show dominance over.

I threw some jabs that he caught with his gloves and I missed wildly with some hooks. He mugged at me, stuck his tongue out, and did the Ali shuffle. I didn't mind getting beat but I did mind getting disrespected. Okay, so the kid was near great and going to be great, but he didn't have to make me into an asshole.

He kept doing this one move where he'd drop his guard, stick his head out, and then lean in, begging me to hit him. Then when I'd move, he'd lean toward me and flash a jab that would stab me on the way in. Those jabs hurt, but it was actually something I'd hoped he'd do after seeing him do it on tape.

"DUFFY, DUFFY."

"DUFFY, DUFFY."

Man, you got to love the Irish. I felt my fist inside the satiny Mexican glove and it was time to give it a shot—probably my only shot. I knew my jab was good but I didn't know if I could pull off what I wanted to do. Who was I kidding—it *was* my only shot.

Marquason started the hands-down-leaning-in routine again. I tightened my fist and waited. He leapt, I stepped slightly to my left and threw the hardest, stiff-armed jab I had, just slightly off-center to his right eyebrow. It caught and I dragged it across his eyebrow and forehead as hard as I could.

It would take a second to see if it worked.

He backed up and circled abruptly, abandoning his showboat style. He stopped throwing punches and looked preoccupied. Then I got my first sign of success. Marquason rubbed his eyebrow and looked down at his glove. There was blood and there was a lot of it.

The expression on his face changed a bit. Blood dripped into his eye and little by little his fancy satin trunks were getting stained. I threw a regular jab that he blocked, but it was hard enough to force his own gloves into the cut. When he pulled back, the cut had spread. It was now almost two inches long and it was a quarter inch deep.

But was it enough?

The bell rang to end the second and there was a surge of activity around his corner. Back in my corner, Rudy iced my shoulders and Smitty was saying something I wasn't paying any attention to because I was trying to see around him into Marquason's corner. I saw the New York Athletic Commission doc come through the ropes.

Oh please, please.

"DUFFY, DUFFY."

"DUFFY, DUFFY."

It was more than a minute between rounds, which meant the doctor was concerned. He looked at Marquason, turned, and whispered something to the ref. And then it happened—it fuckin' happened.

The ref waved his hands over Marquason's corner wildly and I watched. I couldn't breathe. Fred Flintstone was throwing a fit, Marquason pushed the ref and was yelling, and the ref approached the scorer's table. I pushed Smitty out of the way to hear what he told the Commission table.

"TKO on doctor's recommendation," he said.

I froze. Smitty froze.

The handsome ring announcer climbed in the ring.

"On advice of the ringside physician, referee Peter Conboy stops the contest. The winner by TKO, Duffy Dombrowski!"

I jumped in the air and Smitty and Rudy caught me.

"DUFFY, DUFFY."

"DUFFY, DUFFY."

Oh, how you have to love the Irish.

10

Rudy hugged me so tight it hurt, and he wouldn't let go. Smitty smiled his crooked smile and laughed, shaking his head like a guy who just saw a dog riding a bicycle at the circus. He slapped me on the back and left it there as we headed for the dressing room.

Just before I left the Garden floor, there was a group of pasty-faced guys with turtlenecks, wool caps, and bad teeth. They had had more than a few and were hootin' and hollerin' for me behind some security guards.

"'Ere's to ya, Mr. Duff—you done all of us proud tonight, ya know," said the fattest one with the sweater that didn't quite cover the circumference of his belly.

"To Mr. Duffy!" he screamed, and his four friends yelled, "Hear, hear!"

The little guy at the end reached over the Garden security guard and handed me a full beer.

"You could use a pint, Duff," he said.

I couldn't remember smiling harder in my life, and I raised my glass to my new friends.

"To the Irish!" I said, and I headed into the locker room with the impatient inspector from the Commission, who had to take my gloves.

This was by far the biggest win and moment in my boxing career.

I didn't feel real, and although I beat Marquason by exploiting his tendency to cut and by throwing a somewhat questionable punch that utilized the construction of the glove, I wasn't besieged with guilt. See, inside the ropes, there are rules and then there are the real rules.

Fighters operate on a certain code, and I didn't violate that code. The code is you do anything you can with what you have at your disposal as long as your opponent has that same opportunity. We wore the same gloves and I hit him with a legal punch. I didn't lace him in the eye, I didn't kick him, and I didn't bite him in the ear. I didn't hold him and hit him, I didn't hit him on the break, and I didn't put any illegal substance on my gloves. I did hit him in a way that would bust his face open, and that may seem gross, but hey, this is the sport we both chose.

Marquason and his entourage weren't happy but they knew my win was on the up and up. Still, there would be complaints, protests, and undoubtedly a lot said. All of this came with upsetting a prospect and it didn't bother me in the least. It was a great moment and I wasn't in any hurry to get home.

"So, this punch looked an awful lot like that shit you've been doin' on the bags this week," Smitty said.

I smiled and laughed while he shook his head. I sipped my beer.

"It was a thing of beauty, kid," Smitty said. "I'm proud of you."

"Smitty, if it wasn't for you, where would I be—shit, who would I be?" I said.

Rudy came in from getting a beer and joined us.

"Hey, let's get out of here and celebrate. I don't feel like watching another three hours of boxing. Let's get to AJ's," Rudy said, and I couldn't have agreed more.

The hour-and-half ride was the best time I ever spent in a car—a few cold Schlitz travelers and fresh memories of something special. We were almost to the front door of AJ's when I remembered the fact that I hadn't divulged to anyone that I had gotten a phone call from a suspected serial killer the day before. Sooner or later I'd figure out what to do about all that, but for now all I knew was that it was Schlitz City.

Smitty passed on beers, as he often did, and shook my hand before Rudy and I went inside. He pulled away smiling from ear to ear.

"No, I ain't buying it," TC said.

"I'm tellin' you, it's the truth," Rocco said.

"Hold it." Jerry Number One was now involved. "You believe that men think of sex every seven seconds?"

"That's what they say," TC said.

Jerry Number Two was already counting.

"Five ... six ... seven ... All right, Rocco, what are you thinking of?" Jerry Number Two asked.

"That you're an asshole," Rocco said.

"That could be considered sexual," TC said.

"Hey, what are you saying, asshole?" Rocco said.

"He didn't wait another seven seconds that time," Jerry Number One said.

Jerry Number Two was counting again.

"Six … seven … TC, what are you thinking of?" Jerry Number Two asked. TC was in the process of ordering.

"AJ, I need another B&B," TC said.

"Hmm … what does that tell us?" Jerry Number Two said.

"Huh, were you talking to me?" TC said.

"What sexual thought did you just have?" Rocco asked.

"I was just thinking about a drink. You can't count those seven seconds."

Jerry Number Two was into another cycle.

"Five … six … seven … TC, what sexual thought are you having right now?"

"I wasn't ready. Maybe tits," TC said.

"Whatyamean 'maybe tits'?" Rocco said.

"It wasn't a deep thought. Do they have to be deep thoughts?" TC said.

"Define deep," Jerry Number One said.

"Six … seven … Jerry, what sexual thought are you having?" Jerry Number Two said.

"Huh? Uh … uh … tits, I guess," Jerry Number Two said.

Everyone groaned.

"Hey, no one said they had to be original thoughts," Jerry Number One said.

Due to the intense intellectual demands of the discussion, my entrance wasn't noticed until I sat next to Kelley. He did notice me, even though it looked like he'd been around for a while and the Coors Lights had slowed him a tad.

"Hey, Duff. How'd it go?"

"I won."

"No, seriously."

"Fuckin' A—I am serious. I cut him and won the TKO," I said.

"Holy shit! Congratulations!"

The Foursome heard Kelley's exclamation and cut off Jerry Number Two's counting at three.

"What's up, Kell?" TC said.

"Duffy beat the undefeated stud kid in the Garden tonight!"

"Seriously?" Rocco said.

"Yep," I said. "This is cause for a celebration. AJ, set up everyone with a shot of Jameson."

Everyone threw the shots back and slapped me on the back. I let Rudy fill in the guys with the details, which he happily did. I enjoyed the Jameson and the Schlitzes that followed it. Kelley was watching an ESPN Classic hockey game from the '80s and I knew he hated hockey, so I didn't feel that I would be interrupting him.

"What ya hear about Howard?" I asked.

"I think they know where he is."

"Really?"

"Yeah, yesterday I heard something about them being able to trace his calls," Kelley said.

"Yesterday? Shit—"

"Don't tell me."

"He called me at four thirty and I had to get to the Garden. It wasn't like I was going to hide anything."

"Duff, the guy's a fuckin' serial killer."

"We don't know that."

"Ugh…you're fuckin' nuts, you know that? People at the station know you know me, and when you do shit like that it makes me look like an asshole."

"I'll call Morris first thing in the morning. I'm sorry, really," I said.

It was tough to evaluate how pissed off Kelley ever got because he always looked annoyed, but I understood that tonight his annoyance was legit.

It was heading toward five in the morning and I figured I had crammed enough into a single day. I really wanted to stay up and have this day last forever, but I knew it wasn't possible, so when everyone else called it a night, I did too.

11

MARQUASON'S SCREWDRIVER SHOTS STARTED to hurt and between the Schlitz and the endorphins wearing off, sleep didn't come easy. I was in and out, sort of hovering around sleep when the phone rang. I looked up at the nightstand and the alarm clock with Elvis and the hound dog said 7:15.

In general, Al objected to phones and he was not pleased when they rang because they interrupted part of the twenty-two hours he slept each day. The woofing commenced. I tried to answer the damn thing and knocked it to the ground. When I reached over to pick it up, Al half licked, half nibbled on my ear, the sound violently bouncing off my eardrum. The Schlitz-induced blood ran to my head. I tried to say hello but the woofing was getting intense.

I opened the drawer to the nightstand and retrieved my side arm. The rapid-fire Israeli-looking piece was my trusty companion and something I brought out only when absolutely necessary. I aimed and fired, the shots catching Al right between the eyes. He spun around from the force of the blast and laid down whimpering.

The water Uzi was the only thing that would shut Al up. He would try to control his barking for a few minutes after taking fire, but I didn't like to use it because he really did get shot in the head once and I didn't want to bring back any bad trauma for the guy. A Schlitz hangover was an exception.

"Hello," I finally got to say into the receiver.

"Duff?"

"Who is this?"

"Howard," he said, and nothing else, as if he was expecting me to scold him.

"Howard—what's going on? You've got to come see the cops and clear things up," I said.

"Duff, I don't expect you to understand, but I can't. I can't trust the police."

"I know what you've been through, but I have a friend who's a cop and he's a good man."

"I don't think so, Duff."

"Howard, they've tapped the lines and they know where you are. Come meet me and my friend and we'll do this the right way. I'll help you out."

"I don't know, Duff. I don't like cops. You have no idea what I've been through."

"Then you've got to tell me, Howard—I don't like this guessing what's going on stuff."

"Meet me today in Jefferson Park by the bridge when the sun goes down. I'll tell you what I'm going through," he said.

"Look, Howard, I'm not a cop. I—" Before I could finish, he hung up.

What the hell had I gotten myself into?

What I wanted to get myself into was bed. The Schlitz/Marquason hangover was brutal and all I wanted to do was close my eyes and sleep for a week. For once, Al seemed to agree and he jumped up on my bed, did a double 360, and lay down in the center of the bed. I tried to push him to one side, and it was like trying to move a growling sack of sand.

After a Herculean effort stopping just short of a hernia, Al flopped over on his back, immediately fell asleep with all four legs in the air, and almost instantly began to snore. His snoring was proportionate to the size of his nose, so my bedroom sounded like a Southwest Airlines hangar. An IV of Valium wouldn't get me to sleep.

I tried once again to get Al to roll over, but there was something about him being on his back that perverted the laws of physics and made it impossible for him to right himself. I tried to get my hands underneath him to roll him when I was interrupted by a banging on the door. The banging made Al blast off the bed like a black, brown, and white space shuttle, and he headbutted me during his takeoff. Al ran to the door, barking the whole way while I grabbed my head and repeated the word "fuck" loudly.

When the pain subsided enough for me to get to the door, Al bounced up in his excitement and kicked me in the nuts, which normally I've trained myself to parry, but because I was still rubbing the knot that was forming on the side of my head, I didn't see it coming. There were to be no miracle hangover cures for Duff on this blessed morning.

Peering through the curtain of my trailer door, I realized the morning was getting absurdly painful. It was Billy and he had on a brand-new Bad-Breath Karateka pajama set, this one bright red. He also had two new pimples, one on the corner of his mouth and one on the left side of his forehead that appeared to have two heads.

"Billy, it's Sunday morning. What are you doing here at … what time is it, anyway?" I said.

"It's 7:21 a.m., sir," he said and then bowed.

I sort of nodded my head to bow because I didn't want to violate any ancient karate rules.

"Billy, did I say anything about training this morning?"

"No, sir. That is why I am here."

"Uh—"

"I've been practicing a new technique and I wanted to show you my progress as a surprise."

"Great—let's see," I said.

"Permission to demonstrate, sir?"

"What?"

"Permission to demonstrate, sir?"

"Fine," I said.

Billy backed up onto the little front lawn that I had and got into a formal stance and bowed. He stared at me motionlessly until I realized I hadn't returned his bow. I bowed in his general direction and felt the blood rush to my throbbing head.

"WASABIIIIIIIIIIIIIIIII!"

Following his enthusiastic tribute to Japanese horseradish, Billy ran toward the Moody Blue, leaped into the air, threw a front-leg kick, and landed uncomfortably on his shoulder and head. Then he started to scream in pain.

I ran down the stairs to make sure the goofy bastard was all right. He was rolling around in the gravel of my driveway, getting his new outfit all dirty.

"Sorry, sir. Sorry I failed," he said.

"Kid, you did fine. Don't worry about it," I said.

"I failed you, sir. I won't again."

"Kid you didn't fail, you established the wrong way to execute the flying front kick."

He sat up and stopped grimacing.

"Sir, your wisdom knows no bounds—it is clear you are a master."

He jumped to his feet, bowed formally, and thanked me again. Then he started his run home.

I began to wonder if I was hallucinating.

Al interrupted my introspection. He barked and looked up at me and then down between his legs where he had captured my newest TV remote. The life expectancy of my remotes was measured in hours, and I didn't feel like spending my hungover day watching Lifetime because for some twistedly evil reason it was the only channel I got when I had no remote.

I ran toward Al who became Barry Sanders in the open field of the Blue, darting through the living room, to the bedroom, back out, and into the kitchen. He zigzagged like a crazy hound but as he went to go through the living room a second time, he made the mistake of jumping on the sofa. I had him cornered and I went to box him in when he shifted in midair. I tried to cut back but he went right under the coffee table. I made the mistake of trying to shift my momentum in that direction and I went full force into the coffee table, shin first.

I fell to the carpet, holding my shin, and listened to Al chew his new electronic toy. I repeated the word "fuck" over and over.

I spent the day in bed, hovering over sleep—the kind of state that actually makes you feel less rested than if you had just gone on with your day and forgot about getting rested. I began to think that getting punched in the head, followed by greater than moderate consumption of Schlitz may not be the way to a holistic lifestyle. Whether that axiom was true or not, this was a lifestyle I took years to hone, and I didn't really see the utility in trying to move away from it.

I did feel like moving toward AJ's before my rendezvous with my new best friend, the alleged serial killer, Howard. A few Schlitzes and the intellectual stimulation of the Fearsome Foursome was just what the doctor ordered.

———————

"It was in some medical journal," Jerry Number One said.

"Bullshit," Rocco said.

"Let me get this straight." TC tried to add some sanity to the discussion. "If you light up a cigarette from the wrong end it stops the flow of blood to your wiener?"

"Exactly, and if you do that once a month, in about two years you won't be able to get it up at all," Jerry Number One said.

"I wonder if this qualifies for the seven-second rule," Jerry Number Two said.

"I swear, if you start counting I'm going to whack you with this glass," Rocco said.

"There's some sort of chemical in the cigarette that has an anti-Viagra effect," Jerry Number One said.

"You mean you see a color other than blue?" Jerry Number Two asked.

"I'm still thinking of tits—that's all I can come up with," TC said.

"What's the name of the chemical in the cigarette, Jer?" Rocco asked.

"Let me think … it's something like limpfadoraphyl … no that's not it. It was woodrowdeflatus, I think … hold it, it was micoxaphlopin," Jerry Number One said.

"My-cock's-a-floppin'? That can't be right," Rocco said.

"Nothin' right about that at all," Jerry Number Two said.

"Tits—it's all I get ever since Jerry Number Two put this seven-second thing in my head," TC said.

I didn't interrupt the brain trust and instead took my seat next to Kelley who was staring at a retrospective featuring a replay of the time Havlicek stole the ball. The Johnny Most call was probably great the first thousand times I heard it, but now it was getting on my nerves.

"I'm hoping there's no micoxaphlopin in Coors Light," I said.

"Hey, Duff," Kelley said.

"I talked to Howard this morning and promised to meet him tonight. You wanna come?" I somehow thought if I just blurted it out, Kelley would take it easier. I was mistaken.

"You're fuckin' nuts, you know that? Do you realize the kind of trouble you're putting yourself in? I thought you said you were going to call Morris."

"The guy's scared to death and I promised him. I told him you're cool and that I'd bring you."

Kelley didn't say anything. He just stared at me. His eyes almost bore laser holes through my skin. I took a pull off the Schlitz longneck.

"I'm meeting him at sundown at the bridge in the park—you in?"

"Uh geez," was all Kelley said. He turned away and watched Havlicek sink the runner against Phoenix in '77.

12

Jefferson Park is across town from AJ's, and with the lights it's a ten- or fifteen-minute drive. I threw in Elvis's *Promised Land* eight-track and clicked through to the fourth program to listen to "If You Talk In Your Sleep." It's a haunting song about a couple slinking away to have an affair. It was dark and a little sleazy, which was how I felt going to see a man who had murdered four people and whom most folks believed was responsible for murdering four more.

I parked by the tennis courts and walked through the rolling knolls of the park, past the statue of Moses, the modern-art sculptures, and the empty tulip beds. I had hit the cobblestone walkway that led toward the bridge when I heard a voice call me from behind.

"Wait up, nutcase." It was Kelley.

"Hey, what're you doing here?" I said.

"The Foursome started talking about John Wayne's colon again, and I figured meeting Howard had to be more pleasant than that."

"Let's hope so," I said.

We walked the final fifty yards to the bridge and the twilight had given way to the night. The corner of the bridge was dimly lit with one of those retro streetlamps that throw a soft amber hue to everything, which gave the bridge area an even creepier feel. There was no one there yet.

"I hope we didn't miss him," I said.

"Yeah, that would be a shame," Kelley said.

We walked the fifty-foot span of the bridge to check the other side, and there was no sign of Howard or anyone else. The silence Kelley and I stood in made me a tad more nervous, though with Kelley, silence didn't necessarily mean anything. Still, the nervousness gave me a knot in the left side of my chest and my breathing wasn't as smooth as I liked.

After a moment passed, Kelley started to walk around the entrance to the bridge in a way that most people would consider mindless strolling. I knew better. He stopped and suddenly squatted.

"What is it?" I asked.

"Blood," he said.

Kelley was squatting over a pool of blood the size of a Frisbee.

"I should call and get a crime-scene team out here, Duff. You okay with that?"

"Of course."

———————

We hung around and waited for the circus to begin. Morris and his gang came along with the special crime-scene guys who looked remarkably less glamorous and, for that matter, less intelligent, than the people on those *CSI* shows. There were three of them and they scooped up the blood, set up crime-scene tape, and poked around the bushes and the grass. I sort of expected them to wear asbestos suits and have electron microscopes fixed to their heads, but they did most of their work with tweezers and Ziploc bags you could get at CVS. Morris and his guys had their badges clipped to their jackets just like the cops on *Law & Order* do, though it looked more natural and less forced on Jerry Orbach. My best friend Mullings walked by me and shook his head like he disapproved of my existence, which probably wasn't going to keep me from sleeping. I had plenty of things running around my head that kept me from sleeping, but whether or not detective Mullings approved of me wasn't one of them.

Morris, who so far had seemed like a decent guy, was markedly less polite when he finally got around to talking to me this time. He had his hands inside his trench coat when he walked up the bridge to talk to me. He had a look on his face like he just ate something that had spoiled.

"We could arrest you for about eleven different things, you know, Dombrowski," Morris said.

"Look, I was going to call you, I swear. I was here to meet Howard to bring him to you. I knew it was the only way he'd go," I said.

Morris turned toward Kelley.

"Can you vouch for this nutcase?"

"Yeah, Detective Morris, what he said is the truth. He's all right. A little misguided in his energy sometimes, but he's all right," Kelley said.

Morris turned back to me. I took note that both Kelley and Morris had referred to me as a "nutcase."

"This time, out of respect for Kelley, I'm not going to make a deal out of you not notifying us before this little rendezvous of yours, but from here on out—no more bullshit, you understand?"

"Gotcha," I said.

There was another twenty minutes or so of more putzing around by the lab guys and intense posturing by the other cops who had honed their whole intense furrowed-brow, tormented-by-the-criminal-world look. There was just something about people who tried so hard to create an image that I found so contrived—like they didn't have enough inside them to just be who they are. Instead of being themselves, they take on roles and personas to do the work of developing a personality for them.

Kelley and I walked back to our cars through the park in silence. When we got to our cars, I broke the silence.

"That's his blood, you know," I said.

"I know," Kelley said.

Kelley went to get in his car.

"Does it change how you're looking at this whole thing?"

"Yeah."

Kelley didn't say anything, he just went to unlock his door.

"Hey, Kell?" I said.

"What?"

"Misguided?"

13

By midafternoon Monday, Kelley had called me at the office and confirmed that it was Howard's blood in the park. You didn't have to be a brain surgeon to deduce that something went extremely wrong with Howard, but a certain psychiatrist didn't see that kind of obvious reasoning at all.

"It could be consistent with Howard's personality disorder for him to self-mutilate, especially if it could get him sympathy and attention," Abadon said. We were all at an afternoon meeting to discuss his situation.

"Doesn't it make more sense that he was trying to do the right thing but was scared? Then he was assaulted in the park or something?" I said.

"That's what he wants you to believe, Duffy. I think you're being manipulated," Claudia said.

"You don't think there's even a small chance that Howard is frightened about the situation and that he believes there's no way he could be treated fairly?" I said.

"It's likely that Rheinhart is getting off on all the media exposure and the misguided attention Duffy is showing him." Claudia didn't answer me directly but instead talked to everyone.

"If you pray, pray that God protects our community during this time," Abadon said. He had a cross on his lapel today. Dr. Abadon always had a small cross on his jacket lapel but he had never referenced any Christian stuff before.

"Shouldn't we support one of our clients—even a little bit?" I said.

"I believe when a client is clearly perpetuating evil—what I call sin—it is imperative that we don't give him support," Abadon said.

"It bothers me that you're so certain, Doctor," I said. Abadon smiled and looked down at his folded hands.

"We need to move on," Claudia said.

I felt some tension in my hands and noticed that my right hand had balled up, halfway forming a fist, and I had a little twitch going in my neck. I suppose, at least according to Abadon, that what I wanted to do right now was sinful. If you asked me, it was as natural as the day is long.

Though we moved off of Howard, unfortunately for me the meeting wasn't even close to being done. After we finished discussing Howard, Monique and I had other cases to present to Claudia and Abadon for their review. It was two and half more hours of human-services bliss, and the tedium and arrogance got my systolic blood pressure up as high as Star Jones's weight.

When the day finally ended, I needed a comprehensive sanity plan to clear my head. The plan needed to be holistic, and that meant I needed to nurture my inner child with a trip to the gym to hit the bags. Then, I would need to bond with my support group for eight or ten Schlitzes and an order of AJ's toxic wings. It was a plan that would bring me back to my center.

———————

I was heading down the steps to the gym when I heard "WASA-BIIIIIIIII!" followed by a thud that sounded like someone dropped a sack of potatoes from a second-story window.

As I came through the door, there was Billy in another new outfit, rubbing the back of his head as he sat on the floor. Across the way in the door to his office was Smitty, who stood leaning against the threshold, shaking his head.

As soon as he saw me, Billy bounded to his feet, stood up straight, and yelled about Japanese horseradish.

"Bill, again with the horseradish?"

"Sir?" Billy had a giant red zit on his left cheek the size of a Hershey's Kiss.

"Never mind. Look, you and I will train after my workout. Go stretch or something," I said.

"Sir, yes sir!"

"Right."

I walked over to Smitty, who was rolling his eyes.

"Good afternoon, señor," Smitty said.

"That's sensei," I said. "Show some respect, will ya?"

"I got a call today."

"Yeah, another fight already—let's do it."

"This one was a little different."

"Huh?"

"It was the spiky-haired guy. He's interested in you. Liked the way the Irish went nuts for you. Figured you'd bring 'em in in the smaller venues all around New York and Boston, and then he could drape the Polish flag around you and take you to Chicago and Milwaukee," Smitty said.

"You shittin' me?"

"Nope. Talked to him for an hour. He's got a plan."

"Tell me."

"He wants you to get one more win, which will give you five straight. That qualifies you for a shot at the NABU belt. The belt is almost worthless, but it will make you a champion and get you a couple of extra thousand every time you fight. That, and you'll be a small-time headliner."

"What's the catch?"

"None, as far as I can tell. The next fight is to set you up for the title fight, and it will be an easy one. He's got some guy from Arkansas named Jerry Perryman, who you should go through easily."

"When's this going to happen?"

"He wants it in two weeks, while you're still being talked about."

"Let's do it—you up for it?"

"You know I'm not the spiky-haired guy's biggest fan, but I can't see the downside, Duff. This is a hell of an opportunity."

Smitty took me through my workout and briefed me about Jerry Perryman, opponent. He wasn't in great shape but had a fifty-fifty record. That didn't really mean a whole lot because he did most of his fighting down south where boxing gets really suspect. Promoters put fights on every week and a lot of the same guys fight each other all the time. It's easy to get twenty wins in the South in a year and half. It's also easy to get that many losses. Perryman was 20 and 18 and never fought north of Tennessee.

After my time with Smitty, Billy and I did the karate thing. He evoked Japanese horseradish and insisted on practicing his flying kicks, which he performed with amazing consistency. Amazing, that is, by the way he landed on his back every single time he threw one. The kid had zero natural ability, but he did work hard and for that I respected him. We finished up doing some pushups together, stretching a little to cool down, and then, of course, bowing. I said goodbye to Smitty, and Billy and I headed to the locker room together. Just as we were passing the karate room, Mitchell and Harter were coming out.

"Two of life's losers," Mitchell said. He and Harter had stopped on the stairs blocking our path.

"Just different sizes and ages. Hey, Billy, are you learning how to be a bigger loser?" Harter said.

"Is that even possible?" Mitchell added.

I kept walking and motioned to Billy to come along. I walked between the two tough guys, not breaking stride.

"Hey, you guys ought to get a comedy routine in a nightclub or something," I said, and I shouldered my way through the two of them.

"Duffy—watch your back," Harter said.

"Tell you what, guys. Why don't you guys go rent a Steven Seagull movie and whack off to it. It'll be a good workout for those dragons on your forearms."

"Keep it up, Polack," Mitchell said.

"Ooh, yikes. C'mon, Billy, before they start making Bruce Lee noises."

Billy and I headed to the locker room without a word to each other, and I could tell he was still freaked out by the interaction. He got quiet and wouldn't look at me.

"What's wrong, kid?" I said.

"Nothing, sir."

"C'mon, what's bothering you?"

"Nothing, sir."

"Look, Bill, don't let them get to you. They're pussies on the inside where it counts."

"Yes, sir, but don't you think you should be careful around them?"

"That's what they want and we ain't going to give that to them."

I took my karateka home, and even though I tried to kid with him, he was still a little spooked. The fact that these karate guys got into his head to such a degree pissed me off.

Days like this taxed me and I needed to continue to round out my holistic stress management plan. I had exercised, passed on a little of the ancient martial arts, and now it was time I headed to that bastion of New Age feel goodedness—AJ's. In addition to unwinding, I wanted to get the full details regarding Howard's blood, and I knew Kelley would be there.

"She had them taken out and then put back in?" TC said.

"Actually, they were taken out, put in, taken out, and put in again," Jerry Number Two said.

"Can they even do that? Doesn't all the tittage get dispersed?" Jerry Number One asked.

"Tittage? What are you, freakin' French?" Rocco said.

"It has to do with whoever she's married to, I think. Each guy gets to order his own fun-bag size," TC said.

"What do they do with, as Rocco calls it, the leftover tittage?" Jerry Number One said.

"What do you mean?" TC asked.

"Well, when she gets them reduced, where does the tittage go?" Jerry Number One said.

"On eBay—I think they auction it," Jerry Number Two said.

"What do they put it in?" TC asked.

"Mason jars, I think," Jerry Number Two said.

"I might bid on that. It would be a collector's item, and if she got a new boyfriend I could sell it to him," TC said.

"Man, you guys are boobs—they recycle it for insulation," Rocco said.

"How warm could that keep you?" Jerry Number One said.

"It depends what you did with it," Jerry Number Two said.

"There wouldn't be much, at least not enough to cover an attic," TC said.

"I don't know—have you ever seen her in a bikini?" Jerry Number Two said.

"Hey—does this count toward the seven-second thing?" TC asked.

As you might expect, Kelley was turned away, doing his best to watch a replay of a classic women's golf tournament. I'm guessing none of the competitors had any artificial tittage issues.

"It was definitely Howard, huh?" I said.

"Yeah—they checked with the prison and it was his blood," Kelley said.

"What do you think happened?"

"I think Howard got there and somebody didn't want him to meet you."

"Yeah, me too."

"Kell—does this change your view on his guilt?"

"Yeah, to some extent."

"What do we do about it?"

"We? Don't tell me you're getting back in the private-eye business." Kelley rolled his eyes.

"Uh…" I didn't know how to say what was on my mind.

"Oh geez…"

"I just feel like someone has to look out for Howard. Everyone's against him."

"It's tough to get people on your side when you have his history."

"Yeah but—"

"Duff, he brutally murdered four kids."

"Thirty years ago. Doesn't a guy ever get to live that down?"

"Not in my book."

"Maybe in mine. Maybe what was going on inside him was so painful that his choices were narrowed."

"Now you're starting to sound like those assholes you work with."

"It's different. I know everyone's responsible for what they do, but couldn't it be the case that for some people, doing the right thing is just really, really fuckin' hard?" I took a sip of the Schlitz.

"Allow for that and you got chaos in society," Kelley said.

"I'm just talking about one guy—not all of society."

"Look, Duff, I'm not a real complicated guy and I don't do a complicated job. I bust guys who break the law." Kelley took a pull of his Coors Light. "The bigger issue is you getting involved. Last time you did, it wreaked havoc, people died… shit, you almost died.

99

Everything came out okay, but it almost didn't. Use your head and let the cops handle this one," he said.

We sat quietly for a second and I knew he was right. It wasn't my job, it wasn't my role to defend the universe or even to come to Howard's rescue. I was overinvolved already and I had enough going on in my life that I didn't need to play Robin Hood.

"You're right. I need to back off," I said.

"Promise me, you'll stay away from the hero stuff," Kelley said.

"Yeah, it doesn't feel quite right but it makes sense. No more 'Duffy for Hire.'"

"AJ, let me buy Duffy's next Schlitz."

Kelley didn't buy my drinks very often.

14

I CONTINUED TO TRAIN for my bout with Perryman. It wasn't the real intense training you do to get in shape, it was the type of training you do to stay sharp and keep your engine tuned. It's hard for people to understand, but more isn't better when it comes to training. Probably the biggest problem you see with fighters is overtraining—that is, they do too much. Guys will try to work out their anxiety by pushing themselves extra hard, and come fight night they've left all their energy back in the gym. I've been around long enough to know not to do that.

My new spiky-haired promoter called Smitty and let him know that my bout was going on a card featured at the Altamont Fair. The fair is a big county to-do up the Thruway near Albany, and it drew a couple hundred thousand people every year for a week in August. I don't know how he pulled it off, but he had a five-card show scheduled for the weekend and fairgoers would only have to pay an extra ten bucks on top of their fair admission to get in to the fights.

Big-time promoters could make things happen and make things happen quickly. The notoriety the Garden fight gave me was going to be short-lived, so he had to exploit it quickly. I didn't mind; I was used to taking short-notice fights, and besides, Jerry Perryman was guaranteed to be as mediocre as it got. The Crawford newspaper, the *Union Star*, even did a profile of me and explained how the fight was a lead-in to the NABU title fight.

Newspaper stories covering my fights were few and far between. I almost never fought close to Crawford, and most of the time they never covered it. Now I was a human interest story because of my counselor job and my overnight success as a prizefighter. Never mind that the overnight success took fourteen years.

Meanwhile, Al was still making me nuts with all his running around the trailer. It had gotten to be an every-morning thing, maybe because Billy seemed to show up uninvited almost every morning to demonstrate a new way he could fall on his head. Al didn't like the unannounced visits, so even when Billy didn't come he'd bark and run around to ward off anyone who might show up. The bruises and welts on my shins from when Al would duck for cover just ahead of my grasp were piling up like the notches on a cowboy's gun.

I called my old friend Jamal for some canine guidance. Jamal was a fighter who had hung up his gloves after a lackluster pro career and he also was in the Nation of Islam. That's where he met Walanda, a client of mine who was murdered a while back. She was Al's original master after he flunked out of the Nation's bomb-sniffing canine program. It wasn't that Al couldn't sniff explosives—in fact, he was very good at it and even helped me uncover a terrorist aiming to drop a dirty bomb on Yankee Stadium last year.

The problem with Al was that he was always shitting and pissing on everything and that didn't go over too well with the bow-tied and righteous brothers.

I wanted Jamal's recommendations for calming Al down. I got him on his cell.

"Hey Duff—I'm surprised you even talk to little people like me now that you've hit the big time," Jamal said.

"Oh, I'm big all right," I said.

"White guy with an Irish name—shit, you got it made as long as you keep winnin'. Who they got for you?"

"Some guy named Perryman from Arkansas."

"Boy, they takin' care of you, huh?"

"Yeah, I guess—hey, what do I do to get my short-legged Muslim brother to settle down? He's making me nuts."

"Shittin' and pissin', huh?"

"Actually, I've kind of gotten used to that. It's the crazy running all around the house."

"Take him tracking. Have him follow someone around or just take a walk without him and leave a hunk of food at the end of your walk. He loves to find where people went."

"You're kidding me."

"No, it's what hounds are supposed to do."

"So pretty much get lost and have him find me?"

"Duff, people been tellin' you to get lost for years, haven't they?"

"Yeah—I've never done it though."

"No, Duff, no you haven't."

I thanked Jamal and figured, what the hell. I got Al's leash, flopped his fat ass up on my Eldorado's passenger seat, and drove him over to TC's house. TC lived in a cushy suburb of Crawford known as

Londonville, which bordered the industrial section, just a couple of miles from AJ's. On the way over, Al started to whine because I was listening to the sports radio station. I know that whine and it was Al's way of saying he wanted to hear Elvis sing "Can't Help Falling in Love." He was crazy about the tune and there was no use fighting it. If I didn't throw in the *Blue Hawaii* eight-track, the whining would get unbearable.

Elvis just got past the "Wise men say…" part when Al settled in, let out a big sigh, and relaxed.

We got to TC's house and his car wasn't there, so I figured he wasn't home, which was actually what I was hoping. I didn't knock on the door, I just had Al sniff the lawn chair by the garage that TC sits in on those rare occasions that he's home and not at AJ's. Al started to sniff all over the chair like it was covered in sardines and then he looked up.

"Go find!" I said, just like Jamal told me to.

Al bolted along TC's front lawn, nose to the ground like an anteater addicted to cocaine. He continued along the street, pausing at telephone poles and street signs to sniff their bases. Occasionally, he would pause and then run around in a circle like he was creating a whirlpool of scent for his nose. Then, he'd be back on the trail, working his ass off to the point that I had trouble holding on to him. He was definitely into smelling where TC went and he just wouldn't let it go.

He was almost on a dead run for a half an hour and we covered the distance to AJ's in no time. We were coming up on AJ's when he abruptly stopped, squatted, and let go. Nature was taking its course, and Al finished up by proudly kicking gravel over his trophy before sprinting off for TC. In about ten minutes we were at AJ's front door.

I opened the door up and Al bounded through with such vigor that I lost the hold on his leash. He darted for TC, who was saying something about the fact that when ducks quacked it didn't echo, and Al went airborne and caught TC right in the nuts. The B&B left his hands and covered his shirt while Al started to lick his prey's face.

"Ughhhhh! … Duffy—I'm going to get dog-related AIDS … ," TC said.

"There's our favorite basket hound," Rocco said. Al was pushing his ample nose into TC's face, licking and nibbling on TC's ears.

"Dog likes B&B," Jerry Number One said.

"Rocco—he's a basset hound. We've been over this," I said.

"That's right, he's French," Jerry Number Two said.

"He's a frog dog?" Rocco said.

"I didn't think he could swim. Where do they put the tanks?" Jerry Number One said.

"What the hell are you talking about?" TC said, wiping slobbered B&B from his cheek.

"Frog dog—like, you know, like in the Navy. Don't they use underwater bassoon hounds to sniff out explosives?" Jerry Number One asked.

"He can't swim. Basset hounds have the densest bones of all dog breeds and they sink," I said, having watched Animal Planet.

"Shitty frog dogs then, huh?" Jerry Number One said.

"You sure it's not the weight from the tanks?" Jerry Number Two said.

It was a little early for me to sit and pound a few Schlitzes, so I bid the guys a quick early afternoon farewell and walked Al home. Just as Jamal promised, he was remarkably more subdued. Maybe it was the tracking or maybe it was simply the exertion, but it didn't matter to me. If it would mellow Al out, I'd take him for synchronized swimming lessons—with or without the tanks.

When we got back to the Blue there was a message from Smitty. Apparently, Jerry Perryman's license had been suspended and they had to get me a new opponent. The new guy was named Rufus Strife from Oklahoma and his record was even worse than Perryman's. Like me, Strife was a short-notice guy who would get paid more than Perryman because he was taking the fight on even shorter notice. None of it mattered to me; I knew the guy was coming in to be a stiff.

15

For the first time in my professional boxing career, I was excited about possibilities. Don't get me wrong, I loved to fight and I got off on the thrill of it, but I never really allowed myself to believe that it was going someplace. This new opportunity wasn't necessarily for a starring role in the game, but it meant being someone rather than just an opponent.

It's a weird business. I felt like I stepped on the right Monopoly square, and I have to admit I liked what was happening. I've always played the guy who was being sent in for cannon fodder, and now they were finding me a setup. I didn't feel bad over that—Strife would get his paycheck and go home just like I've done lots of times.

I couldn't remember being in better shape. I wasn't fooling myself, I knew the NABU was not a real championship, but even marginal titles meant more fights, more TV, and more money. I had been a pro for eight years and getting to wear a championship belt, even a goofy one, was a big deal to me.

The promoter loved the response I got at the Garden from the Irish. In boxing you can become a folk hero if a nationality gets behind you. He was talking about plans for Chicago, Milwaukee, Boston, and even Belfast or Warsaw down the road, maybe not as a headliner but as a co-feature or added attraction that would get the crowd going. It sure beat fighting in front of disinterested crowds who had no idea who you were and cared even less. Irish and Polish fans came out for their countrymen because of their nationalistic pride and because of the fact that the beer was pretty cheap at the fights. That was cool with me.

So it was pretty clear: win this fifth fight and get a chance to fight for a belt. Win the belt and every fight means a bit more money. The fight with Strife at the fair was going to be broadcast on the Gotham Cable Network, which featured weekly TV fights that weren't what you'd call "world class." Honestly, a fight card where Duffy Dombrowski is the feature attraction is not exactly world class—not yet anyway.

Fight night came and I was walking on clouds. There were several thousand fans from the area and for the first time ever, Crawford was seeing me as their guy. It felt a little weird but I loved it and it charged me up. I got to the fair a couple of hours before my bout during one of the early prelims and found our makeshift dressing rooms were in the cinder-block building in the center of the fairgrounds.

Smitty wrapped my hands in his usual deliberate fashion, all the while reciting his mantra of fundamentals. They were the same pre-fight things he's said for the last fourteen years to me and to everyone else he's trained. It's not that he's not creative or doesn't know the game inside and out—he definitely does. He believes down to his bones that boxing is a matter of doing the right things over and over, every training session, every round and every fight. He, of course, was right.

Strife had the dressing room right next to mine and, unlike a lot of fighters before fights, he was quiet. I saw him briefly at the weigh-in and the pre-fight physicals, and let's just say, he was less than imposing. Simply put, he was fat, slow moving, and he looked disinterested. These weren't the characteristics of a champion, which was okay by me. If ol' Rufus wanted to get a payday and go home, that was going to be just fine.

While the preliminaries were going on on the Gotham Network, announcers came into my dressing room to get some comments they could air during our introductions. It was the usual TV shit—actually, who am I kidding? I've been on TV a couple of times but never as a feature fighter, so this was hardly usual for me. What was usual were the idiotic questions about my strategy, what the fight meant, et cetera, et cetera. My strategy was to hit the other guy more than he hit me, and the fight meant a chance to make some cash. Of course I didn't say that, but that was the real deal. The commentator was a guy named Bobby Briggs who had held the middleweight title for a month or so in the '70s. He was a fighter and a decent guy.

"Duffy, can you tell us what this fight means to you?" Briggs asked.

"It means a chance at a belt but more importantly it means a chance to show my hometown who I am and what I can do," I said.

"Do you have a game plan to handle Strife?"

"Well, he won't have to find me—I plan to be right in front of him, pressing the action."

"Thanks, Duffy. Good luck." Briggs finished up with me and spoke with the camera guys about some technical stuff before moving on. They left me and I presumed they went over to talk to Rufus, who was still silent in his room. He didn't even bring a cornerman, instead he was going to use a local guy and pay him fifty bucks from his purse. That wasn't unheard of, but it was pretty sad even by boxing standards.

Smitty started to have me loosen up with some pad work. Before fights he spent most of the time drilling the recoil again and again to burn it into my mind even more just before I went in the ring. The goal was to get me to break a light sweat before I went in the ring and it was a good strategy. Guys who went in cold and dry often got caught with a punch they weren't expecting.

Smitty had me take a break and I heard Briggs outside the door arguing with some producer type wearing a head set.

"I don't care what you say," Briggs said. "It ain't right and I ain't using it."

"C'mon, Bobby it makes great stuff," Headset said.

"The fuckin' guy's mom dies two days ago and he takes the fight for funeral expenses and you think that's cool? Fuck you." Briggs said.

The headset guy walked away with his arms up in the air for maximum dramatic effect. I walked over to Briggs against Smitty's protest.

"Kid, get your head where it belongs," Smitty said.

"Hang on," I said.

I walked up the hallway to find Briggs. I called to him to slow down.

"Hey, Bobby," I said.

"Yeah, Duff?"

"That shit about Strife's mom—is that true?"

"Kid," Briggs said. "It's not your concern. Go warm up," he said.

"But—"

"Look, Duff, I got to get to the ring."

He walked away and I stood there, not sure what to think. I turned just in time for Strife to leave his dressing room to make his ring walk. Handwritten on his terrycloth robe was "For Momma."

Smitty scolded me back to the dressing room and told me to get my head into the fight. I tried and got ready to walk out to the ring. I felt sick to my stomach, but it wasn't the usual pre-fight jitters—this was different. I walked out to the strains of Elvis's opening, the *2001: A Space Odyssey* theme, and tried to get ready. The crowd cheered my entrance and I heard them, but it was like I was removed from it at the same time. Something wasn't right.

In the ring, Strife's robe was off and it was clear he wasn't in any kind of shape at all. His gut hung over his trunks and he had "Laney RIP" written on his beltline. The sickness in my stomach grew. The ref brought us together for instructions and Strife looked to the ceiling. Tears trickled down his cheeks, and we touched gloves and went back to our corners. As he turned he said, "Momma, for you."

I almost threw up.

In the corner, Smitty put my mouthpiece in and told me to concentrate. The bell rang for the start of the fight, and I came out of the corner doing my best to be instinctive. Rufus was fat and didn't move well. I hit him with the first jab I threw and his knees actually wobbled a bit.

"Move in!" Smitty yelled. "He's hurt!"

I didn't move. I threw another jab. Strife wobbled again.

"Move in, God damn it!" Smitty yelled.

I stepped toward Strife but no punches came. He threw a hook that missed and he went off balance. I have no idea who this guy had been fighting, but I couldn't picture someone losing to him.

My third jab landed on his nose pretty hard and it forced him back to the ropes. This time I did move in, and as I did I heard Strife let out a wail, like an exhausted cry. I tried to go on automatic.

"Finish, Duff, finish strong!" Smitty yelled.

I hit Strife twice to the body, which doubled him over, and then I hooked him to the head with my right and he wobbled into the corner. I loaded up with my straight left to put him out and I threw it hard and straight. He was hurt and there was no way he was going to last, but just when I thought the ref might call it, the bell rang, ending the first round.

Back in my corner, Smitty was furious.

"What the hell are you waiting for? You had him, now take him out!" he said.

Round 2 started and Strife was breathing heavily; he already looked exhausted. I tried not to think and I moved forward. My jab went through his gloves and sent his head back. I followed with a body shot that made him moan and double over. Then, I caught him with an uppercut. I knew the end was near and I threw my straight left.

I never saw it land.

I never felt it land.

Instead, the world went from vertical to horizontal instantly. A light shot through the inside of my head from side to side and there was a loud ringing. Noise sounded different and things looked like they were underwater. I blinked hard four or five times. I was looking at the lighting stanchions above the ring and they made me squint.

I realized I was on one knee and the referee was in front of me. He was in an exaggerated counting stance and the first number I heard was seven.

I went to get up. Nothing happened.

"Eight," the ref said.

I went to push off my knee and my gloves slipped off.

"Nine."

I tried again but wobbled backward in an awkward crouch and landed on the seat of my pants.

"Ten."

The ref was above me waving his hand back and forth. The state doctor was shining a pen light in my eyes, there was a lot of crowd noise, and Smitty was lifting me onto the stool in the middle of the ring.

Across the way, Rufus Strife had fallen to his knees and was crying into his hands.

There were ring announcements, then the interviews, but the announcers spent most of their time with Rufus, who shouted and cried and hugged everyone he could. I congratulated him and he hugged me just before I went to the locker room. My head had cleared and I was fine. I've taken harder shots, much harder shots, but when you don't see it coming, ten seconds isn't a long time to recover.

The quiet in my dressing room was uncomfortable. Smitty didn't look at me, Rudy left to get a beer, and I dressed in silence. I showered and dressed as fast as I could because I wanted to get out of there. It felt weird.

As was the tradition, Smitty drove me home after the fight. We were in the car for forty-five minutes before either of us spoke.

"Duff," Smitty said. "How many years I been training you?"

"Fourteen, Smitty, you know that."

"In the last fourteen years, you've lost a fair number of fights, right?"

"Yep, you know that."

"In all those fights you lost, when have you ever been knocked out from a shot because you didn't recoil your left?"

"Never," I said.

"Uh-huh," Smitty said.

We drove the last twenty minutes in silence, and I felt lousy about ten different ways, most of all because I let Smitty down. You see, winning fights and moving up is moving up for him too. It was a validation of all the work he's done. And I lost.

He pulled up in front of the Moody Blue.

"Duff, for the last fourteen years, what have I told you after every fight?"

"That win or lose, you're proud of me."

"That's right. I'm proud of you tonight too, Duff."

"Tonight? You sure? I fought like shit," I said.

"Yep," Smitty said.

16

I WAS DRUNK BY noon.

Legally, AJ's isn't supposed to open until noon, but a lot of times AJ will stay open all night for the guys who work the graveyard shift in the cookie factory around the block. At noon, the Foursome started to come in, and I was praying they wouldn't grill me about my performance.

They had all gone to the fight, as did Kelley and some of the people from the office. It pissed me off—I finally got to a point where I get some hometown attention and I lose in the most embarrassing fashion imaginable. There was a lot on the line, I was fighting a fat, out-of-shape guy with a shit record, and he beats me in front of my hometown crowd. Check that, he knocked me out in front of my hometown crowd.

AJ's always had the paper and it had a photo of me on the front section of the sports section sprawling to the canvas after I tried to get up. The cute banner above it read, "Dombrowski Falls Back to Palookaville."

Sweet.

TC and Jerry Number One came in together like they often did. They didn't come in the same car nor did they call each other, they just wound up always coming through the door at the same time. Less than fifteen minutes later Jerry Number Two arrived, followed by Rocco. They always came in the same order, always spaced by the same amount of time.

I was braced for questions about how it happened or suggestions on how they would have done things differently. I waited for some cockeyed philosophy about how getting knocked out was a good thing followed by a two-hour discussion about the brain science involved in rendering someone unconscious.

The guys greeted me, said hello, and ordered their drinks. Then, they just watched the TV and the pre-game show for a preseason football game. I waited and they never mentioned anything about the fight.

It made it worse.

I decided that the Schlitz wasn't getting me where I wanted to be, so I ordered a Beam on the rocks. I saw Jerry Number One look at my drink from the corner of his eye like he was trying not to get caught. I thought to myself just how pitiful my existence had become when the Fearsome Foursome had begun to feel sorry for me.

By three o'clock I had that woozy drunk feeling where it becomes difficult to think about your own thoughts. Things kept coming in and out of focus and nothing stayed in my head clearly for more than a thought or two. I remembered the ref counting seven through ten and how I wanted to get up but I couldn't. I remembered how it felt to have my body not respond to my brain's commands. That's what happens when you get knocked out—time goes by quickly and it takes a while for your body to get your brain's messages. It's why you always see fighters arguing after they've been counted out. Besides being embarrassed, they don't believe enough time has gone by and they're pissed off at their bodies for not doing what the brain told them to do.

At four o'clock AJ hesitated when I ordered my bourbon. Even as bombed as I was, I knew it took a lot to get AJ to hesitate. The Foursome were back to talking and they were kicking around something about whether cows lay down when it rains because they're tired or because of the dew point. TC thought the dew point had something to do when the cow had to move its bowels. It faded off after that.

At eight, I awoke in a puddle of my own drool, my face flat on the bar. Kelley had come in to watch the Yankees game, which was being shown on the ESPN *Sunday Game of the Week*.

"Welcome back," Kelley said.

"What time is it?" I said.

"Eight."

"Shit."

"You all right?"

"Yeah."

"Sorry how last night turned out."

"Yeah."

That was all he said, but I appreciated him saying it. We sat mostly in silence watching the Yankees lose to Boston eight to nothing. The Yankees got just two hits in the whole game. I nursed a few Schlitzes during the game, and I was probably still drunk by some official drunkenness measurement. It wasn't a fun drunk or even an escapist drunk, but rather it was the shitty part of being drunk without any of the positive aspects of it.

I still couldn't walk right and I couldn't think clearly but I felt sick to my stomach, not from the booze but from the fight. It was the type of feeling that drinking will numb a little for about a half an hour while you're building your drunk. After that there's no use and you know it, but you keep drinking anyway to avoid feeling that feeling that will now be worsened by the shaky feeling of losing your buzz.

Kelley took me home and I didn't argue about him giving me a lift. Al kicked me in the nuts when I came through the door and just like the night before with Strife I didn't move quick enough to defend against it. My drunkenness was probably scarring Al and I was sure it wouldn't be long until he would soon start attending BOA meetings—that's Bassets of Alcoholics meetings.

I grabbed another Schlitz to help me be drunk enough to sleep. I spilled some down my face trying to drink it with my head on a pillow. Al jumped into bed with me and walked up the length of my body making sure to stride right on my left testicle on the way up. He licked my face and stuck his tongue in my ears and chewed a little. Then he spun around twice and paused with his ass in my face for effect and finally laid down next to me, his back spooning into my gut.

Apparently, Al didn't care about me getting knocked out by a fat guy.

17

DRUNK SLEEP SUCKS.

I was in and out of it most of the night and somewhere around four in the morning I think enough of the alcohol had left my system that I could get some quality sleep. That gave me four or four and half hours of sleep, if I pushed it, before work.

It wasn't meant to be.

First there was the yells, then the loud *thwack* sound going on outside the Moody Blue. Finally, there was Al's objection.

"WOOF, WOOF"—*thwack*—"WOOF, WOOF."

Oh, how I hated life.

I sat up in bed and got a rush of that queasy, not-quite-pukey feeling. I stood up and realized my equilibrium was off and thought for a second that I was going to blow my cookies right there on my bedspread. Al didn't help by running circles around me and incessantly offering me his opinion on the yelling and the thwacking.

Al did one last circle and stopped directly in front of me.

"WOOF, WOOF, WOOF, WOOF," Al said, clearly upset that he wasn't getting the response he wanted from me. Then he jumped up and kicked me in the nuts. I decided that now was as good a time as any to go barf. Al followed me with a steady chorus of WOOFs.

Having heaved through the basset din, I thought I'd go check out the five a.m. commotion in front of my house. There he was, decked out in yet another Karateka Bad-Breath ninja getup. He was yelling about horseradish and throwing something at the tree in front of the Blue. Against my better judgment, I opened the door.

"Sir, good morning, sir," Billy said.

"Billy, we've been over this," I said.

"Sir?"

"Never mind. What are you throwing against my tree?"

"Sir, permission to demonstrate, sir?"

"Knock yourself out."

"Sir?"

"Throw the fuckin' things, will ya!"

"Sir, yes sir."

Billy reared back, yelled "WASABIIIIII!" and threw a metal object into my tree from about forty feet.

"Nice, kid, what are they?" I said.

"Sir, they're Karateka-Brand Titanium Throwing Stars. This one is the six-pointed Okinawan Starfire and the one I just threw is the Yomiuri Four-Pointed Annihilator."

"Kid, that shit is illegal as hell."

"Actually, sir, as a practicing martial artist, I am allowed to practice with them."

"If you say so. Look, kid, I'm going back to bed."

"Sir, when will we train again?"

"Kid, I'll let you know. I'm taking a bit of a break."

"A break, sir?"

He looked at me in disbelief and sadness. It was tough to handle, but I didn't feel up to heading to the gym and going through the motions with this kid. I didn't feel like facing Smitty, and I certainly wasn't up to the sensei routine.

"Yes, sir," he said. He bowed and turned to head home, but today he walked.

I went back to bed and tried to sleep, but it was useless. Hungover and pissed off was not the ideal way to go to any job, but it was definitely not the best way for me to face the Michelin Woman and Abadon. On this particular Monday, we had a treatment team meeting and that meant a double dose of Claudia's officiousness and Abadon's patronizing arrogance.

The queasiness didn't get better as the early morning wore on. In fact, it got worse. I felt carsick driving to the clinic, and I felt carsick walking to my cubicle.

"You all right?" Monique asked when she got a look at me.

"It wasn't the best weekend I ever had," I said.

"Didn't you have a big fight?"

"Yeah, I got knocked out. Suffice to say, it didn't go well."

"I'm sorry, Duff," Monique said.

I tried to round up the files I needed for the meeting, but I just couldn't muster the energy or work through the apathy. I grabbed a handful of some of the charts and headed in ten minutes late. Claudia was at the head of the table with her ultra-cool clipboard with the calculator built in, and Abadon was at her right hand like some sort of twisted version of that last supper painting. I sat down, trying to minimize any attention, and Michelin flashed me a dirty look for being late.

Monique continued to present the case that I interrupted and updated us on Sabrina Shakala, a woman who was mandated to treatment for beating the shit out of her drug-dealing boyfriend. She was on probation and the boyfriend wound up in jail and frankly, I thought Sabrina was functioning pretty well. Anyone who can knock out a dealer's front teeth with a portable CD player was all right with me.

I must've let my eyes close because I heard Abadon's voice and it startled me.

"Duffy, are you with us or are you still on the canvas?" he said.

"What did you just say?" I felt my neck twitch.

"Sometimes an individual who has had a concussive episode will have delayed neurological reactions—like narcolepsy."

Both sides of my neck twitched and my face felt on fire. Monique kicked me twice under the table. When I get angry enough it's tough for me to speak, and that's not a good thing because I wind up expressing myself physically.

"C'mon, Duff, or I'll start counting to ten … ," Abadon said.

That was it.

I threw my hot cup of coffee at Abadon's head. I missed but it smashed against the wall and splattered all over Claudia. I was on my feet and on my way toward him when Monique got in between me. At five foot four and a sleek 130 pounds, it wasn't her physical presence but her innate authority that stopped me. Abadon was on his feet, beet red and breathing heavy.

"C'mon, asshole. I'll show you some fuckin' neurological damage," I said, my ability to speak returned.

Abadon gritted his jaw and flexed his weight-room muscles but before he could say anything, Claudia ordered me into her office. Her big blousy polyester top was splattered with coffee. I didn't move right away and neither did Abadon, but Monique touched my shoulder and sort of steered me out of the conference room toward Claudia's office.

"Effective immediately, you are suspended pending termination approval from the board of directors. You are to go home immediately and not be on these premises until you are notified in writing," Claudia said. She was even more humorless than usual.

I didn't feel like saying anything.

Instead, I signed the suspension form and headed home. My blood pressure was up from the combination of alcohol withdrawal and dealing with Abadon. It wasn't Claudia's authority that kept me silent, it was the desire to get the hell out of the office and go home. I knew the consequences were significant, but in the immediate moment it was good to get out of there. I grabbed my keys and split.

I would've joined the Foursome for an early start on drinking, but the thought of it made my stomach flip. That, and I wasn't crazy about the potential future I was developing as an alcoholic. I figured the safest thing to do would be to head home, get kicked in the nuts, lie on the couch, and do nothing until I could think straight.

Al was confused by my early arrival, but he quickly adjusted and we watched *Hawaii Five-O* together. It was one of the episodes where McGarrett is pitted against his archrival, Wo Fat, who was played by the same guy who I think wound up as the funky blind

Kung Fu master on David Carradine's *Kung Fu* TV show. I thought about why I knew that and also about how unfair it was that just because an actor was Asian it meant he was limited to playing stereotyped roles. Then, I thought, when you're a short, fat, bald guy with slanted eyes, you really would struggle to get the Cary Grant roles, wouldn't you?

I went in and out of sleep until about four when I must have really fallen out, because it was a knocking on the door followed by Al's alarm system that rousted me at about eight thirty. I came to and dreaded seeing my pizza-faced ninja falling on his head on my front lawn. It took me a while to get off the couch, but when I went to the door I was pleasantly surprised. It was Trina.

"What are you doing here?" I said at the door.

"There's a sweet greeting," she said.

"Sorry, I'm just surprised. C'mon in, the place's a mess."

Al ran to Trina and snuggled up to her. Trina and I have a bit of a history. On more than one occasion we've gotten involved, usually when one or both of us has just gotten out of a failed relationship. My relationships failed regularly and Trina's weren't much better.

"Where's Todd?" I said referring to her current BF.

"Todd's an asshole," she said.

"I always thought so, but I didn't want to say anything."

"How about Marcia?"

"She's in therapy and her therapist says she can't go out with me."

We found our way to the couch and I wiped Al's slobber off the cushions before Trina sat down.

"Duff, you've really done it this time, you know. I don't know how you're going to save your job," she said.

"Yeah, I fucked up royally," I said.

"I'm sorry about the fight. I was there, you know."

"I thought you hated boxing."

"I do."

She touched a small raspberry on the side of my head. It was the only remnant of the knockout.

"God, I worry about you," Trina said, looking into my eyes. I could feel what was about to happen. She put her hand gently on my knee and let it stay there. I put my hand under her shoulder-length chestnut hair and lightly rubbed her neck.

Instinctively she leaned into me and kissed me hard. I took her roughly into my arms and in one motion turned and laid her down on the couch. She stopped kissing me for a moment and let out a breath that was filled with something that was part emotion and part desire. We went back to kissing and her hand slipped inside my shirt and grabbed at the muscles in my back.

Trina pushed me off her just enough to start struggling to get my shirt over my head. She got it halfway and I did the rest, propping myself up on my knees. She undid the buttons on her white tapered blouse with fury and then the front clasp of her bra. We rolled over and she was out of both her blouse and bra. She was a sight, her hair softly falling on just the top of her shoulders, her flat waist, with just a hint of muscle and maybe, most of all, a glint in her eye showing that she was totally in the moment.

She reached to the snap on my jeans and I felt my heart race while I closed my eyes. The tongue was warm and wet and just a bit rough against my side, and I felt Trina shift off my lower body. I kept my eyes closed to heighten the anticipation. Again, with the tongue, only this time it felt scratchier.

"Ewwww. Make him go!" Trina shouted, startling me out of my bliss.

"WOOF, WOOF, WOOF, WOOF," Al said, frightened by Trina's yelling.

I looked up and there was Al's nose. He was poised to lick me in the face to make sure I was all right from whatever it was that this intruder was about to do to me. I tried to shoo him away but instead he climbed up on my bare chest and sat on it with his back to Trina, who was now sitting on the couch with her head in her hands.

Al had a satisfied look on his face, as if he was experiencing a sense of success in protecting his master. Trina's expression was less than satisfied as she fumbled to put on her clothes. Just a moment ago, when she was fumbling to get out of her clothes, she looked incredibly sexy. Now, with the process in reverse, she looked incredibly awkward.

"I'm sorry," I said. "I really don't know what to say."

"That's okay, I got carried away. It probably wasn't a good idea anyway," Trina said.

I didn't know how to respond to that because the whole thing seemed like a swell idea to me, but I realized women aren't like men. It was one of those things where if I disagreed I think I would've come off like a sexually desirous pig—which of course I am. I just didn't want to state the obvious.

In an effort to ease the awkwardness, I got Trina and myself a drink even though she didn't ask for one. I threw on the TV just to have some noise other than our silence. The Crawford station was in a special report. The attractive female correspondent was live at the McDonough High football field next to the bleachers. There was police tape, flashing lights, and a lot of activity.

"Crawford appears to have another murder victim on its hands. The victim is seventeen-year-old Elisa Madnick and though police officials and the FBI are releasing very little information, News Channel 13 has learned that the victim was sexually assaulted, sodomized, and then stabbed repeatedly in the neck and chest."

"Oh my God," Trina said.

"Yeah." It was all I could think of to say.

The reporter continued.

"Police still have not determined the whereabouts of Howard Rheinhart, the serial killer who was recently paroled from prison. Rheinhart disappeared around the time of the murder of Connie Carter, the McDonough High cheerleader who disappeared several weeks ago," she said.

"How many is that now?" Trina asked.

"Five, I think," I said.

"Oh my God."

18

THE NEXT MORNING WAS the start of my unofficial vacation. I didn't have to go to work and I didn't have a fight to train for, but I didn't feel like working out either. My new karateka was conspicuous by his absence, which was a bit of a relief but it also made me sad because I hadn't wanted to hurt his feelings.

I was into my third cup of coffee and trying to ignore Al, who was whipping around the house like I spiked his dish with Sudafed when the phone rang. It was Hymie and I dreaded talking to him.

"Son, what is this latest mess you've got yourself into? That Claudia is meshugenah with anger, you know," he said.

"Yeah, I know, Hymie. I'm sorry. It's my fault," I said.

"You threw a coffee cup at the doctor?"

"Yeah."

"Son, I'm sorry about your fight. It's okay, there'll be others."

"I'm not sure there will be, Hymie."

"Son, you've got to let it go. You're a crazy Irishman and the Polish doesn't help, but you know better."

"Yes, I do, Hymie."

"What did this doctor do?"

"He believes Rheinhart is the murderer. That, and he took a shot at me about my fight."

"Isn't this guy, Rheinhart, the guy?"

"I don't think so, Hymie."

"Son, you have a soft heart—this Rheinhart, he has had it rough, no?"

"Yes."

"Son, I'll see what I can do with Claudia, but I don't know this time."

I thanked Hymie and I signed off. At this point I didn't particularly care about the job and I didn't care about my boxing career. There wasn't much I gave a shit about, but I didn't like the thought that Howard was getting screwed. Of all the shit swirling around my toilet of a brain, that was the one piece of shit that just wouldn't flush.

Sure, I promised Kelley I'd back off, but with all this time on my hands it certainly wouldn't hurt anything if I poked my head around a little bit. It would give me something to do and it would be a way not to think about everything else. I definitely could use the diversion and I was betting that Howard could use someone— anyone, to look out for him. After all, he asked me for help.

In the meantime my Muslim brother was on my last nerve. I grabbed the leash and tried to get him hooked up but he thought it was an opportunity to practice his open-field running. Again, he was running crazy as dog shit all over the Blue, dying for me to give chase. I'd try to stop and pretend like I wasn't going to chase him, thinking he would feel guilty and relent to the leash. Apparently guilt wasn't an emotion that Al struggled with, because when I'd pause he'd stay just out of reach until I took a step toward him and then he'd fake left and go right. Finally, out of frustration, I ran as fast as I could after him and got real close when he shifted direction and ducked under the coffee table.

My shin was actually bleeding and the thin skin over the bone was a dark purplish red. Al crawled out from the table with his tail wagging, ready for his walk just as soon as I stopped hopping around repeating the f-word. I'm man enough to know when I've lost.

I lifted Al's fat ass into the passenger side of the Eldorado and switched tracks on the *Blue Hawaii* eight-track until "Can't Help Falling in Love" was cued up. Al curled up, belched, and went to sleep. I drove toward Smitty's house, not to see him but instead to have Al pick up his scent and follow it to the Y. Smitty was almost never home, except late at night, so I figured I'd let Al nose around, see if he could pick up some Smitty aroma, and see if he could find his way to the gym. I guess in some ways I knew I had to see Smitty and maybe I was setting up a scenario to bump in to him accidentally on purpose.

Al huffed around Smitty's front lawn, his porch, and settled on a bench where Smitty read. I gave him the "Go find!" command and he was off with his nose working the ground and the pavement like an Electrolux on overdrive. Al kept a steady pace, stopping and raising his nose in the air, pausing to think from time to time, and then getting back to the ground to do his work. He worked the trail for a couple of miles and he was more intense then I'd ever seen him. Trailing was clearly in his blood and it was what he was meant to do, at least in addition to eating and farting.

About a block from the Y, Al stopped, crapped, and then sprinted to the parking lot right to Smitty's car. He was jumping all over Smitty's Oldsmobile, happy as could be with me praising him when I heard voices a couple of rows behind me in the parking lot.

"That would be a fitting dog for you. A dog that looks as pathetic as your life."

It was Harter, the karate guy. I looked up and he was standing there with Mitchell and, of all people, Dr. Abadon. They were standing in front of a shiny black Escalade with gold chrome all over it.

"Maybe floppy-ears would like to play with Seagal," Mitchell said, and with his remote he lowered the driver's-side window just a bit. The head of a pit bull emerged with its snarling mouth almost foaming and its teeth barred. Al got behind my legs and whimpered.

"Ha, just like his master!" Harter said. "Hey, nice job at your last fight … loser!"

I was taking it all in and feeling several of the veins in my neck twitch, but I didn't want to subject Al to any more of this. The whole episode seemed so out of context, especially with Abadon joining these two, that I felt a little off, like something was wrong or something was about to be wrong.

Even though it would have been my nature to get into it with them, I walked away with Al without saying anything. Al's jubilant mood from the trailing was gone and he looked a bit ashamed.

19

WHEN I DIDN'T KNOW what else to do with my time, I went to AJ's. With very little going on in my life, but a lot of things racing through my head, I needed the group therapy that AJ's offered.

"It's all based on shittin' the bed when you're a kid," Rocco was saying.

"I thought it was wetting the bed," TC said.

"Why would shittin' and pissin' in the bed make you a serial killer?" Jerry Number One asked.

"How would you like to sleep in a shitty, wet, and uriney bed every night?" Jerry Number Two said.

"That would stink," TC said. "Hey, doesn't setting small animals on fire have something to do with it too?"

"It must be a big bed," Jerry Number Two said.

"I don't think they have to set the animals on fire. I think those are two separate categories," Jerry Number One said.

"Separate from what?" TC said. "What if they sleep with an animal that wets the bed? Does it still count if they kill that animal? It could be justified, you know."

"When I was a kid I had a hamster that slept with me," Jerry Number Two said.

"So?" Rocco said.

"He caught fire accidentally," Jerry Number Two said.

"In bed?" TC said.

"Yeah, there was pot involved. He survived though," Jerry Number Two said.

"How?" Rocco said.

"I pissed all over him," Jerry Number Two said.

"That's disgusting," Jerry Number One said.

"You're telling me," Jerry Number Two said. "You ever smell urine-soaked, burnt hamster?"

"That's enough to put a guy on a killing spree," Jerry Number One said.

Kelley was in his position watching a profile on NASCAR legend Richard Petty. Kelley would have watched sex tapes of Golda Meir if it meant drowning out Jerry's drowning hamster story.

"So, are you picking up educational credits by listening in on the brain trust's discussion on serial killer forensics?" I said.

"Yeah. But I'm going to need another few beers to rid my mind of the visual of Jerry in bed pissing on that poor, flaming hamster," Kelley said.

"Has anyone heard from Howard?"

"Not that I know of."

"You're not going to like this, but I'm going to start looking into this."

"You're right. I don't like it at all. Didn't we have this talk?"

"Yeah, we did, and it didn't sit right. Besides that, I ain't got much going on these days and I'm kind of pissed off."

"What you talking about?"

"I'm suspended from work and probably getting fired."

"Isn't that almost always happening?"

"Yeah, but I don't like the way the so-called helping profession is throwing Howard in."

"That's why you're pissed off?"

"Partly."

"Wouldn't have anything to do with anything else, would it?"

I didn't say anything.

"Be careful," Kelley said.

We went back to watching the TV in silence, at least silence between the two of us. The Foursome was still jawing.

"I guess you'd have to say that Manson was the best," Jerry Number One said.

"The best? What makes him the best?" TC said.

"You know, for sheer terror and attention," Jerry Number One said.

"You know he was in the Beach Boys," Rocco said. "He started killing people because he got obsessed with that 'Help Me Rhoda' song. It made him nuts," he said.

"He did hang out with Brian Wilson and he was definitely nuts," Jerry Number Two said.

"Whatever happened to that crazy broad that tried to shoot Nixon? Stinky Fromage was her name," Rocco said.

"Wasn't she Squeaky Fromme?" TC said.

"I never heard her speak or knew where she was from," Rocco said.

20

I FIGURED I'D START out by trying to find out as much as I could about Howard's life. Seeing as though he spent most of his life in prison, it made sense to find out what his time inside was like. I didn't have many prison staff connections that would've known Howard when he was inside, but I sure had plenty of connections of clients who used to be inmates. It was just a matter of heading down to the Hill and seeing who was on the corner.

Jefferson Hill was the old Irish neighborhood where a lot of my family lived generations ago. Today, it was almost entirely black and Latino, with the exception of some old-timers who were too old or stubborn to move. The houses need painting, there was always litter being blown around, and the whole section just seemed dark, like even the sun didn't want to come around anymore. Even though I'm a very white guy, I could hang on the Hill, partly because of my job but mostly because I was known from the gym. There was something about the fight game that brought down the barriers. I'm not saying boxing never had a racist element, but when baseball and football didn't allow blacks or Latinos, boxing had champions of those persuasions. Sure, it was harder for them and they didn't let a black guy fight for the heavyweight title for a long time, but it was still better than the other sports.

I parked the Eldorado near the corner of Steuben and Albany Streets and headed up Albany to see who was around. Up by Craig Street three older black guys were passing around a brown paper bag. I knew two of the guys, Carlisle Jackson and Chipper Poston, because both of them had been to the clinic and had dropped out several times. Both of them were alcoholics and heroin users.

When I walked toward them they instinctively hid the bottle until Chipper recognized me.

"Duff—what's up?" he said.

"What's up, Chip?" I said.

"Hey, Duff," Carlisle said.

Both guys were gray and weathered looking. They were kind of like the jakey-bum version of Laurel and Hardy, with Carlisle at about six foot three and rail thin and Chipper a rounded five foot six. They had run together for the last thirty years, and they were somewhere between fifty and seventy-five. There was no way to figure out how old they were by looking at them.

"Duff, this is Silk, from Brooklyn. He's Chip's second cousin," Carlisle said.

I exchanged silent nods with Silk.

"Duffy, what you coming up here for?" Chipper said.

"I'm curious about something," I said.

"Curious? You comes to the Hill, you gotta be pretty fuckin' curious," Carlisle said.

"You guys were inside when Rheinhart was in, weren't ya?" I asked.

"Crazy, skinny-ass white boy who killed all them kids? Yeah, we both were," Chipper said.

"Boy kept his mouth shut and the rest of him buttoned up," Carlisle said.

"You remember anything about him?" I said.

"Yeah, he was the only motherfucker who didn't OD in that part of the tier," Chip said.

"Eight motherfuckers died, another eight all fucked up vegetablewise in the head. Crazy white boy had death all around his skinny ass," Carlisle said.

"What was the story?" I asked.

"We was both away from that shit, but the word was one of the hacks was sellin' some bad acid trip, 'cept it wasn't regular acid, it was some new shit I never heard of before or since. They called it 'Blast' or some shit," Chipper said.

"Shit was bad and no hack ever got caught. It was all swept under the fuckin' carpet. Who care if inmates dyin' anyway?" Carlisle said.

"Why didn't Howard get into it?"

"Boy was straight-laced, man. He was no hardened criminal. I think the motherfucker flipped for a short period and then went back to be just a skinny-ass white boy," Chipper said.

"You guys ever try 'Blast'?" I asked.

"No man, shit came and went fast. I heard it was fuckin' crazy shit—like meth and acid and dust times ten all at once," Chipper said. "I'm a down head. I ain't lookin' for no fuckin' Ferris wheel ride," Carlisle said.

We kicked around some small talk and I let them know how they could get a hold of me if they needed me. With guys like this you didn't come on too strong about getting help, but I always wanted them to know where they could find me if they had to.

I thanked the guys, gave them a ten, and headed back to the Eldorado. On the way back to the Moody Blue, I threw in the *On Stage* eight-track and listened to Elvis do "Walk a Mile in My Shoes." I was thinking about Howard's shoes and how his whole life he'd been stepping in shit with those shoes, and probably how the one time he fought back against it in his life it was the biggest mistake he ever made. I also wondered why he wasn't getting high in prison. I knew if I ever had to live that life I would have done anything and everything to alter my consciousness away from the reality.

It felt to me like the "Blast" overdoses had something to do with something, but that just might have been my mind's way of making something fit. It could just as easily have been one of the many fucked-up events that had occurred during Howard's thirty-year stint in our culture's hellhole. Elvis had moved on to "Sweet Caroline" as I was pulling up to the Blue when I saw Billy chucking his throwing stars into my oak tree. He sprang to attention as I pulled in.

"Sir!" he said.

"Hey, Bill," I said, returning his bow with just a slight nod.

"Sir—I am anxious to resume training, sir."

"Yeah, well Billy, uh, I haven't felt like going to the gym much."

"Sir, I will train anywhere."

"Okay, Billy, but I've been a little fucked up lately, so I'm not sure how good I'll be as a teacher."

"Sir?"

"Uh … it's just … well … never mind."

Billy looked at me with his eyes wide open and his head tilted. It's the same look Al gives me when I take away a shoe he's been chewing on. I figured it would be easier to just give Billy a half-hour workout than to try to explain it to him.

"All right, Billy. C'mere," I said. He sprang up, ran over to me, came to attention, and bowed.

"WASABIIII!" Billy screamed, snapping his fist down into a ready position.

For the next half hour I worked him on throwing good punches and pretended it was a special karate technique when in reality it was fundamental boxing. I'm not entirely sure why, but I made him drill his recoil every time he threw a punch, and I did it so much I could tell that even Billy was getting bored with it. To me, it was like some sadomasochistic medieval mantra I was doing to punish myself because I had misplaced my hair suit. I kept with it though, like it was an infected itch that I should've stopped scratching a long time ago.

After I dismissed Billy, Al greeted me at the door with a jump toward the nuts that I was able to dodge. He did two 360s and then lay down on the floor and farted. I wasn't sure how to take that as a greeting, but with the way things had been going I didn't feel like interpreting it.

I hit the machine and there was a message from Marcia.

"Hi Duff, it's me." She sounded full of energy, which wasn't like her at all. "I've been doing a lot of work with my therapist, and she says that I need to have some closure. So I wanted to let you know we won't be getting back together. I just needed to say that."

Well, I'm glad she's making progress.

You know you're getting to a fairly low point in your life when even the women you don't really like much are breaking up with you. Actually, Marcia had already dumped me and this call was to make sure I really got it. If nothing else, therapy was teaching her to be thorough.

Something told me to turn on the TV, and when I did I wasn't surprised to see that all the local stations were in special-report mode. There were shots of crime-scene tape, what looked like forensic teams, and guys in windbreakers that said "FBI" on the back. In the middle of the camera shot was a large gray bag, what I guessed was a body bag. The reporter was having a very official conversation with the anchors back in the studio.

"Liz, do the authorities have any idea of the whereabouts of Howard Rheinhart?" Lance Justin of Channel 10 asked his live, local, late-breaking correspondent.

"Lance, they do not, but I have an unconfirmed source that Rheinhart's blood was found at the scene," Liz Priest said.

"There have been suggestions that this murder was more gruesome than the others. Can you tell us anything about that?"

"Yes, Lance, though I'd like to warn our viewers that some of the details I'm about to share are quite disturbing. This victim, a still-unidentified teenage female, had several fingers removed and inserted in other parts of her body. There were also strange puncture wounds up and down her sides as if she was being drained of blood, Lance."

They continued the banter back and forth, saying essentially the same things over and over. This was getting crazy weird, and to have it so close to me gave me a queasy feeling like I had woken up in an alternate universe.

I actually felt sick.

21

WITH THE LATEST MURDER I had this feeling that I needed to pick up my pace and stop spinning my wheels. It seemed like every day I didn't find Howard put some high-school kid at risk. This whole thing felt like a puzzle, and the only thing that seemed to make sense to me was to pick one of the pieces and start seeing where it might fit.

I'd never heard of this Blast and I've been working with street addicts for a long time. Sometimes drugs come and go but more often drugs get new names, or slightly different versions of them appear mixed with something new that alters the high. I met some guys once who combined Benadryl with some prescription narcotic, and they said it was their best high ever.

With not a whole lot clogging up my day planner, I dropped by Rudy's office at the hospital. His office was buried back in the corner of the second floor, and it was filled with stack after stack of papers, textbooks, and interoffice envelopes. I walked in without knocking.

"Excuse me, Doctor, I have this hemorrhoid I'd like you to look at," I said.

"Geez, you are a hemorrhoid," Rudy said without looking up from his desk.

"What do you know about prison medicine?"

"What are you, making a documentary? Look, kid, I'm really freakin' busy—why aren't you at work?"

"There was an incident."

"There always is with you—it didn't have anything to do with my new tenant Sanchez, does it? I can't believe you had me lie to social services."

"No, it's not that. Rheinhart was on my caseload and I'm trying to find out about what his prison time was like. A bunch of his tiermates OD'ed back then on something they called 'Blast.' You ever hear of it?" I asked.

"Yeah, as a matter of fact I have. A guy in my practice did some rounds at the prison during that period. It was a synthetic hallucinogenic with some narcotic characteristics. The high was supposed to be like a combination of acid, heroin, and crank," Rudy said.

"Wow, now there's a trip for ya. Where'd it come from?"

"That's the thing, no one could ever figure it out. The other thing was that once it built up in the system it was very quickly fatal. Turns out that it metabolized into something very similar to strychnine. The inmates who died had only done it three or four times."

"Could they've made it themselves?"

"Unlikely. This wasn't a bathtub crank, it was more like graduate-chemistry shit. Some of it broke down with different half-lives and that prolonged the high while something else broke down more rapidly to accentuate something else. It was pretty complicated shit."

"Have you ever seen it turn up since then?"

"No—hey, Duff, this is all pretty interesting, but unless you want to go check on the seventy-four-year-old guy with the colostomy with me, I got to go."

I thanked Rudy and got the number of his doctor friend. As he was leaving he gave me the rundown on his friend.

Dr. Manuel Pacquoa was about sixty-five years old, four foot eleven, and had an expression on his face like he just took a huff of a rotting fish. His specialty was infectious diseases and in his home country of the Philippines he was seen as a deity for the work he had done with the poor people. He still traveled back there three times a year to treat as many of the street people as he could. Later in his career, he added psychiatry and his work in the prison was part of his certification process.

He greeted me in a friendly way that was more customary politeness related to his friendship with Rudy than it was because he was glad to see me. Rudy had explained to me that when Dr. Manny had some visa problems he had lent him a hand, and the Filipino never forgot his gratitude. He brought me coffee and fussed a great deal about making me comfortable.

"Dr. Rudy tells me about the favor you did for your patient without a home," Dr. Manny said. I was surprised that Rudy would've bothered to share such information.

"Yeah—it was nothing really. I hate to see a guy get screwed by the government for stupid reasons," I said.

"You are a good man. I understand the man is from my homeland?"

"I think his mother was, anyway."

"Thank you for helping him." It was an interesting response. He clearly saw a favor to a member of his country as a favor to him. "Someday, if I can return your favor, I hope you allow me."

"I'm good at allowing people to do favors for me," I said. The doctor didn't laugh.

I asked him about his time in the prison, what he remembered about Howard, and about the deaths related to Blast overdoses.

"This Blast was very addicting and very exciting, especially to those with thrill-seeking tendencies. I believe the monotony of the prison life made it appealing." He took off his wire-rim glasses and ran a hand through his thin black hair.

"It was like the crack drug that is popular now, but it had hallucinogenic qualities as well."

"Do you have any idea where they got it?"

"We never found out because the inmates died, all within three days of each other. Then, it abruptly stopped."

"Any guesses?"

"It would be only a guess, but there was a graduate assistant that left without notice during that same period. I never saw or heard from him again."

"Do you remember his name?"

"It's not that I don't remember it, it's that I didn't ever know it. I only came in two times a week and then I saw patients back to back. I just remember the rumors."

I thanked the doctor for his help, and he thanked me again for helping Sanchez.

"Please remember me when you need a favor," he said.

22

IN ALL THE YEARS I've been training in either karate or boxing, I never took much time off. I never saw it so much as dedication as just something I did, like taking a shower or going to the bathroom. Not going felt weird, and I felt out of sorts both physically and mentally.

On the way back from Dr. Pacquoa's I found myself down by the Y. I didn't get there on purpose or totally by accident—it was more like I got there on instinct. I went past the parking lot and saw Smitty's Olds, and I got a sick feeling in my stomach, kind of like when you see an old girlfriend with someone new. He wouldn't call me; I'd have to show up or call him, not because Smitty was stubborn but because he always contended that boxing wasn't for everyone. He'd often say that it wasn't the healthiest way to spend your free time and the minute you wanted to leave it behind that was okay with him. He didn't like guys who were ambivalent, but he respected people who made clear decisions based on their conscience.

Right now, I was feeling ambivalent and that's what was keeping me out of the gym. I circled the block to kill time and to think, and as I came around Union Street on the back side of the Y, I came across the karate guys again. This time they were talking to someone in another SUV, and I parked far enough away so they wouldn't see me. Both their heads were close to the driver's side window so I couldn't see whom they were talking to. They kept up the conversation for a few minutes and then the driver handed Mitchell a shoebox. The three shook hands, and as the driver pulled away I got a look at him.

It was Abadon.

I followed him as he drove off, making sure to stay back a fair distance so he couldn't spot me. He headed onto I-90 and then to 787 and took it as far as it would go. At Waterford he went up Route 44 and turned down a country road called Schemerhorn Lane. I didn't make the turn because there was no way I could follow him and not get spotted, so I pulled over on the shoulder and waited five minutes. I knew there was a good chance that I lost him, but I had nothing better to do, so after my break I went down Schemerhorn.

The road was lined with swampland and heavy brush with an occasional farm but otherwise it was pretty much uninhabited. I was the only one on the road, and after about four miles or so I started to think about turning back. Before I stopped, I came upon a homemade wooden street sign at the end of a dirt road called Toachung Road. I remembered *toachung* from my karate days as the Korean word for sacred training area.

I slowed down as I passed it and all I could see was a long dirt road that eventually wound through the brush. I didn't want to chance driving down it, so I drove ahead and parked the Eldorado on the side of the road in a dirt area behind some trees. I set off on foot toward Toachung Road.

I stayed to the side of the road so that if I needed to I could dive into the brush for some cover. I was on the road for a full twenty minutes when I came upon a clearing and what looked like a training camp of some sort. There was a log cabin, a pavilion with free weights and weight machines, and a corrugated steel building with a single pipe chimney emitting smoke. To get in the steel building, you had to enter an area that was covered with stones and gravel and surrounded by a ten-foot-high fence. The stone area was set up with a large statue of the Buddha, maybe six feet high and four feet around. Surrounding the statue were heavy stone benches. The whole area was circular with a locked door at one end that was the entrance to the steel building. It was about thirty feet in diameter, and there were several other Asian-themed stone figures of dragons and tigers.

When I looked closer, I could see that Mitchell and Harter's pit bull was asleep on the gravel just in front of the Buddha statue. Abadon's SUV was parked just outside the fence, and after a few minutes he came out in a sweatshirt and shorts and headed over to the weight-training pavilion. I watched him lift for a few minutes and decided to head out before I got caught trespassing. The place had an eerie feel to it and I wanted to get out.

So, Abadon and the karate guys were training buddies, maybe close training buddies? What the hell would a self-proclaimed Christian be doing with friends like these guys? Who knows, but maybe they were into the whole Christian thing too. The place gave me the creeps, as did this bizarre friendship. I was walking out of the place, feeling a bit uneasy, and I noticed a half-pungent, half-sweet odor in the air.

It added to the creepy feel of the place.

At AJ's, the brain trust was discussing several topics at once.

"Ripken was so upset, they canceled the game," Rocco said.

"They canceled the game because his wife was having sex with Kevin Costner?" TC said.

"Were they humping on the mound?" Jerry Number Two asked.

"It was on her mound anyway," Jerry Number One said.

"Maybe it was in the batter's box," TC said.

"Costner was clearly in the batter's box and Ripken was on deck," Jerry Number Two said.

"You know Marilyn Monroe had six toes on each foot," TC said.

"What does that have to do with Ripken's wife?" Rocco said.

"She had six toes too?" Jerry Number One asked.

"I don't know, but you could see the extra toes in that scene where she's standing on the subway grate," TC said.

"Who was looking at her toes?" Jerry Number One said.

"Certainly not DiMaggio. He was pissed because you could see right through to her mound," Rocco said.

"Hey—grass on the infield. Play ball!" TC said.

"That's what Kevin Costner always said," Jerry Number Two said.

"You know one of the Bond girls used to be a guy," Rocco said.

"Huh?" TC couldn't keep up. "A transmitter?"

"Yep," Rocco said.

"How many toes?" Jerry Number One asked.

"I bet you didn't see her mound in that movie," TC said.

"I would cancel a game over that," Jerry Number One said. "I'd refuse to even get in the batter's box."

"You screwball," Rocco said.

Kelley was in his usual spot, turned away from the Foursome. ESPN Classic was showing that old home-run derby show and Hank Aaron was up against Moose Skowron.

"Hey, who's on the mound?" I said.

"Please . . . ," Kelley said.

AJ slid a Schlitz to me and a Coors Light in front of Kelley.

"Any news about Howard?" I asked.

"No, they don't have anything new."

"I think it might have something to do with that prison overdose. Dr. Pacquoa said that around the same time that the inmates died, a graduate intern abruptly stopped coming to the prison."

"What the hell are you talking about?"

"Rudy knows a guy who did some psychiatric consultation in the prison during that time and I went to talk to him. He's a Filipino doc and he told me about some things."

"Oh really?"

"Maybe you could suggest to Morris and his bunch that they should look in to that?"

"Maybe you should go screw that Bond girl—what are you, nuts?"

"Hey—I'm just trying to help."

"That's the problem. Once again you're out of your league and in over your head. They have no interest in proving Howard is innocent; they're interested in finding him as fast as they can. Until kids stop showing up dead, the cops and the general public don't find Howard a terribly sympathetic character," Kelley said.

Clearly, Kell wasn't in the best of moods and I didn't feel like getting scolded, so I shut up for a while. I went back to drinking my beer and AJ flipped the TV to Channel 13 for the news. The local stations were milking the hell out of the murder story with nightly updates even when they had very little new information.

"New developments in the Crawford Slayer case," the pretty rubberized female anchor said, starting the news. "Toxicology reports indicate that victims Connie Carter and Alison Mann both had traces of illicit drugs in their system. The State Laboratory did not recognize any of the drug's metabolites and they did not fit any of the usual drug categories."

"What the hell does that mean?" I said.

"It usually means that the subjects were using a designer drug like ecstasy, except it's a new version or some sort of derivative," Kelley said.

"Hmmm…"

"What 'Hmmm'?"

"Well, what do you think that does to the case?"

"The fact that a high-school kid was getting high? I don't think it does anything. High-school kids being high, when did that become news?"

"Yeah, I suppose."

I decided that I had gotten my recommended daily dose of Schlitz and started to head out. On my way to the door, I couldn't help but hear the Foursome looking for some sort of resolution to Cal Ripken's problems with Kevin Costner.

"That's why he played in all those games," Rocco said.

"Because his wife was doing the guy from *The Untouchables*?" TC said.

"Apparently, he wasn't untouchable in real life," Jerry Number Two said.

23

AL, THE LONG-EARED ALARM clock, went off at just after five on Sunday morning. In between the steady stream of WOOFs there was the familiar *thwack* sound.

"Good morning, Billy," I said as I stood on my front stoop. It dawned on me that it had been a couple of days since I put the kid through his paces, which probably accounted for his early morning visit. He was throwing his stars into my tree from about forty or fifty feet. The kid couldn't throw a kick without landing on his backside and he couldn't string together more than ten pushups, but he was pretty accurate with the stars.

"Sir, yes sir." He snapped to attention when he saw me despite the fact that I was wearing ratty old sweats and a dirty wife-beater. Today's zit was at the point of his chin and he had a dollop of Clearasil on it. "Sir, we haven't trained in a few days."

"Sorry about that, Billy." The kid looked at me with a face sadder than Al's. "We can train tonight if you want."

"Sir, yes sir!"

"One 'sir' is more than enough, kid."

"Sir?"

"Never mind. Meet me at the Y tonight, but not in our usual place. Let's meet in that aerobics room on the second floor around eight."

"Sir, yes sir."

"Geez… Hey, Billy, let me ask you a non-karate question."

"Sir."

"How has this crazy shit going on in school with the killer affected things?"

"Sir, kids are scared."

"Did you know any of the kids at school?"

"Sir, I keep mostly to myself. The girls that were killed were cheerleaders."

He said it like the fact that they were cheerleaders made him unworthy to be in their presence. I remembered what high school was like for guys like Billy. Teenagers weren't a kind, accepting bunch, especially if you were a little goofy—ask Howard Rheinhart—and Billy was more than a little goofy.

"I'll see you tonight, kid," I said. He bowed and ran down the street.

———

I brought Al with me to the Y and took advantage of his low profile to sneak him past the front desk. The disinterested teenager knew I was a regular and didn't look away from the TV as I waved to him. I had seen Smitty's car was in the lot, like it always was, but I wasn't ready to say hello yet. Smitty was a lot of things and in many ways a complex man, but he didn't trouble himself with small talk. He didn't care for bullshit ambiguity and I was ambivalent about just about everything going on in my life. He would look at me and I'd divert my eyes and stutter. For the time being, I decided to avoid him.

The Y was a sniffer's paradise, and the combined aromas of bad BO, talc, and liquid soap had Al a little overactive. There was just a bit too much for him to process, so by the time we got to the aerobics room he collapsed on a mat, rolled over on his back, and started to snore with his four legs in the air.

It was five after eight and my karateka was no place to be found. Billy had never been less than half an hour early for anything. When he was fifteen minutes late I started to worry, and at half an hour, I began to panic a little bit. Something was wrong.

While I sat there and grew more anxious, it dawned on me that I knew very little about the kid. His dad was dead and his mother worked a lot, but I didn't even know an address or a phone number. Whenever I gave him a lift he asked me to leave him a mile from his house so he could run home. I don't know what that was all about—maybe he was embarrassed about his house or his mom. Shit, maybe he was embarrassed about me. Maybe he just wanted to run. I swear, working in human services screws you up for life.

It wasn't like I ever needed to contact him—God knows, Billy made himself available. At eight forty-five I figured he wasn't coming, and I left the Y more than just a little nervous.

As we walked out Al pulled me all over the Y, once again overwhelmed with the sniffles. When we hit the parking lot he was like a burning man who had jumped in a swimming pool. He seemed to relax and say "Ahhh..." We walked past Smitty's Olds and were headed toward the Eldorado when we came upon Mitchell and

155

Harter's SUV. At first Al paused like he didn't want to encounter the pit bull, but then he proceeded over to it.

There was no barking, so the pit bull probably didn't take the ride that night. Al was back, sniffing like a mad hound. He went up one side and down the other and then focused his attention on the back gate. He got up on his hind legs and sniffed all over the handle, pulled back, and barked twice. Then he sat at attention staring at the back of the SUV.

I pulled him and he strained his neck, but he wouldn't leave his position. There was no point in looking in the vehicle because the windows were tinted. I called to him and pulled hard enough to shake him out of his stance, but he continued to resist to the point where I nearly had to drag him. As we walked away, he whimpered.

I knew something was up the second I got to AJ's. The Foursome weren't talking and they were riveted to the TV screen. Kelley was there too, but no one paid any attention to me when I walked in. The TV was on MSNBC and they were in a special report.

"... It is a sign of ritualized murder, a thought-out process and one in which the murderer is expressing more confidence. He's actually thumbing his nose at the authorities trying to apprehend him," the head profiler said.

"The draining of blood from the bodies, is that a particular sign of something?" the anchor said.

"Draining a human body of blood takes a level of expertise. It takes a particular commitment to totally drain the life out of an individual, if you will, and it also indicates to everyone involved that he has the power to control others."

"Holy shit," I heard myself say.

"Two more teenagers. Throats slit, blood drained from them and discarded in a field. This is getting beyond sick," Kelley said.

"This isn't Howard. This is something else," I said.

Kelley didn't say anything, which told me a lot. All of AJ's sat in silence for a long time, which gave everything an even more surreal feel. AJ's and silence just didn't fit together. When my thinking got back to normal I thought of Billy and got scared.

I borrowed Rocco's cell phone and called my machine. There was a message from Marcia asking me why I haven't called and just because we weren't going out anymore we could still be friends, but that was it—nothing from Billy.

Then I called Jamal. He was never without his cell.

"Jamal." It was the way he always answered.

"It's Duff, J. Salami and bacon," I said.

"*Salaam alaikum*... Why you got to fuck with Allah?"

"Sorry. Hey, tonight Al did something really weird."

"Duff, that all that hound ever do."

"He sniffed all over this car, jumped up sniffed the handle, barked twice, and then sat at attention. He wouldn't move."

"Uh-huh. You remember what I told you Al was trained for?"

"He sniffed explosives."

"Yeah, but he was trained as part of the Fruit of Islam's security team."

"So, what's that mean—he guarded Al Sharpton's pomade?"

"Nope—it means the crazy-ass hound knows how to sniff out illegal drugs."

24

I WENT IN AND out of sleep that night, worried about Billy. Sure, he was a goofy and annoying kid, but I didn't want anything to happen to him. I also didn't know what to make of Howard, his life in prison, and what if any role this Blast shit had to do with anything. Then there were the karate guys, their drug dealing, and why a God-loving guy like Abadon would hang around with them. Maybe it was as simple as the fact that he trained with them; after all, I've boxed with some of society's real pariahs and enjoyed my time in the gym with them. People are rarely one thing and I do my best to see them that way. Don't forget, Hitler loved dogs.

Of course, I don't know if he put up with them barking at five a.m. like I did. Al rousted me out of my restless slumber with his attention to the door. I was hoping it was Billy, but this was a bit on the early side, even for him. Then Allah-King spun around and sat, relieved to know it was the karate kid he was familiar with. I opened the front door and there he was, at attention and looking kind of pale.

"Sir, my apologies for not making practice, sir. No excuses sir, and I will do one hundred pushups as a suitable discipline," Billy said.

I looked at him closer and what I thought was a pale pallor was really a mess of Clearasil on the whole left side of his face. I stepped off my stoop and walked toward him to get a closer inspection.

Billy dropped into his knuckle-pushup position and began to count out.

"One … two … three …"

"Kid," I tried to interrupt him at four but he kept on going. "Attention—on your feet!" I tried to give it as much authority as I could.

Billy stood in front of me, hyperventilating from the pushups. I wiped at the Clearasil with my thumb and as a big goop of it came off Billy winced. The whole side of his face was black and blue.

"Who did this to you?" I said, almost to myself.

"It was an accident."

"Who did this to you!" I returned to my karate command voice.

"Uh, sir …"

I could feel the vein in my neck twitch.

"Who?" I realized I was shouting.

"Jake, my mother's boyfriend." A silent tear ran down Billy's face.

"This isn't the first time, is it?"

Billy shook his head and more tears came down his face.

"To your mom too?"

Billy nodded and sniffled the accumulating tears back. His cheeks were streaked.

"What does Jake do for work?"

"He works out of town, construction. He's only around some weekends."

"Is he in Crawford this week?"

"No, he'll be back on Friday."

I took a second to think. Billy had stopped crying and was standing at attention.

"Meet me at the Y tonight at eight, you understand?"

"Sir, yes sir."

I bowed and dismissed him, and he did his usual run down 9R.

The vein in my neck wouldn't stop twitching. I wasn't exactly sure how I was going to do it, but I was going to make sure that Jake never harmed Billy again.

———————

I chose to look at my suspension as a semi-retirement. One of my heroes, the fictional Travis McGee from John D. MacDonald's pulp novels, used to say he was taking his retirement on the installment plan. He also lived on a 110-foot houseboat and had endless chicks and a best friend who was an economist. I lived in a 27-foot Airstream, got dumped regularly by women in therapy, and my best friend was a short-legged, long-eared slobber machine. Me and Travis had a lot in common.

I poured some coffee and flipped to MSNBC. They were doing their daily update on the "Crawford Slayer," which they did every day regardless of whether there was new information. The former FBI profiler was talking via satellite to the blonde, very attractive, but not very intelligent anchor.

"With the second and third victim's toxicology reports indicating drug use, is the evidence now pointing to cult involvement?" the blonde asked.

"We're talking about a repeat serial killer, and we often see feelings of grandeur and delusions of almost godlike qualities. I think it's a very real possibility that these killings, especially with their gruesome characteristics, and now drug use, could be pointing to cult involvement," the profiler said.

"Does the evidence point to Rheinhart as the cult leader, and what role do drugs play in a cult leadership?"

"Drugs become addicting or at least pleasurable, and cult leaders use them as a way to control followers. The ritualistic slayings further indicate that the murders mean something to the killer."

"How so?"

"The decapitation, the writing with blood, and the draining of blood demonstrate anger and a complete dehumanization of the victim. The fact that the high-school students met such a dramatic end may suggest that they were involved in the cult but lost the approval of the leader. That, or he no longer had any use for them."

The pretty head continued with more of the same nonsense banter that I just couldn't buy. First of all, I don't think I ever met anyone who was less of a leader than Howard. He was a painfully shy loner who freaked out for a few days thirty years ago—this Hannibal Lecter shit just seemed like bullshit to me. The fact that high-school kids had drugs in their system just didn't seem at all like news to me. I would've been shocked if a cross section of high-school kids didn't have drugs in their system.

The question I wanted answered was where was Howard and why was his blood spilled in the park. Who was he afraid of and why would they want to get him?

25

WITH A BIT OF forceful prying on Billy, I found out his mom's BF was Jake Sofco. And with Kelley's help, I found out he's a two-time felon with a history of assault, DWI, and drug dealing. With even more pressure on Billy, I learned that Jake hangs out at a roadhouse called the Insideout just past the Crawford county line. He'd get primed there and show up at Billy's mom's apartment and start terrorizing them.

Not having enough to do is probably dangerous for me. My mind isn't a place I should head into on my own, but that's exactly where I found myself, thinking all week that this man had to be stopped and I was the one to do it. Billy let me know that Jake drove a red Chevy pickup with rusted fenders and a gun rack, so I figured if I just hung out at the Insideout on a Friday afternoon, eventually Jake would show up.

On Friday afternoon, I got to the parking lot around four o'clock, brought a box of eight-tracks, a six-pack of Schlitz, and Rudy's cell phone. The Schlitz would make doing what I had to do easier, the eight-tracks would get me psyched, and the cell phone was just in case I needed to call Kelley.

Elvis was singing the "Where Could I Go But to the Lord/I'm Saved" medley, and I was looking down at my fourth empty when I saw the red truck pull in. Both sets of knuckles went white around the steering wheel and my neck began to spasm. Jake was a big boy with a mop of curly hair, a fat face, and a layer of hard fat that pushed out his flannel shirt just over his belt. He had the build of a pretty good Division III football guard, ten years out of the game. He could've been Michael Strahan and it wouldn't have mattered tonight.

I slammed the door to the Eldorado and headed toward the entrance. The gravel kicked up as I walked, and I became aware that both my hands were balled into fists. I thought of Billy, a goofy-ass kid without a dad, and what it would be like for him to watch his mom get slapped around. Sofco couldn't get beat up enough.

I got within ten feet of the door and I found myself stopped in my tracks. My neck was twitching all over the place, but there was an invisible force keeping me from moving forward. My rage was there but I couldn't move.

I went back to the Eldorado and opened another beer. I held the cold can to my forehead and wiped the tears off my face with the back of my hand. I was shaking.

I called Monique, who I knew would still be in the office late on a Friday afternoon. I gave her the background on Billy and Sofco.

"Let it go," she said.

"I can't let it happen again," I said.

"That's not for you to decide." Her voice remained in the same gentle but forceful tone. "This is a dynamic that will go on despite any beating you give this man, Duffy. There needs to be a change of permanence for Billy and his mom to make a difference," she said.

"I want so much to hurt this man."

"Is that about you or helping the Cramers?"

She was right. She always was.

I headed to the Hill to take care of some business that I would need to do to get this project done. There was a creep whose reputation I knew from the gym named "the Caretaker," who the street kids talked about. He was really kind of a street broker who dealt in situations more than product, but if you needed something he either had it or knew where to get it. The rumors were that he did enough dealing to make a living but that he was obsessively careful not to rise above law enforcement's radar screen.

I only saw him once but I remembered him. He was a black man but he had that weird condition that Michael Jackson claims to have where patches of his skin become almost bleached white. Three-quarters of his face were blotched white and his kinky hair, which he wore tight to his scalp, was reddish. Strangely enough, he dressed like a preppy even though he did all his dealing deep in the 'hood.

He had an office of sorts in the back room of a place that sold DJ tapes, and I knew enough about how it worked to know that I had to ask up front and give my name to get an audience with the Caretaker. I did just that with the black kid with the ridiculously baggy white jeans up front who did his best to look disinterested as he called on the phone. With a real economy of words and a head gesture he directed me to the back of the store to a curtain. I went back beyond the curtain to see the Caretaker.

He was wearing one of those pink golf shirts with the guy riding the horse on it and a pair of neatly pressed khakis. Loafers with no socks filled out the outfit that made as much sense on this individual as Nell Carter in a thong.

"How can I help you … Duffy … right? You're the fighter," he said.

"Yeah, that's me. I need a gun and some heroin," I said.

"Hmmm … The devil's right hand for the pug and some of the white vacation …"

"I have something difficult to do and I'm going to need some help."

"Yes, apparently you do. How big of an army would you like?" The Bond-villain-speak was getting on my nerves.

"Army?"

"Caliber?"

"Whatever, it doesn't matter. I hate guns."

He rummaged through his desk and handed me a handgun.

"Tres ocho por Señor. Now for the whiteness, I'm hoping you're not looking for volume. The Sky Pilot has not landed this week."

"Sky Pilot?"

"My … uh … distributor. He's somewhat not of this earth."

"Yeah, a couple of bags would be fine."

I gave the Caretaker what he asked for and didn't hang around for small talk. I had shit to do and frankly, the guy creeped me out with his looks, what he did, and his affected James Bond speak. I kept waiting for Dr. No and Pussy Galore to come around the corner and offer me a martini before they forced me into some sort of diabolical death machine. Still, you couldn't accuse the Caretaker of being your run-of-the-mill ordinary Crawford citizen.

I made a quick trip to AJ's to get help from the guys and as usual, if the favor involved free drinks, they were up for it. I led them all out to the Insideout and they knew their job and they knew it well. When it came to getting bombed, no one, and I mean no one, did a finer job than the brain trust.

I sat in the parking lot with another Schlitz and felt uneasy in the presence of the gun. Having a few bags of heroin on me didn't sit quite right either but I was definitely going to need it. Elvis was halfway through "How Great Thou Art" and I was finishing off the six-pack. I got out of the Eldorado and went over to the red pickup.

Sofco may have been a real asshole, but his timing was impeccable. He came out of the bar just as I was through and he passed me as I walked back to the Cadillac. He was staggering a bit—two hours with the Fearsome Foursome on a mission would do that to anyone. I started up the Eldorado after I made the call and let Sofco get a fifteen-minute start on me. Hopefully, that's all it would take.

I eased out of the parking lot and headed down Route 55, which headed toward Crawford and the side of town Billy lived on. The twitch in my neck let me know that Sofco wasn't going to make it there tonight.

I was only driving for about ten minutes when I saw the flashing lights and the Crawford police cruiser. The number on the back of the car, 9261TS, told me it was officer Mike Kelley. The handcuffed Sofco told me he blew the wrong numbers into the breathalyzer.

And the fact that officer Kelley was looking in the glove box told me that Billy and his mom would be safe tonight.

You see, two-time felons, guilty of DWI, with an illegal handgun and heroin in their possession don't make bail.

26

AL MUST'VE SENSED THE twitching in my neck and my elevated blood pressure because he went extra nuts when I came through the door. I got him his sustenance and cracked open another can of sustenance for myself.

My hands were shaking and I wasn't sure if it was my flirtation with the underworld, the illegal shit I did that could've caused me a world of trouble, or the fact that I just set up a man to go to prison for a long time. It might have been that stuff or it might have been the fact that I didn't get to beat the shit out of Sofco.

Or it might have had more to do with me being away from the gym. Since I took up karate at age eleven, I haven't gone two weeks without sparring or fighting someone. I've had a handful of street scraps, not very many, but I always had the outlet between the ropes. My self-imposed avoidance of the gym left me with a gap, and that gap was sending adrenaline, anger, or Schlitz-induced rage through my veins. Maybe it was all much simpler. Maybe I just wanted to beat the shit out of a bad guy.

Al calmed down and I went through the mail. Six credit card companies were offering me their business, there was the cable bill and a solicitation from the Polish American Club, and there was a letter from the office, which I opened. It read:

> This is to provide you with written notification from Jewish Unified Services that we intend to terminate your employment on September 2. You will have until that time to appeal this termination.

It was signed by the Michelin Woman, and it finally seemed like she had won. The hardest part for me to accept was the fact that I had made it easy for her. Sure, I could appeal, but that was a futile formality that would just serve to further embarrass and demean me, and that was a pleasure I didn't want to give Claudia.

It had been a hell of a month.

I hit the button on the machine to see who had called and I had three messages. The first was a recorded sales message about aluminum siding, which I found particularly absurd considering I lived in a steel tube. The next message was from Marcia.

"Hi Duff, I just wanted to let you know that I've met someone new and very special, and even though my therapist thinks it's too soon for me to get involved, I really feel something special for this man. I just knew you'd be happy for me. Take care."

That really was special.

The third call was from Dr. Pacquoa.

"Duffy, I called an old colleague about our days in the prison. The graduate student who disappeared shortly after the deaths was named Victor Gunner, and he was in the doctoral program at the University at Albany. No one knows what happened to him since. Don't know if this helps. Thank you."

Hmmm…that felt like something important, though I wasn't completely sure how or why. Suffice to say, between the evening's events and the Schlitz I wasn't firing on all cognitive cylinders at this point. Of course, it was nice to hear that Marcia had found somebody special. Geez.

I was drifting off on the couch when the phone rang. It was Kelley and it was now close to one in the morning.

"You up?" Kelley said.

"Uh-huh," I said.

"You're drunk, aren't you?"

"You say that like it's a bad thing."

"Hey, this DWI you tipped me off to. The Foursome tells me that you gave them cash and drove them out to the Insideout to drink with him."

"Yeah, so."

"So, bullshit. Those four leave AJ's every time there's an eclipse. What's up?"

"The guy's abusive to a goofy kid I'm teaching karate to."

Kelley paused. He didn't know anything about me and Billy.

"The kid you teach karate to…let's just leave that alone for a second. You knew this guy had a record of DWIs and drug possession."

"Yeah, you told me that, remember?"

"So you get him drunk on the outside of town and call me when he's on the road?"

"Yep."

"I probably don't want to know if his claim that the gun and the drugs weren't his is true, do I?"

"Uh, Kell, the guy was regularly beating the kid and his mom."

"You're fuckin' nuts, you know that, don't you?"

171

"Yeah—tell me something I don't know."

I hung up and the next morning I woke up on the couch with my head using Al as a pillow. I was hungover but otherwise I slept pretty well.

27

ACCORDING TO THE UNIVERSITY at Albany, Victor Gunner graduated and got his license to practice psychiatry in 1997. There was no mention of his abrupt departure from the prison internship, and after he got his MD he went to a medical center in Seattle in 1998, then to a prison in North Dakota in 2000, then to a hospital in Mississippi in 2002, and then finally to another hospital in Wisconsin. Then it appeared he left the country. They didn't have any further information than that on him.

When I Googled his name on Rudy's computer, nothing came up. I checked into some serial-killer websites and was disturbed at the shear number of them available. Some of them were straight reference sites but others were like fan clubs for the murderers. Slashanddie.com had a listing of unsolved creepy murders by state and I checked in to the places Gunner had been to. In 1998 there were three murders of teenagers in Seattle in which the victims were drained of blood. In Grand Forks, North Dakota, in 2002 there were four slayings that involved the disfiguring of the corpses and sexual mutilation of teenagers, two male and two female. In Natchez, Mississippi, they found a teenager's headless body drained of blood, and she had been sexually assaulted. There were four other teenagers murdered by puncture wounds who had lost significant amounts of blood.

A blood-drained, female, teenaged body was found in Oconomowoc, Wisconsin, in 2003, and another was found in Waco, Texas, in 2005. The website didn't speculate on whether any of these slayings were related. In fact, they listed blood drainings and decapitations as categories like they were hardware products or groceries. It's a strange world.

The one section that did catch my eye featured pages of pages of copycat murders. There were at least eleven separate slayings that mimicked Manson's work, complete with bloody messages written on walls, women with shaved heads, and weird devotion to the Beatles. Jeffrey Dahmer had some fans too, with eight different murders since his arrest in which the victim's body parts were left in acid to decompose. Even that age-old favorite Jack the Ripper had scores of fans doing whatever they could to be like Jack. All of a sudden I felt pretty comfortable with my idolization of Elvis Presley.

I called the three medical centers in an effort to find out about this Dr. Gunner and asked their human resource departments for information. I claimed to be from a local college where Dr. Gunner had applied to teach. I did my best to sound like a disinterested human resource worker going through a formality. In both cases they gave the standard information that he was employed on such and such dates and that he was eligible for rehire. They wouldn't give me anything else.

From there, I checked the New York State Department of Health registry and there was no record of a Dr. Victor Gunner at all. Ol' sawbones Gunner had either died or quit the doctoring business and disappeared. Somehow Gunner was able to vanish from the face of the earth.

———————

The stress of living and the stress of metabolizing Schlitz was getting to me. I needed to work out but I wasn't quite ready to box. I wasn't ready to see Smitty and the idea of preparing for a bout just kind of gave me a sick feeling in my gut. Still, it would be good to blow off some steam, so I decided to head to the Y to lift some weights. Weight training wasn't my favorite, but over the years I mixed it in, especially when I was training to fight a heavier boxer who I'd need to push off me. It wasn't the same release, but it was a place to channel some of my frustration.

Mostly, I didn't go into the Y weight room because the bodybuilders and the power lifters got on my nerves. Sure, they could push enormous amounts of weight, but they couldn't do anything useful with their bodies. They would do their bench presses and then they'd look in the mirror and scowl at the other people in the gym like they were tough. The thing was they weren't tough and they couldn't fight—they had huge muscles but those muscles were specifically trained to lift a bar, not throw a punch.

Every now and then one of these guys would drift into the boxing room and announce that he wanted to become a fighter. Then sooner or later he'd get in the ring and get his ass kicked by someone with a far less impressive body and you wouldn't ever see him again. I took special joy in smacking around a guy who could bench press a refrigerator.

I headed to the corner of the weight room by one of the alcoves and brought some thirty-five-pound dumbbells with me. When I lifted I went for high reps with relatively little weight. This way I built some muscle endurance, which would help my boxing, when and if I ever got back to it. On the opposite side of the gym were four huge guys taking turns working on the bench and they were making a lot of noise, grunting and growling.

It was kind of like a bad car wreck in that I didn't want to stare but I couldn't help it. Luckily, my trance was shaken when I heard a familiar voice.

"Yo Duff, salaam alaikum," Jamal said.

"Hey, J, what's up?"

"You know, trying not to get too fat in retirement," Jamal said. It was about the silliest thing he could say. Jamal had the body fat of an Olympic sprinter.

"Hey, shouldn't you be down with the bags?" he said.

"Taking a break."

"Sorry about that last one. It happens."

"Yeah. Hey, how's the high-school gig working out?" Jamal was currently a hall monitor and assistant football coach at McDonough.

"This weird shit with Rheinhart has made the adolescent years even more fucked up than usual."

"How so?"

"Well, you got your kids who are panicked—that you could count on. You got your macho types sayin' they're gonna find Howard and fuck him up. But the strangest shit is the Howard fan club."

"What the hell is that?"

"There's a group who dress all in black—what's the word they used for them crazy-ass Columbine motherfuckers? Disenfranchised? They got suspended for wearing pro-Howard T-shirts. This, while their classmates are getting murdered."

"Holy shit…"

"Yeah, holy shit is right."

"Are the cops looking at them?"

"I hope so." Our conversation was interrupted by the four bovine weightlifters. They were grunting and groaning so loud that you couldn't hear yourself think.

"Ah, the juiceheads are here," Jamal said.

"Juiceheads?"

"You know, on the shit. You don't get that big from taking vitamin E, you know." Jamal smiled. "Look at the jaw bone, the acne, and the foreheads bigger than a billboard. That ain't powdered protein doing that."

"Really? What the hell would these guys be doing that shit for—just to look good?"

"There you go, Duff. Ain't no more complicated than that."

"How hard is that shit to get?"

"You thinking it would help you in the ring?"

"Shit, no, I'm just curious."

"You don't have to go any farther than up those stairs to the karate room. The dragon brothers are taking care of everyone at the Y."

"No shit…" Now Al's parking lot behavior made sense.

"Oh yeah, no small market for it these days either," Jamal said.

Well, there was another reason to hate Mitchell and Harter.

After a less than satisfying workout with the weights, I headed to AJ's. Elvis made the ride easier with the 1960 post-army hit "Such a Night," a tune originally recorded by Clyde McPhatter and The Drifters. It was one of the best swing numbers ever recorded, and an Elvis song you seldom hear on the radio. Besides that, anytime I could work the name "Clyde McPhatter" into a conversation, I did.

I pulled into the parking space just in front of AJ's in the shadow of the cookie factory, which tonight was producing those sugar cookies with that little dollop of red goo in the middle. I could tell by the sickeningly sweet smell in the air. It made you feel like a molecule-sized being trapped in the middle of a sugar-cookie universe. Man, you start having thoughts like that and you know it's time for a Schlitz.

I was flipping my keys around my index finger when a shadowy figure came around the corner in a bike. I really do mean shadowy because whoever it was was all decked out in black. As a reflex I could feel my posture brace up a bit and with it came a slight tingling in my neck. When the figure spoke I relaxed.

"Sir, good evening, sir," Billy said.

"Kid, geez, you scared me. What's with the outfit?"

"It's my Evening Darkness Karateka Nu-Breath Ninja suit, sir. It helps me blend into the dark of night." Tonight's zit was where the cleft of Billy's chin would be if he had a cleft. Billy was cleftless so the whitehead didn't do anything to make him look like Kirk Douglas.

"It sure does, but be careful on your bike. You don't want traffic to see you blending in with the night."

"Yes, sir. One needs to be careful when stealth training, sir."

"What? ... Stealth—never mind."

"Sir, will we train soon, sir?"

"Sure, tomorrow night in the aerobics room, if you want."

"Sir, yes sir!" Billy said. Then he got off his bike to issue me a very official bow, but the bell-bottoms of the Stealth Bad-Breath suit caught on a handlebar and he took an ugly fall. He bounced right up and tried to hide the stinger in his hip.

"See you tomorrow, Bill," I said. The Schlitz was going to taste extra special tonight. The first few steps brought me from the sublime to the ridiculous. Actually, I've never understood what that meant, and it was probably more accurate that it brought me from the ridiculous to the really fuckin' ridiculous.

Rocco was down on all fours and Jerry Number One was on Rocco's back. TC was on all fours facing the opposite direction. Jerry Number Two was out in front examining the weird formation like Monet must've when he stepped back from his water lilies.

"Still doesn't seem right," Jerry Number Two said.

"I told you this wasn't it," Rocco said.

"This doesn't seem humiliating enough," TC said.

"That's 'cause you still have your clothes on," Jerry Number Two said.

I wasn't sure that I wasn't hallucinating.

"Fellas, you're scaring me a bit. Can you fill me in?" I said.

"We're trying to recreate that pose in *Newsweek* of the Iraqis in that Camp McCrabe," TC said with confidence.

"That's the Abe Miban prison, the Israelis built it," Rocco said.

"I don't think that's it," Jerry Number One said.

"Why were we doing this?" Jerry Number Two asked.

"I forget, but my knees are killing me. I need a B&B," TC said.

The human pyramid disassembled and I joined Kelley at the end of the bar. He was watching the Yanks and the Jays game.

"Didn't feel like getting in the scrum?" I said.

"Nope," Kelley said.

"What's new on the street?"

"If you're asking about Howard, not a thing, at least that I know." Kelley sipped a new Coors Light. "Some kid from McDonough was taken to the hospital after OD'ing, and they have us interviewing kids, teachers, and administrators at the school. It's a pain in the ass."

"What did the kid get high on?" I said.

"Something new, that's what has everyone extra worked up. They're afraid that, whatever it is, it's going to be the new crack."

"Is the kid going to make it?"

"No, Duff, he's already gone. Good kid too. Class president. What a waste," Kelley said.

"What about these kids who are worshiping Howard?"

"Yeah, that's some fucked-up shit."

"You think there's any chance they're doing these murders?"

"Duff—you watch too much Court TV."

"C'mon, Kell. There's all sorts of copycat murders related to serial killers."

"I'm sure it has dawned on the FBI. It's a little outside my jurisdiction."

I finished my beer and changed the subject. Thirty years ago one of Howard's victims was the class president, and now another class president was dead. That, and there were a gang of kids who thought Howard's killing spree was cooler than skateboarding. Too much had happened recently for me to figure out if all or any of that meant anything. It was easier just to go home.

28

ALL I WANTED TO do was avoid getting kicked in the nuts and go to bed. Before I hit the sack, I grabbed the mail, blocked Al's assault, and hit the button on my machine.

"Duff, it's me, Howard. I've been lying to you. I am the slayer and you need to stop looking into things or you may be next. It's imperative that you stay away."

So much for me getting some sleep.

That was all there was to his message and he hung up. I sat back on the couch and Al jumped up next to me. The silence we sat in made Al a bit uneasy and he started to hum. Howard's message sounded different than the previous ones, more controlled, more calculated. I didn't know what to make of the series of calls, but I also remembered my last encounter with Morris and the other cops and decided to call them.

The gang of them was there within fifteen minutes, and Al objected in what could probably be described as uncivil disobedience.

"AHOOOO…hmmmm…woof, woof…AHOOO…grrrr…," Al said. He was staring at my friend Larry Bird.

Morris directed the crime-scene guys to examine the machine and the phone. I wasn't sure what they were trying to accomplish, and I hoped they didn't believe that Howard lived inside my answering machine.

"AHOOOO…hmmmm…woof, woof…AHOOO…grrrr…," Al said.

Morris asked me about the time of the call, if he had called any other times, and if I had called him. I told him the truth, that is, that I hadn't. Bird was walking around the Blue, picking things up, looking at my mail, and generally being nosy. This didn't please Al.

"AHOOOO…hmmmm…woof…woof…AHOOO…grrrr…grrrrrr…grrrrrrrr," Al said. The extra "grrrrr's" concerned me.

Apparently, they concerned Larry Bird too, because he pulled a can of mace out of his suit jacket and aimed it at Al.

I broke away from my conversation with Morris.

"Whoa, what the fuck do you think you're doing?" I said, with my neck tendons dancing.

"Your dog needs to—"

He didn't get to finish. As Bird turned to yell at me, Al pounced and went after his shin like it was a TV remote. Larry yelped, Al increased the intensity of his bite, which made Bird sing in pain, and then everyone's favorite white hooper dropped the can of mace. Al scooped it up and ran into the bathroom.

While the all-time greatest shooting guard was jumping up and down on one foot, holding his bloody pant leg, I went to the head, grabbed the mace from Al, and closed him in.

"Now, what was it you were saying, detective Morris?" I said.

"You son-of—," Bird said.

"That'll be enough, Mullings. Go out to the car and put something on that," Morris said.

Larry gave me a menacing look behind his bright-red face and limped out of the Blue.

"We're going to have to take the tape out of your machine. I'm sure you understand," Morris said. He directed the crime scene guys to dust a few things and poke around here and they all left soon after that. Mullings never came back in. I let Al out of the bathroom and fixed him his dinner, treated with a few extra sardines.

I met Billy in the aerobics room, and I was glad to see he made it on time, or, more accurately, his customary thirty minutes early. Today he had a zit on one ear lobe, which in some ways made him look a little hip, like he got it pierced or something. Billy was warming up by practicing his flying kicks, and each and every time he landed on his back. I decided to just not mention anything about Sofco.

"Billy, what was up with the class president over at McDonough?" I asked.

"Sir, he was a jerk—I mean, I'm sorry he's dead, sort of, anyway, but he wasn't real nice," Billy said.

"How so?"

"He made fun of people a lot, sir."

"Did he make fun of you?"

"Yes, sir." Billy tried to put his energy into a technique, but I could see he was uncomfortable.

"What did he say?"

"Sir, he said it looked like my mom put out a fire on my face with my dad's golf shoe ... then, he once nominated me for some award just to tease me. He was a jerk, sir."

I guess the more things change the more things stay the same. Teenagers can be real a-holes. When I was Billy's age, my pizza face had gotten me into my share of fights, which at the time led me to my share of getting my ass kicked. In turn that got me into karate and then ultimately into boxing.

"Was he known to be into drugs?" I asked.

"I didn't hang with him but he was in the crowd that thinks they're cool, so I wouldn't be surprised."

"Are there a lot of drugs at McDonough?"

"Yes, sir. I know I hear about the dealer 'the Caretaker' and the guys they call 'the Caretaker's men.'"

"Have you ever seen this guy they call the Caretaker?"

"No, sir. I've just heard about him."

"What about this fan club for the serial killer?"

"They're really weird and, if you ask me, sir, very disturbed."

"How so?"

"There's rumors about them torturing stray animals and doing things to little kids."

"Damn, Billy, high school has gotten pretty weird, hasn't it?"

"Compared to what, sir?" I didn't have an answer for that, so I decided it was time for a workout.

I put Billy through his paces, trying my best to disguise fundamental boxing technique as karate. It wasn't easy; there isn't anything complex or fancy about throwing good punches. You could spend a lifetime learning the nuances of the most fundamental techniques; it was simple and complex at the same time.

I got to thinking of the Caretaker and his involvement at Mc-Donough. I didn't know a lot about him, but dealing at the high school didn't seem like it was his game. The risk was too high, the penalties too great for a guy known for being in total control to take. It's not that he necessarily had any honor, it was more like he just didn't want to go to prison.

I dropped Billy off and headed to the DJ store to get another audience with my new bleached-out friend. I wasn't even sure what I was looking for, but I wanted to see if I could get some answers. There was a different kid up front, and his boom box was blasting an angry rap song that referred to my sister and my mother and a series of unnatural acts that the singer desired to do to them. It took a while to get the kid's attention, but he made the call and motioned for me to go back.

Mr. Caretaker was wearing a blue blazer, lightweight cuffed gray pants, and a red-striped shirt. He had his reddish hair awkwardly parted and he had on horn-rimmed glasses.

"My pugilistic *ami. Bonjour*," he said when I came through the curtain.

"Hey, how you doing?" I said. With this cartoon character, having anything near a normal conversation seemed bizarre.

"What are you in search for?"

"Today, just some information."

He laughed, sat, and crossed his legs in that affected way that talk show guests do.

"I don't handle information," he said.

"Word is you're dealing at McDonough High. That kid who OD'ed was yours," I said.

"Mr. Duffy, do not be a provocateur. You do not know me well enough."

"Then I am right?"

"No."

"Who then?"

"Why the fuck should I tell you?" For an instant he lost the preppy, Zen, Bond-villain façade. This was all street.

"Kids are dying."

"Kids are always dying, my man." He sat back and went back into his character.

"If not you, why are you letting it be said that it is you?"

"Hmmm … first of all I'm not letting anything. The microwaves from that have yet to hit my radar. Second, I choose to keep my profile low."

He rubbed his chin and looked at the ceiling. I let the silence happen.

"Duffy, I am telling you the following not because you asked or because you intimidated me, but rather because it will serve my interests." He had his fingertips lightly touching in front of his face. "It is my feeling that it is the Sky Pilot's doing, and I am not at all pleased that he would bring my name into it."

"Who the hell is the Sky Pilot?" I said.

"I never deal in surnames. Do your homework." He stopped doing that thing with his fingertips and just stared at me. It wasn't exactly an intimidating stare, it was more a stare of absence. It was like the Caretaker was there but not really. At least, not for me.

I got out of the Caretaker's storefront and headed around the corner to see if I could find Carlisle and the boys. It had started to drizzle a bit and that meant the guys would be under the pavilion in the park next to the basketball court. It was just four blocks, and as I walked up the street I could see the guys there.

Carlisle was there with Chipper but his cousin wasn't with them today. I exchanged pleasantries and before long they asked me what I was looking for. Being accepted in the ghetto wasn't the same as being expected and we all knew I wasn't just walking through Jefferson Hill because I enjoyed the scenery.

"What you need, D?" Carlisle said. He didn't look good—his skin was ashing and he had dried saliva on the corners of his mouth. The salt in crack has brutal drying effects on the skin.

"You all right? You're into that shit, aren't you?" I said.

His eyes got shifty and he started to stutter. Chipper put his head down.

"No man, I—"

"Carlisle, I'm not here to bust you. You know I ain't about that, but that shit will kill you."

"I know, I know…" He got a sad look to his face. It happens when an addict knows he's been called and his defenses drop. It doesn't mean anything's going to change, but it's where anything starts.

"Come see me at the clinic, will ya?"

"Yeah Duff, I'll try." He looked sincere but the chances were slim he'd come by. It was time to change the subject for a couple of reasons.

"Hey, Carlisle. I was talking to the Caretaker and—"

"What you doing with the Caretaker?" He looked at me like I said I had just met with Jesus.

"Long story. He said something about a 'Sky Pilot.' What's he talking about?"

"Shit—that funky-ass motherfucker could be talking 'bout any shit."

"C'mon, what could it mean?"

"Yo, Duff, it ain't like all us brothers pass around a dictionary to keep up with each other's rap," Chipper said.

"No ideas?" I looked back and forth between the two of them.

"I don't know, it's pretty old-school shit, but the Caretaker is all up funky into that shit." Carlisle shook his head as he thought.

"A guy I knew inside used to talk that same rap … Sky Pilot? … Hmmm … I think that's what he used to call the chaplain. I guess a Sky Pilot is a preacher or some sort of man of God," Carlisle said. "That sound right?"

"Yeah, yeah it might," I said.

29

ELVIS ROCKED ME OVER to AJ's with Glen Campbell's "Gentle on My Mind." There was never any use in trying to convince anyone that Elvis could make a goofy Glen Campbell cool, so I didn't even bother. Besides, with the unfolding series of events running through my head, there wasn't really anything being gentle on my mind.

Thank God there was no bicycled ninja ready to confront me at AJ's front door, but that didn't mean I was going to be able to slip right into a bar stool next to Kelley to give him the lowdown. The brain trust was busy problem solving and I got sucked in.

"I'm telling you, you can get high on nutmeg," Jerry Number Two said.

"So how come we don't see guys in back alleys trying to smoke egg nog?" TC said.

"I hate egg nog. I puked on egg nog once," Jerry Number One said.

"Actually, if you're trying to get high on nutmeg, you're likely to get sick to your stomach first," Jerry Number Two said.

"Talk about your bad trips," Jerry Number One said.

"What about banana peels?" Rocco asked.

"What about them? Cartoon guys are always slipping on them, and in my whole life I've never come across a banana peel that made me trip," TC said.

"You weren't using them right," Jerry Number Two said.

"Huh?" TC said.

"If you didn't trip then you obviously weren't doing them right," Jerry Number Two said.

"What the hell are you talking about? Why would I want to trip on a banana peel?" TC said.

"To alter your consciousness," Jerry Number Two said.

"By banging my head? No thanks, I'll stick to the B&B," TC said.

"Ask Duff. He works with dope fiends," Rocco said.

"Duff, can you trip on a banana peel or nutmeg and do they make you puke?" TC said.

"In college I got drunk and tripped in a guy's puke. It was disgusting," Jerry Number Two said.

"I think you can on nutmeg but not on banana peels," I said.

"There," Rocco said.

"There what?" TC said.

Kelley was watching one of those strongman contests. Two guys were racing while carrying the engine block of a Ford van, and both of their huge heads looked like they were ready to explode.

"Talk about altering consciousness … ," I said, nodding at the strongmen.

"I'd have to smoke a lot of nutmeg before I tried something like that," Kelley said.

"Bananas. You eat the nutmeg, you smoke the bananas."

Kelley gave me a look and I decided that I didn't need to explain any further.

"Hey, you know what I heard?" I said.

"What?"

"That those karate guys down at the Y are dealing steroids."

"Wouldn't surprise me. That shit's all over."

"Do you guys ever go after steroid dealers?"

"It's a low priority. It doesn't have the same ramifications of, say, crack."

"I think the shrink from work is on it. He works out with those guys."

"Could be. You'd be surprised how many people are on the juice."

Kelley finished off his Coors and slid the empty in front of him. AJ had a new one in front of him without a word.

"I was talking to the Caretaker and—," I said before Kelley interrupted.

"You what? What are you doing with that scumbag?"

"He was telling me that the guy dealing drugs at McDonough is a preacher or a priest or something."

Kelley just shook his head and watched the TV. The strong guys were now trying to bend perfectly good iron bars.

"You have any idea who he's talking about?" I asked.

"You're the private eye. You figure it out," Kelley said without taking his eyes off the strongmen.

That was my cue to change the subject or, in Kelley's case, move on to no subject at all. We watched in silence as the strong guys put harnesses on and got prepared to try to move an eighteen-wheeler twenty feet before they herniated their nuts all over the pavement. I settled up with AJ before that happened and headed home.

———————

The next morning I took a ride over to the high school. I wasn't sure why I was going or what I was trying to accomplish, but I thought if I immersed myself in the school atmosphere I might get a better feel for what's going on. Call it wanting to feel the school spirit.

I parked the Eldorado and walked around the block to the front of the school. There were cops on every corner scanning the playground and keeping an eye on everyone coming and going. I noticed there were far fewer kids mulling around and everything was much quieter than I had been accustomed to. I didn't feel like being labeled a suspicious person of interest, so after a cop looked me up and down from a half block distance I decided not to try to talk to any kids or go in the school. Instead I just observed what was going on and tried to make sense of it.

I was thinking back to when I went to McDonough and how being a teenager really sucked. Oh, you'll hear people tell you it's the best time of your life, but I think that's a bunch of horseshit. I had a face like a pizza, I was terrified of girls, my armpits were soaked by nine fifteen every morning, and I went through the day with one boner after another. No wonder kids do drugs.

I was almost back to the car when I saw a familiar SUV pull into the faculty lot. It took me a few seconds to place, but then I realized it was Dr. Abadon. Since the steroid thing, I wasn't sure what to make of him. I mean, he was a clinical psychologist, an expert in human behavior, and a devout Christian, and he was into steroids—it didn't fit. The fact that he even associated with the karate guys didn't register with me either. There was no question that Mitchell and Harter were assholes, and for that matter not real bright, and I couldn't understand why they would become friends. It seemed to me that Abadon's education and religiosity should put him on a higher plane, but the more I thought about that the more I reasoned that there was no real reason that had to be true. Maybe it was something simpler—like he liked Mitchell and Harter's workout equipment.

Regardless, I had some work to do. The last time I saw the doctor I threw a cup of coffee at his head and that wasn't right. Sure, I didn't need to hear the shit about being knocked out, but my response was out of proportion.

"Doctor, hey wait up," I yelled. He froze for a second and then turned toward me. He looked braced for something.

"Look, Doc, I want to apologize for the other day. I was way out of line." I extended my hand.

He looked down at my hand and half smiled. Then, he paused for what seemed like a long time.

"The Lord tells us to forgive others as we will want to be forgiven," he said, and he finally shook my hand. He smiled with his mouth but not with his eyes.

"Yeah, well, like I said, I was out of line," I said.

"Yes." He continued to smile with his mouth while his eyes looked through me.

"What are you doing here, Doc?"

"I do a weekly consultation and supervision with the social work staff. As you might imagine, there's been more work to do lately."

"Yeah, I guess."

There was an awkward silence while neither of us said anything.

"How do you like working with teenagers?" I said for no other reason than to break the awkward silence.

"Teenagers are in the midst of God's development. It's imperative that they get set in the right direction," he said.

"Yeah, I guess. Look, Doc, I gotta run."

Abadon just nodded. As I walked away, I noticed that he had the cross pin on his tweed suit coat.

I'm not sure what I accomplished, but I know I didn't feel right in that way that is tough to identify. It feels a little dirty, a little guilty, and a lot confused. I decided to do my best not to think at all and threw in Elvis. I headed back past the high school and thought how wrong it is that the police would have to guard a school to this degree. I thought about the fear the kids and the parents must be living with, and I thought something had to be done.

Elvis was into the chorus of "One Night of Sin" when I made the left up Albany Street and headed toward 9R.

30

I CALLED RUDY AND had him meet me for lunch in the park. I sweetened the deal by promising him a Big Dom's Double Special sub, which delivered on its ad-copy promise to "Bust any belly!" We met at a bench by a fenced-in area designated for dogs. I figured Al could use some quality time with his peers.

Just outside the gate of the dog run there was a very well-put-together woman who looked to be in her late thirties. She wore a pink velour sweatsuit, the kind that isn't really designed for sweating, and her shiny shoulder-length black hair formed a nice contrast against the powder pink. She was on a mat in the grass doing some sort of yoga-Pilates-who-knows-what routine, and it didn't really matter because she was lying on her back scissoring her legs wide open before closing them. I did my best not to stare.

"Excuse me," I said in my softest nonthreatening-male voice. "Is it okay if my dog goes in with your dog?"

"Sure." She gave me a halfhearted smile and about a millisecond of eye contact.

Her dog was a Corgi, one of those low, cute, and sissified dogs that are favored by British royalty and about the same height as a basset. She had a pink collar, the same color as the scissor kicker's suit. I looked back over at her master who was now on all fours doing some sort of kickbacks, and I suddenly felt a little perverted at the imagery that popped onto my mental movie screen. The first reel was only slightly blurred by the glint bouncing off the ring on her finger that featured a stone bigger than any doorknob in the Moody Blue.

"What's your dog's name?" I asked.

"Matisse, after the artist," she said, this time with zero eye contact.

"I love Matisse," I said. This failed to get a response. I loved Matisse without knowing him, as I love all of mankind.

The dogs were done sniffing each other and Al had moved on in a different direction to do some olfactory forensic work on a pile of organic material left by a previous visitor. Thank God, that's when Rudy showed up.

"All right, kid, what is it this time? You sprang for a Double Special, you must want something," Rudy said while he manhandled the wrapping the sub came in with a force that might have gotten him charged with assault.

"What happens if a doctor is caught dealing drugs?" I said.

"He gets arrested and loses his license forever."

"Why would a doctor making a zillion dollars take that kind of risk?"

"Well, first of all, your premise is off. Doctors don't make that kind of money anymore."

"Yeah sure . . ."

Rudy's second bite got him into trouble. The oil dribbled on his chin and a spiral of an onion slapped up against it. It didn't seem to bother Rudy at all, and I could tell he really loved his meal—his face was starting to sweat.

"Look, kid, we have a gazillion dollars in student loans to pay, we have a gazillion in liability to pay, we have to pay dues in every organization we're in, and insurance companies do all they can to disallow payment. You add in an ex-wife, like in my case, and what you have to pay attorneys to defend you and your staff to support you and I'm not much better off than the guy who made this sub."

The oil actually dripped off his chin and onto his shirt. Rudy shifted the sub into one hand and used the other hand to run through his hair. He now had kind of a Big-Dom's-meets-Pat-Riley coif thing going on.

"So a doc might deal for the money?"

"Of course, but there's something else. A lot of guys get into doctoring because of messiah complexes. They feel they deserve tons of money, and when they don't get it, they get resentful and they start to take. With some it's insurance fraud, with others it's becoming an easy touch for prescription hounds."

"But why illegal drugs?"

"I don't know, they see how easy it is to become addicted and they see an easy market. They see how they can control people."

I sat and thought or at least tried to think. Rudy was chewing with his mouth open and it reminded of the second-grade trip I took to the Bronx Zoo. I remember we got to the pen with the wildebeests right at feeding time and watched and listened to them devour a bunch of cabbages and apples.

"I think the shrink at work, Abadon, is dealing to the kids he's counseling at McDonough. He hangs out with the steroid heads, and a dealer I was talking to said his supplier was a man of God or something."

"Kid, slow down." He wiped his face with the back of his hand and smeared oil over one cheek. "This is the guy you threw the cup of coffee at?"

"Yeah, he's a self-righteous, born-again type."

"Hey, I'm not crazy about the born-again crowd either, but—"

Rudy was interrupted by screaming from Scissor Legs.

"Get him off, get him off!" she screamed.

I jumped off the bench and saw Al furiously humping away at poor Matisse. He was lost in the moment and failed to respond to the shrieks from Lady Scissor Legs. She was traumatized, but I didn't pick up trauma from Matisse. Actually, Matisse looked like she was having an okay time.

I bounded over the fence and ran toward Al who, for the first time, actually gave me a menacing growl. I grabbed him by the waist and pulled him off, but as I did it, Al's head snapped around and nipped my little finger. I dropped him and he ran after Matisse, who by this time had been scooped up by her traumatized master.

"Matisse, Matisse!" was all that came out of her mouth. She was too traumatized to see Al running toward her.

Al muddied her pretty pink suit in an effort to get after his new true love, and as her master turned away to shield her, Al did the next best thing—he started to hump away at her leg. Hey, at least he had good taste.

I pulled Al off and apologized profusely. I got a teary "hrrmph" and the pair hurried away.

"Kid, you lead an interesting life," Rudy said.

I had Al back on a leash but he wasn't in a good mood. He sat and I had to pull him over to the bench.

"So how do I turn this doctor in?" I asked.

"Turn him in? It's like any other criminal activity. You can't just turn him in, the cops have to get proof. Usually, docs who get involved in this short of shit cover their tracks pretty well. They're smarter than the average street jerk."

"Ahh shit."

Rudy thanked me for the sub and patted Al on the head as he got up to leave.

"Al, sometimes it is better to have loved and lost than to have never loved at all," he said as he headed to his car, oblivious to the oil spots that made an asymmetrical polka-dot pattern on his shirt.

31

BEING A MODERN-DAY Robin Hood was complicated. I had set out to graciously defend my buddy, Hackin' Howard, from the injustice of being falsely accused only to be thanked by him confessing and threatening me. Now, I'd uncovered what I believe is a dirty shrink dealing drugs, maybe even to the kids under his care. So do I continue to search for Howard with the legions of law enforcement professionals doing the same thing, or do I try to expose the born-again criminal poisoning the kids? These are the tough decisions facing today's superheroes.

I cracked open a Schlitz and lay down on the couch, propped up enough to not dribble my beer. I flipped through *SportsCenter*, *Law & Order*, *Law & Order SVU*, and *Law & Order Criminal Intent*, past Lifetime, which was showing a movie about a guy who disguised himself to seduce his ex-wife and steal the kids, and to an infomercial about a product in which you could put your clothes in a plastic bag and suck all the air out to make it really flat. Then there was a show about really cool motor homes, a black comedienne's special, and a show about animal cops in Detroit. VH-1 was showing something about the best one hundred booty songs, and Bravo had that guy with the bad beard interviewing a skinny actor with greasy hair whose name I didn't know. Finally, I turned to the local cable news channel, my default channel to nap to.

Al had joined me, making a fort out of the crook in my knees and rolling up in a ball. The news was doing a traffic report, which I found absurd because Crawford was a medium-sized town without any real traffic problems, but the reporter did everything he could to emphasize that everything was moving along without any major slow-downs. The enthusiastic traffic guy was about to turn it over to the up-to-the-minute-Doppler weather guy when the anchor abruptly broke in.

I got that weird chilly feeling.

They split the screen with an on-scene reporter. She was in a field with an ambulance, several police cars and a lot of activity behind her. You could see guys with those windbreakers with the big "FBI" on the backs milling around her. She was a bit shaken, more so than a reporter should be.

"…One body recovered consisted only of a torso, and it was drained of blood through a series of punctures on the sides of the torso. It was the body of a teenage girl. The second body was decapitated and emasculated but the limbs were intact. In both cases, the missing body parts were not found by the bodies…," she said.

I sat up, which forced Al to do the same. I could feel the sweat on my palms and I had the instinct that I had to rush and do something, I just had no idea what. I grabbed my coat with the intention of heading to AJ's when the phone rang. The chilly feeling, which hadn't gone away, multiplied, and I had a weird premonition about who it was going to be.

"Duff? It's me. What I told you was the truth, and it is imperative that you mind your business," Howard said.

"How—" It was too late, he was gone.

———————

I flew the Eldorado to AJ's and didn't have a cogent thought the whole way. It was like my mind overheated and couldn't function properly. I was going to see Kelley; I didn't even care about drinking.

The Foursome were at it, having been watching the special reports all afternoon. Even their mood was somber, but it didn't make their conversation any less idiotic.

"I thought it was because Berkowitz's father was named Sam," Jerry Number One said.

"No, it was his neighbor's Rottweiler," Rocco said.

"Labrador," Jerry Number Two said.

"Rottweiler," Rocco said.

"His father was a dog?" TC said.

"Son of a bitch," Jerry Number One said.

"No, he was psychopharmic and believed the Labrador was talking to him," Jerry Number Two said.

"Rottweiler," Rocco said.

"What did the Rottweiler say to him?" TC asked.

"Labrador," Jerry Number Two said.

"He didn't say anything to him. Dogs can't talk, stupid," Rocco said.

"What about those dogs that sing the Christmas carol?" TC said.

"That was spliced," Rocco said.

"Most dogs are today. It helps with the overpopulation," Jerry Number One said.

———————

Kelley was there and he wasn't watching TV, he was just staring straight ahead drinking his Coors.

"He called me," I said.

"You need to call Morris right now, no bullshit," Kelley said.

"All he said was that he was telling the truth and that it was imperative that I stay away."

"You need to call Morris, now."

"Why would he call me moments after doing this?"

"Call Morris, now."

"Fine," I said.

———————

I went home and called Morris and he came over, this time by himself. He asked *what*, *where*, *when*, and *how* questions and left. Al remained calm and I guess Morris's fascination with me as a source of information had diminished. It was now heading toward eleven; I didn't feel like heading back to AJ's and there was no way I felt like sleeping. The Yankees were off and there was nothing on the tube and I didn't feel like drinking much, so I decided to take a ride.

Al came along and we headed out Route 11 West just to go someplace different. Elvis was doing his rocking gospel number "I've Got Confidence," from the early '70s, and he was doing an outstanding job. Forty-five minutes into the ride I decided to head over to where they discovered the bodies just to see. A half an hour later, I pulled up to a field lit by portable spotlights that, along with the misty late-summer rain, cast a surreal glow over the entire area. It looked like an alien landing spot or a spot being preserved for something supernatural. It just looked out of place.

I parked on the side of the road and walked with Al toward the yellow tape until a uniformed cop stopped me.

"Crime scene, sir. You'll have to move on," he said.

"Sure, I couldn't sleep and just wanted to see this," I said. The cop didn't say anything at all. Though there were a handful of police types around it didn't look like anyone was doing anything.

I moved along and started to head back to the Eldorado when I thought of something. I stopped and Al looked up at me.

What could I lose?

I looked back down at Al and our eyes met.

"Go find!" I yelled.

Al's nose went to the ground and he worked around a circle. This was weird because although I gave him the command, I had no scent source. Al could pick up the smell of a rabbit and I could wind up in the woods for the rest of my life. What the hell, I wasn't going to sleep and I didn't have to get up for work tomorrow.

Al circled, paused, looked up, put his nose back to the ground, and moved forward. Al had a scent and he was after it. He took me down to the road ahead of the Eldorado and stopped. He looked up, looked left and right, put his nose down, looked back up, and wrinkled his brow. Then, the nose went back down and he moved forward slowly and deliberately with his tail straight out, which I think meant he was on to something. He moved ahead steadily, if not quickly, but stayed in a straight line along the road.

A mile and half ahead there was a crossroads, and without hesitation Al made a left. He moved on, never lifting his nose from the ground, and he kept going. There was a light mist falling, and little by little I had gotten soaked all the way through my T-shirt and jeans. My watch told me it was a quarter to two in the morning and Al had been on this trail for two hours. I couldn't have stopped him at this point if I wanted.

Forty-five minutes later, Al stopped and took a crap. Then, he resumed for ten more feet, stopped, sniffed, looked up, looked down, looked left and right, and put his nose back down. There were tire tracks in the mud in the side of the road. In fact, there were what appeared to be two sets of circular tracks that headed back in the direction we came, like someone met at this spot and then turned around together. I was still looking at them when I felt Al tug me in the exact direction we came from. Retracing the same path, we were back on the scent.

At three fifteen, we were at the crossroads and Al got confused. He started to take the left, hesitated, and went in the direction we originally came from but started looking back and walking with his nose up. Before long his nose left the ground and it was clear he was off whatever he set out after. If there were two cars maybe one made the turn and one didn't, or maybe they got out on foot, or maybe there was a rabbit that ran around and doubled back. Shit, maybe a pizza-delivery guy spent the night looking for a house, turned around, and then got back on track by making a left at the crossroads.

It was after four when I got back to the Eldorado. Al was moving pretty slow and it had been a long night. The spotlights were still shining and I headed up the brushy knoll for another look at the scene. The cops weren't milling around, and I figured they had finally got permission to call it a night. That seemed weird to me, but I didn't get a chance to think it through because Al had given me a wicked tug. He pulled me hard for about twenty feet through the wet, high grass, sniffing like crazy.

Al stopped and I saw what was making him crazy.

The cop we were talking to earlier was lying in the grass with half of his face blown off.

32

A WHILE BACK I had seen some dead people. Kelley shot a guy in the back of the head as the scumbag was about to rape a little girl. The term "blown his head off" is so overused that it's meaningless until you're standing in front of someone when it happens. There was blood all over, and the image of what was a breathing human being now was right there for you to contemplate, shattered and oozing life. For whatever reason, I remember the smell.

There was a smell of gunfire and there was the almost metallic smell of blood, and there was something else—what I perceived was the smell of death.

I was going in and out of the present while I looked down at the dead cop and the video of the other death I saw played in my head. The corner of the top of his head and the eye on that side of his face was gone while the other eye remained closed. A wave of the smell reached me and I puked without having a chance to bend over.

The yakking brought me back into the present as only barfing can do, but I knew I was going to be battling nightmares and what

I called "daymares" all over again. I didn't feel real and I had no idea how much time had elapsed. Al was sitting at my feet, at attention, sensing something untoward and important was happening. His nostrils never stopped moving even while the rest of him remained still.

I started to breathe heavily and I could hear my heart beating when a voice shook me back to the moment.

"Help me … help …" The voice came from the field, and it was close.

Al ran twenty feet ahead and stopped, his tail straight out.

I followed and came across another uniformed cop bleeding hard from the chest. He was a light-skinned black guy with a weightlifter's build, and his uniform was soaked with blood. A deep scarlet hole to the left side of his chest seeped blood like a sump pump.

"Oh God … ," I heard myself say. I didn't have any idea what to do, so I ripped off my T-shirt and placed it over the wound. The cop sucked in a few painful breaths, but otherwise he was barely breathing.

"Call … call …" He pointed to his radio.

I pushed the yellow button on the side and said "hello" several times until some sort of dispatcher responded. I don't know what I said, but he said something about ambulances and not to go any place.

I kept my T-shirt in place and my head drifted away. I think I threw up a few more times and I know I was shivering, but everything that was happening was blurry. Then there was some activity and I remembered seeing Kelley's face and the look on it. Then a detached voice said, "They're all dead."

The next morning I came to in the spare bedroom in Rudy's house. Al was sleeping next to me and I awoke feeling half drunk. Rudy poked his head in the doorway; he was wearing a ratty robe that probably used to be white. He was sipping coffee.

"Valium, kid. Trust me, you needed it," he said.

I tried to talk and it didn't make much sense to me, but Rudy handed me a cup of coffee. Al sat up and just looked at me. He didn't fuss or bark, which was weird enough on its own.

"You remember much from last night?" Rudy asked.

"I remember dead cops ... one still alive, lots of blood. What the hell happened?" I said.

"They were ambushed. All four are dead. You blacked out and went into shock when the cop you were helping died."

"How'd I get here?"

"Kelley brought you around eight."

"What time is it now?"

"Four."

"Who did it?"

"They have no idea."

The coffee was helping and so was the conversation. I didn't feel like things were real.

"What's it mean to go into shock?" I asked.

"Your body shuts off when it's had too much either physical or psychological shit happen too fast. It can be dangerous but you're fine ... physically, anyway."

"What the hell does that mean?"

"Kid, take it easy for a while. Read some books, rent some Elvis movies, walk the dog ..."

"Uh-huh."

"Yeah, I know. Like there's a chance in hell of that happening," Rudy said.

––––––––––

By nine that night the Valium was out of my system, so I decided to add some Schlitz to it. I didn't feel like sitting around the Blue by myself getting weirder by the minute. I headed to AJ's, and Elvis and "One Broken Heart for Sale" on the way helped—Elvis always helped.

I was heading in the front door when I heard Billy's voice.

"Sir!" he said, wheeling his bike out from behind the side of the cookie factory. I could see the spokes of the bike but I couldn't see Billy.

"Billy?"

"Here, sir." He pulled his ninja mask down to show his face. I thought to myself that life couldn't get much weirder.

"What's going on?"

"Are you okay, sir?"

"Yeah, why?"

"I heard about your night, sir."

"How did you hear about my night?"

"I have a police scanner, sir."

"Yeah, well, I'm okay. Shouldn't you be home?"

"Sir, I wanted to check on you, sir."

"Billy, you don't need to check on me. Go on home."

"Sir, yes sir," Billy said and then peddled away.

––––––––––

Well, it was good to know I had a ninja guardian angel/stalker looking out for me.

The boys were in and at it. Tonight they were absorbed in the Kennedy assassination.

"The mafia was up there in the suppository," Rocco said.

"I think you mean 'depository.' The Texas School Book Depository," Jerry Number Two said.

"What the hell was that, anyway?" Jerry Number One asked.

"That's where they kept the books for kids in school," TC said.

"But it was November and the kids were in school. Why did Texas have so many extra books?" Rocco asked.

"I don't know, but that's where Lee Wilkes Booth shot him," TC said.

"You mean Lee Harvey," Jerry Number One said.

"Lee Harvey? That's the guy who does the radio news and says 'Lee Harvey ... Good day!'" Rocco said.

"That guy shot Kennedy? When did that come out?" TC asked.

Kelley was drinking and looking straight ahead, oblivious to everything else.

"Sorry, Kell." It was all I could think of.

"Jackson's wife is pregnant with their second. They have a three-year-old," he said.

"Do they have any idea who?"

"No, none. It's gotten very strange. They tried talking to you and you gave them what you knew in between passing out. You okay?"

"Yeah—it brought back some of the shit from last time."

"Don't mess with that shit, Duff."

"I know."

We sat in silence through two more beers each. Finally, Kelley broke it.

"I know this goes against everything I ever say to you, but if you come up with something, make sure you let me know," he said.

33

THE NEXT MORNING FOUND me far less than bright eyed and bushy tailed. I guess a Valium/Schlitz double-header will do that to you. Al joined me for coffee and he still continued to look me up and down like he didn't know what to make of me. There was no Walter Payton runs through the Blue, no barking like crazy, and no remote teething. He just kept an eye on me.

"I'm fine, now leave me alone," I heard myself say to the basset hound I shared my life with.

I sat at the kitchen table, drinking a pot of coffee and thinking about what I had learned in the last couple of weeks. I had set out to save Howard, who was letting me know he was being set up only to have him change up in a matter of days and not only confess but threaten me if I continued to try to help him. I found out about this drug, "Blast," that killed a bunch of inmates years ago when Howard was inside, and a suspicious graduate student that disappeared around that same time. That grad student later became a psychiatrist named Gunner who traveled around the country from job to job, and whatever city he appeared in there were unsolved murders. Then, as of a few years ago, Dr. Gunner fell off the radar screen completely.

So either Howard is the vicious murderer everyone tells me he is and I'm a big sap, or this Gunner guy had something to do with the Blast and the murders and is somehow in Crawford killing people because, well, that's what he does. The fact that some of the current victims had drugs in their systems may actually fit in with that. Of course, kids having drugs in their systems could mean what it does all over this country—that kids do a lot of drugs.

There was a third alternative. Maybe it wasn't Howard and it wasn't Gunner and it had nothing to do with drugs. Maybe it was a group of copycat murderers who had taken their fascination with killing to the next level.

I was doing my best to be as logical and as strategic as absolutely possible. The Schlitz and Valium notwithstanding, it felt good to organize it into arbitrary categories even if all it gave me was the perception of logic. The fact of the matter was that Howard was missing, and even though he periodically contacted me, he never spoke long enough for anyone to trace the call and his cryptic messages gave me no real information, especially lately. The last several messages repeated the same message and tried to warn me off.

That suggested to me that I should do as much research on Dr. Gunner as possible. I knew employment dates and I knew the unsolved murders during his tenure, but I knew little else. I wasn't clear exactly what I could find out that would be helpful, but it felt like the direction I should head toward. Rudy had tipped me off to a national registry for physicians and their license history, which I ran down in the hospital library. Gunner's license had no sanctions or censures, and he didn't have any lawsuits during his time as a doctor.

He kept up with his continuing education credits and there were positive citations or awards. He sounded like your run-of-the-mill psychiatrist. I decided to call his previous employers again just to see what kind of feel I could get for the guy. The place in Seattle refused to disclose any more information than they already had. The Mississippi hospital referred me to administration, and they said they'd have to get back to me. I began to realize that if I continued to go the quasi-legitimate route then I was likely to get no useful information.

I tried a different strategy when I called the place near Milwaukee. I described myself as an old med-school buddy who was getting a reunion trip together and said that I wanted to find my ol' buddy "Guns." The HR director thought about it a bit and transferred me to the hospital medical director, who only knew Gunner as an acquaintance but seemed to remember an OR nurse he was friendly with. She now worked in a clinic off-site from the hospital, and I waited while he found me her number.

Leslie Roy worked at a women's health center, and I called her right around lunchtime.

"Sure, Dr. Gunner and I were … uh … close for a while. I mean we dated and it didn't work out, but we remained friendly," she said when I reached her.

"Do you ever hear from him? We're trying to get the guys together for a cruise. You know, to remember the old days in med school," I said, trying my best to sound like a carefree, fun-loving doc.

"He left here to care for a friend who was dying. He was a very committed friend once you got to know him."

"Geez, what happened?"

"There was another doctor who worked here at the same time about the same age as Dr. Gunner. They became close friends when the doctor was diagnosed with an aggressive form of pancreatic cancer. Dr. Gunner left to take care of him."

"Wow, are they still in the area?"

"I don't believe so. I think he moved him to Arizona or New Mexico. The other doctor was estranged from his family, so Dr. Gunner was all he had."

"I don't know how to ask this but—" She interrupted before I could finish.

"I never did hear if the other doctor died, but it has been a few years now, so I don't see how he could've made it this long."

"What was the other doctor's name?"

"God, it's terrible, but I can't remember. He was some sort of specialist, so we didn't see him a lot. I can't remember."

"Well, Guns doesn't show up on any medical registries so it's really hard to find him. If you think of the other doc's name that might help a bit. Call me if you think of it, okay, hon?" I said.

She agreed to and I gave her good ol' Dr. Dombrowski's home phone number. I'm not sure what all of this told me except that Gunner disappeared and the funky murders where he lived stopped. That, or wherever he was in the interim had a series of unsolved gruesome slayings, but that was impossible to prove or disprove. The only thing that traced him back to this area was grad school, and he fled after suspicious circumstances. It didn't make sense that he would come back here.

Not that the lifestyles of serial killers ever made any sense.

I flipped on the TV just to try to let my mind think of something—anything—else for a while. The TV turned on to MSNBC, the channel that I was watching last, and they were in the midst of a "Crawford Slaying" report.

"Would you say this is the first break in the investigation?" The pretty brunette with the huge brown eyes was saying to a correspondent next to the Crawford courthouse.

"The police officer had, I believe, a T-shirt believed to be Howard Rheinhart's with Rheinhart's blood stained on it. It was in the back of the officer's personal vehicle with an assault-style knife that would be consistent with the weaponry used in some of the slayings, and at least one source is saying the police officer was at the scene of the latest killing before the 911 tapes show the murder was called in. The police officer's name is Brendan Mullings and he has been placed on administrative leave."

"Is there speculation that he is the slayer?" Brown Eyes asked.

"Not yet. It may be that he was just involved in unauthorized activities, but either way the Crawford PD just isn't saying."

While the two continued talking, the TV screen was filled with the official cop photo of Mullings.

It was the guy I had been calling Larry Bird.

34

CRAWFORD WAS A MESS. There were services for the policemen who were murdered, there were yellow ribbons all over town to signify city mourning for the teenagers who were slain, and there was the constant presence of the national news people. Howard Rheinhart's image was on wanted posters, and a fair number of them had been defaced with messages about how he should be tortured when he was caught. Now Mullings was getting his fair share of sound bites, and there was speculation that he was way too close to everything and his suspension was soon to turn into an arrest.

The *Union Star* front page was a tribute to the policemen, and they began a new section of the paper dedicated just to the slayer. There was a day-by-day section, complete with a timeline and full biographies of all the victims. The special section made the situation that much more bizarre, like it was a media opportunity. I wondered if advertising in the "Slayer" section came at higher prices.

In the regular local section there was a short piece on the back page about the McDonough kid who overdosed last week. The coroner was unable to identify the specific drugs that he used; he was only able to list the metabolites of whatever was in the kid's system. In other words, whatever he was taking was not related to any current drugs of abuse that came up on current drug screens. That, the article said, was quite unusual because although new designer drugs are always being tinkered with, they almost always are derivatives of some already-existing popular drug.

The metabolites, the stuff the body breaks the drugs down to in our metabolism, were new and different from anything anyone had ever seen. It appeared as though the kid had taken the drug for about two weeks before OD'ing, and they couldn't tell if he took too much of the substance on one occasion or if the buildup of the stuff in his system did him in. I had some questions for Rudy.

"Rudy," he said when he answered the phone.

"Geez, you're gruff," I said.

"Kid, I'm busier than a one-legged man in an ass-kicking contest."

"All right. Quick question. When someone OD's, is it more likely because they took too much at one time or that they've been taking too much over the course of a few days?"

"Uh. If I understand you right, it can go either way, but it's more common for addicts just to do too much. Drugs that build up over time usually don't make it to market, or for that matter even the black market. People tend to frown on drugs that will kill them if they take a dose for a few days."

"Do you know the coroner?"

"Stanley? Sure. He has a pig roast every summer."

I tried my best to not conjure up the image of Rudy at a coroner's pig roast for about fifteen different reasons.

"Call him and ask him about the toxicology reports of the slaying victims."

"Kid—"

"C'mon, Rudy, this is important."

"You should be resting or doing arts and crafts or something. I'm not kidding—you shouldn't fuck around with PTSD."

"Call me as soon as you know something," I said, and I hung up before I got the argument.

I got Al his breakfast and added sardines for being such a good boy. I was listening to the soothing sounds of him snarfing it all down when the phone rang.

"All the victims had some sort of unidentifiable designer drug in their system," Rudy said.

"I figured. One more question—was it the same designer drug in each kid?" I asked.

"No. It was slightly different in each case. How did you know that?"

"One more question."

"You just said that."

"Was it poisonous if it built up?"

"He didn't say. I'm not even sure he could tell something like that."

"Call him right back and ask him."

"Kid—"

"Rudy, call him."

I hung up and sat back on the couch. My neck vein was doing its thing and my knees were going up and down. I think I had figured something out but I needed it confirmed.

The phone rang.

"Yes, the shit in all of them was poisonous and very similar but not exactly like the shit that killed the McDonough kid. How'd you know all this?" Rudy said.

"Rudy, these murders aren't what they appear to be. They're about something else entirely."

"What?"

"You remember the guys who died while Howard was in Green Haven?"

"Yeah, they were taking that 'Blast' shit, right?"

"Yeah—how fast did they die?"

"I don't know, they all died within two weeks of taking it, I think."

"And then the grad student disappeared."

"So?"

"Suppose the grad student was trying to perfect a new get-high drug. He tests it on the inmates but finds out they die when they take it."

"Yeah..."

"Suppose that same guy is still trying to perfect the drug. So he test markets it on a bunch of high-school kids."

"Yeah, but those kids were murdered before they died from the drug."

"Exactly. Whoever the guy is, he's taking the kids out before they can OD and implicate him."

"But why all the weird shit? The blood drainings, the decapitating…"

"Two reasons. One, so he can frame Howard, who conveniently was discharged just in time. I'm betting the guy studied when Howard would be paroled and set this plan up for a perfect cover."

"Huh?"

"He picks Crawford because he knows Howard will be there. Decides to use McDonough kids as his human guinea pigs and knows if the drugs don't work, he can kill them and blame Howard. In the meantime, he kidnaps Howard so Howard can't defend himself."

"What's the other reason for the murders? You said there were two reasons," Rudy said.

"The sick bastard likes it," I said.

35

"You think Mullings did it?" I asked Kelley. We were promulgating a stereotype by meeting at the Dunkin' Donuts. I had a toasted coconut and a glazed and Kelley was just drinking coffee.

"Look, Mullings is an asshole, everyone knows that, but that hardly makes him a murderer," Kelley said.

"What about the kids at McDonough, the ones in the fan club?"

"They're keeping an eye on them. Two got picked up for smoking pot, and they had some strange kung-fu-type weapons on them."

"What are you guys making of that?"

"Creepy pothead kids with toys to make them feel tough."

"Did they do forensics on them?"

"Forensics? Duffy, go back to boxing, will ya?"

"Humor me for a second. What if we looked into this guy Gunner a little closer?"

"So, all we have to do is find a guy who left the area a decade ago and who there's presently no record of ... anywhere?" Kelley said.

"Aren't there records I can go through—death records, driver's license, shit like that?" I asked.

"Yeah, but unlike on TV, it isn't that easy. I can try, but I have to have a reason to start requesting that sort of thing."

"A reason? You're kidding, right?"

"Not really. There's two ways of doing this. I can present the whole bit to Morris, who can then take over. That's the legitimate way."

"What's wrong with that?"

"Maybe you've forgotten, but Howard has confessed. Why would anyone expect anything different? There's a confession, a history, and clearly a means, in that he's done this sort of thing before."

"What's the other way?"

"I sneak around and get the information."

"You up for it?"

"You're nuts, you know that?" Kelley said and then shook his head. He said he'd have whatever he could by the end of the day or sooner.

———————

Around three thirty Kelley called and let me know he came up with absolutely zero. He was able to do it quickly because nothing at all came up on Gunner. The best we can tell is that he ceased to exist, at least in this country, about five years ago. No medical license renewal, no driver's license, no credit card, and no mortgage. There was also no record of death.

As a last-ditch effort, I called my new friend back in Wisconsin. I think I had gone to that well enough, but I had nothing left to do. I remembered her extension and dialed her directly.

"Leslie, it's Dr. Dombrowski. How are you?" I used my best too-cool doctor voice. "Hey, hon, I'm still striking out on ol' Guns. You didn't think of anything else, didya?" I said.

"Hi Doctor. No, I really haven't," she said.

"How about the doctor who Guns left to take care of, the sick guy with no family?"

"Ah, it was a long time ago now. Hang on, some of the other nurses are here today. Let me see what they know."

She pulled away from the receiver but didn't cup her hand over it. I heard her yell to the others if they remembered Dr. Gunner and the other doctor. There was the usual banter.

"Oh, what's his name?" a nurse said.

"He was kind of cute," another said.

"You think? I didn't think so," the first nurse said.

"Wasn't it Dr. Richardson?" a different one said.

"No, Richardson's in California. He's a jerk," another said.

"Ask Julie, she remembers everything," the first one said.

Leslie returned to the phone.

"Hang on, Doctor, we're going to ask the unit secretary," she said. I heard her call to whoever was the unit secretary.

"Dottie, who was the doctor that had pancreatic cancer that was friends with that Dr. Gunner?" she said.

Dottie must've gotten up and joined the circle of nurses.

"Oh, yeah, what was it? It began with an A. Avalon, like Frankie Avalon," Dottie said.

"Abadon, not Avalon," one of the nurses said.

"Yes!" they all chimed in together.

Leslie got back on the line.

"Did you hear that, Doctor? It was 'Abadon.' We all remembered at once."

"A-B-A-D-O-N?" I said. I felt a chill.

"Yep," Leslie said. "But I don't know where he went."

"I think I do," I said to myself but out loud. "Thanks," I said, and I hung up.

That night at AJ's, I laid it all out for Kelley. Gunner is alive and well, living in Crawford after stealing the original Abadon's identity. Kelley wasn't as positive as I was.

"So how does he just take the guy's identity?" Kelley asked.

"He had the perfect cover. This guy was dying, so Gunner could quit his job on the grounds of being distraught and no one would suspect a thing. He takes him someplace, tells no one, kills him before he dies, and takes his identity. They're about the same age and he's privy to all of Abadon's personal information and he just takes his identity."

"Then why does he come to Crawford?"

"To have Howard as a patsy."

"I don't know, Duff." Kelley sipped his beer. "Why would he risk it?"

"One, because he's deranged, but there's probably a more logical reason. He knew Howard was due to be paroled, and he knew Howard could identify him from his time in Green Haven."

"Huh?"

"If Howard could finger Gunner as the graduate assistant with the fatal drug, then he could put him away. If Gunner wanted to pursue his drug experiments, he could choose the kids from this area as well as kids from any other area. Then, if the experiments didn't go right, he could kill them and make it look like Howard did it."

Kelley's eyebrows went up and down and he looked straight ahead. After a moment he turned back around.

"Duff, it's a little out there," he said.

"Tell me it doesn't make sense," I said.

"No one's going to buy this, you know. All you really have is a name and a missing guy," Kelley said.

"How many Abadons you know?"

Kelley just sat and looked straight ahead.

"I'll tell Morris and he'll laugh," Kelley said.

"I know," I said.

"That means you're not only in the private-eye business again, but you're also going after a serial killer."

"Yeah, I guess."

"You sure you want to do this?"

"Nobody else will," I said.

36

MY FIRST THOUGHT WAS to wait for Gunner to leave the clinic, whack him in the back of the head, take him to the police station, and tell my theory. On deeper reflection, I decided that would get me arrested and keep him out on the street. In order to really put Gunner away, I was going to have to have hard evidence on him. Howard had confessed and he was still the obvious suspect.

In the meantime, I had to keep an eye on Gunner so he wouldn't kill again. I took a ride to the clinic and spied the parking lot, but there was no sign of his SUV. Then, it was over to McDonough while I sat in the idling Eldorado, listening to Elvis do his *Aloha from Hawaii via Satellite*. Elvis always introduced the band about three-quarters of the way through the show, and it was right about that time that I got sick of waiting and headed back over to the clinic. The eight-track kicked around to the second track for the second time, and there was still no sign of him.

I drove until I found a pay phone, which took a while because since everyone has gotten wired or whatever the appropriate geek expression is, there's no need for public ones. The old-fashioned diner on Pearl Street, about two miles from the clinic, still had one and I went there to call Monique.

"Monique," she said when she answered.

"Be honest, the place isn't nearly the same, is it?" I said.

"All kidding aside, which is never the case with you, no it isn't. You add spirit to the place," she said.

"Yeah, yeah..."

"There you go again."

"Hey, is Abadon in?"

"No, as a matter of fact he had to leave town kind of abruptly. We're not sure when he'll be back."

"Shit..."

"Why would you care about him getting out of town? I thought you'd be happy."

"I'll tell you later. Thanks, 'Nique. Give the Michelin Woman a kiss for me."

"Duff, you know she's gunning for you. Said something about you not being able to save yourself this time."

"Yeah, she may be right too."

I signed off and tried not to think about getting fired. For one thing, I had enough on my mind at the moment and, for another thing, I was always just about to get fired. After a while you get used to it.

I took a ride to the Y and didn't see Gunner's car, so I headed out to their compound on Route 44. I kicked around the idea of why Abadon would need to abruptly take some time off. With the kind of jobs he had, clinic and high-school consultant, it would cause a lot of chaos for the staffs there to do without him on such short notice.

Something had to be up.

I left the Eldorado up the road and walked into the training camp. The sweet odor that I picked up the first time I came was more pronounced today and it wasn't pleasant. I moved carefully down the side of the long dirt driveway because my latest revelations about Gunner/Abadon suggested he wasn't a kind person. The fact that he constantly spewed a bunch of born-again crap just made it worse.

The pit bull was guarding the stone garden, pacing back and forth, his paws rustling the stones with each stride. Just to the left of the steel building there were three SUVs all exactly like Gunner's. There was no sign of Mitchell or Harter, and I had no idea how they figured into this. For that matter, I didn't really have any idea what "this" was.

I stayed about fifty feet away, fairly certain I was undetectable in the circle of brush I chose. For the longest time I just watched and waited. Then the doors opened.

Two Asian men wheeled hand trucks to the separate SUVs with Gunner, walking a few strides behind them. The Asian men were the same height and dressed almost identically, the one on the left wore pressed black slacks and a red silk T-shirt and the one on the right had the same getup except for a purple T-shirt. They both had on wraparound sunglasses with orange lenses. They shook hands with Gunner and headed out the driveway. I ducked down to ensure I was out of their view.

Ten minutes later, Gunner came back out of the building and this time he had a skinny redheaded man whose hands were hand cuffed behind his back with him. Gunner shoved him into the back seat without a word and started the vehicle.

The man was Howard.

Gunner was in a hurry, and he blew past me on his way out. There was no way I was going to be able to get back to my car and follow him, so I decided to take a look around the compound. The pit bull first snarled, then showed his teeth, and then barked. I looked it in the eye and he ran toward me and jumped, seeming not to care that there was a fence between the two of us. It was hard to believe this animal was of the same species as Al. He continued to snarl and bark, but I think because I showed no interest in entering his area he soon lost much of his aggression. He continued to pace and keep an eye on me, but he stopped hurling himself against the fence.

The area he was guarding was a strange sort of stone garden. The Buddha statue was more than life size and had to weigh a ton. The stone benches with their ornate legs were also substantial, and the various stone dragons and tigers and whatnot were all heavy pieces of stone. These guys went to a lot of trouble to create this and it didn't fit. I just couldn't picture a serial killer, drug pusher, and a pair of narcissistic karate wackos spending time in deep meditation.

The only doors into the steel building were through the fenced-in area and I didn't really want to get up close and personal with my four-legged friend, so I walked around the other side of the building. There was one window, but it had smoked glass and I couldn't see anything through it. I began to realize that my nostrils were picking up an irritation, and I imagined that whatever it was that they were concocting in this place wasn't good for you.

37

It was time to visit my new best friend, the Caretaker. It wasn't like I was warming up to the guy, but so far he had dealt directly with me and hadn't done anything underhanded. Clearly, he was motivated by self-interest and greed, but if we stripped away a lot of life's bullshit double talk we'd probably find that there were quite a few people who fit into that group.

I headed straight for the Hill and, now that I was a semi-regular, I got my audience with the man almost as a matter of routine. The young brother with the obnoxious baggies was in, and he barely looked up from his Martin Lawrence DVD when he gave me the nod to head toward the back.

"My pugilistic acquaintance, what can I provide you with today?" the Caretaker said. Today, his sartorial ensemble included gray flannels, a pinpoint button-down white shirt, and a rep tie in blue and white, which I believe are Yale colors, no less. His black loafers had the cutest little kilt on them.

"I took a trip and found your 'Sky Pilot,'" I said.

"Fellow of interest, no?"

"Yeah, especially now. Between me and you, he's got Howard Rheinhart with him and I think Abadon is the man doing all the killing."

"His evil spreading of malicious rumors is of more concern to me." The Caretaker's use of the passive tense made me crazy.

"I thought we could help each other out."

"Ha. I avoid reciprocal sharing. It tends to cloud the balance sheet."

"I'm looking to ruin Abadon and get him put away. I want the killing to stop and I want the innocent to be exonerated."

"Noble of you."

"Yeah, I'm swell. If I can get Abadon, you don't have to worry about the heat from the OD's that they're trying to pin on you."

He sat back and crossed his legs talk-show style, putting his fingertips together as he thought. I wondered if this asshole ever did anything that wasn't contrived.

"And you want exactly what from me?" he said.

"Right now, information."

"Listening..."

"Abadon was loading packages for two Asian guys today. Identical SUVs—"

"The Lees, Hun and Sun, they are brothers. They traffic in New York. 'Distribute' is probably a better term."

"New York guys coming up here? Isn't that backwards? Isn't all the drug business in the city?"

"The Sky Pilot does wondrous things. His concoctions will make crack look like potato chips."

"It's that big?"

"It will be. Word is that my man of God has worked the kinks out and his new product won't kill the user. New York is where things happen first. If he turns on the city that doesn't sleep, the word will be out and right now he is the only man that can cook this special Sunday dinner."

"How do you know the shit isn't fatal anymore?"

"The Sky Pilot is a man of science, my friend. You might say his clinical trials have been completed."

"Dead kids?"

The Caretaker half shrugged and half nodded.

"What are Mitchell and Harter in all of this?"

"Security; they are not players. The word is they enjoy the muscle formulas that the doctor fashions for them. They are quite protective of that."

"Is Abadon a threat to you?"

"Is Toyota a threat to GM? Better yet, if Toyota could put out a better product and then restrict the raw materials from GM, that would cause GM's stock to plummet, would it not?"

"Sure."

"I no longer put my faith in the Sky Pilot."

"In effect, then, if I can take him out, I would be doing you a favor."

"It would save me the trouble."

"Caretaker, this looks like the beginning of a beautiful friendship."

"I've always loved *Casablanca*," he said.

———————

We spent the next hour working out the details of what we were going to do. It was a mess, mostly illegal, and, if I screwed up, deadly. Kelley wouldn't be proud of me and what I was about to do, at least not until it was over. If everyone lived through it, he might shake his head, tell me I'm nuts, and then crack a smile.

Maybe.

38

THE CARETAKER PULLED OUT of his condo complex in London-ville, not far from TC's house, and headed out of town toward Gun-ner's karate compound. In his new Saab, the Caretaker didn't look like your average brother from the 'hood. I guess when you live in a condo in the city's richest suburb you're not really from the street at all.

I followed him on the twenty-minute drive out to 44 and pulled off to the side while he went down the compound's dirt drive. I angled on foot across the open fields leading to the compound with the goal of coming up on the back side of the steel building. I didn't count on the field being semi-marsh and that every stride would take me two inches into muck. It took me close to forty minutes to get into place, and I hoped the delay didn't screw up the plans.

I squatted in the mud and looked in between five-foot-high cat-tails with my binoculars to see what was happening. The caretaker's Saab was parked by the gate to the stone garden and the Lee broth-ers' SUVs were there, parked farther up the drive. While I waited,

Mitchell and Harter came down the drive to join the party, and when they got out they opened the back door and pulled out Howard. Perfect, everyone was in place.

Howard looked awful. His hair was long and a tangled mess and he hadn't shaved in a long time, which gave him one of those really fine kinky beards that redheads get. He had a blank look on his face, and through the binoculars I could see the deep circles under his eyes. Mitchell and Harter were talking to him and laughing, but Howard's face remained blank like he was incoherent. He began to walk with them to the weight-training area and he shuffled like he was sedated. When they got to the weight area Harter motioned for him to sit at a bench while they did their workout.

The door to the steel building opened and out came the Lee brothers, followed by the Caretaker and then Gunner, who was pushing a handcart. The Caretaker brought his thumb and forefinger to the bridge of his nose to wipe his eyes and I received the signal. I pulled out Jerry Number Two's video cam with the zoom and started filming. The Caretaker by now had started recording his conversation. The video camera worked remarkably well and I filmed as Gunner spoke to his audience, talking with his hands and smiling the whole time.

There was a pause in the conversation, and the Caretaker reached into his blazer pocket and pulled out the envelope. Gunner was smiling from ear to ear and the Lees turned and gave each other high-fives. It was Gunner's peak experience and his shining moment of success, and now he was getting the financial reward that came at the expense of who knows how many dead kids and inmates.

The Caretaker still had the envelope and now he was speaking, prolonging the transaction and probably setting up Gunner to say the exact right words. He was doing this with no risk to his own career, as I had promised him he would not appear in the video that I was going to send to the police and that his voice would be disguised. The Caretaker was smiling and holding the envelope for Gunner when the group of them was startled by an awful metallic clanging coming from the weight-training area.

I looked up and Howard was sprinting as fast as he could toward the woods. While Mitchell was bench pressing and Harter was spotting, Howard had hurled a ten-pound dumbbell that hit Mitchell right in the nuts, causing him to drop the three-hundred-some-pound bar and plates violently on his chest. It was perfectly timed because Harter was struggling in vain to pull up the weight to keep Mitchell from suffocating. The bar tipped to one side while the plates flew off and then, like a kid's teeter-totter, it slammed back in the other direction. There was screaming and clanging and the perfect distraction for Howard's getaway.

It also ruined my project.

Howard, the man who was the patsy for every crime Gunner committed and a witness to every dirty deed, headed for the thick woods. The meeting with the Caretaker was abruptly closed while everyone ran after Howard into the woods. Howard had a two-hundred-yard head start and a straight forty-foot run to the dense brush while the others had to get around the rock garden and over the training area. By the time they got past the weight area there was already no sign of Howard.

Meanwhile, the Caretaker was pulling out in his Saab, probably figuring that nothing good was going to happen if he were to hang around. Gunner had stopped running and he yelled at Mitchell and Harter to go after Howard. Mitchell, however, couldn't move yet and

Harter was trying to help him. Gunner clearly didn't want to leave the compound. The problem was, Howard grew up in these woods and it wasn't going to be any easy trick finding him.

Gunner stepped into the shed next to the weight-training area and came out with two handguns, which he gave to Mitchell and Harter. Mitchell was moving again, albeit slowly, and he and Harter headed to the woods. I was reasonably confident that Howard could avoid them for a while.

Although I had never spent any time in those woods I was even more confident that I would be able to find Howard easily. But I was going to have to head back to the Moody Blue. Howard probably could stay out of trouble for thirty or forty minutes.

Probably.

39

AL GREETED ME AT the door and I let him know that we were in a hurry. He had a way of sensing when something was important and he quickly settled down. His tail stood straight out on the way to the car, and he sat straight up with his brow furrowed over his brown eyes as he stared straight out the windshield.

I drove like a madman and I was back to the compound in just under thirty minutes. That meant Howard was out there for a total of just over fifty minutes. I hoped it was enough. I drove past the dirt driveway, pulled up just north of the compound, and entered the field just after the weight training area where Howard left the compound and entered the woods. All the cars were gone now and the place was deserted, but I didn't trust the feeling that I was alone.

I got Al to the center of the field and I identified one of Howard's tracks. I pointed to it and gave Al the command.

As soon as I said "Go find," Al was off sniffling and snuffing his way to the woods, knowing where he was going, even if I didn't. When we hit the real heavy brush, Al paused to sniff and to point his nose skyward. Then he brought it back down and was back working the trail. Before long we were in brush so dense I couldn't tell which direction we were headed. Al was on his trail but it was absolutely impossible to tell where we were going.

Al stopped and lifted his nose again. Then he stood still while his nostrils flared in and out. While we were standing still I heard a rustling from behind us and it dawned on me that I was in the woods with Al, unarmed, looking for Howard with at least two other armed men who weren't supportive of my cause. In my excitement, I had forgotten that detail.

Al's life was Howard's scent, and he showed no fear. He kept on zigzagging through the brush and sometimes through the mucky marsh. In the moments he stood still, I could hear the rustling behind me but now it was closer. Al went back to work and we headed forward, picking up the pace. The sun was setting and pretty soon we'd be doing this in the dark of night.

Al was on to something and we were now in a full run, heading toward a patch of trees. He stopped to shit, which was usually a sign that he was very close. While he curled his haunches, I could hear the rustling behind us—now it was clear enough to hear actual strides running through the brush. I turned and heard something but saw nothing.

Al finished up and moved toward the patch of trees, gaining acceleration. The sun had set and it was actually hard to control him as he darted in and out of the trees with his nose to the ground. Those short little legs may make some people laugh, but out here they were perfect equipment. He was now humming and snorting, heading to the trees, when there was a flash of light. Actually, it was two sets of lights coming from forty-five degree angles, and Al sprinted to the vortex of the lights.

"Hold it right there, Duffy."

It was Gunner and he was pointing a gun right at my head. The light was coming from Mitchell and Harter's SUVs. They both had guns drawn and pointed at me.

Howard was tied to a tree.

Gunner stuck his pistol into his belt and went to Harter's car. He rummaged for a second or two and then came out and walked over to me. Whatever he was holding shimmered in the cars' light. I couldn't make out what he was carrying until he got closer. In one hand was a knife with a blade that was easily over a foot long. The blade was serrated in a zigzag pattern on top. In his other hand was a thin, cylindrical, metal pole, almost like an arrow, though a little bit thicker with a very sharp point.

"I'm going to enjoy spilling your blood, Duffy," Gunner said with no expression. "Do you know how long it takes to bleed to death when your fingers get cut off one by one?"

"Harter, take the dog and let him play with the pit bull while you watch the product," Gunner said. "Mitchell, tie the loser up."

I watched Al get pulled into the SUV and I was powerless to do anything. Gunner was showing me the sharpened tip of his steel weapon.

"Oh, how I'm going to enjoy this," he said.

40

"Too bad you'll miss the show your dog puts on with Seagal," Mitchell said while he duct-taped me to the tree ten feet from Howard. Howard was gagged but I could see the terror in his eyes.

Gunner came right up to my face.

"I'm going to lop off your fingers, Duff, one by one. I've learned to do it carefully though, so that you'll not pass out. I don't want you to miss the experience. Bet you're wishing you didn't throw that cup of coffee at me now, huh?" He laughed and I could feel my stomach wanting to heave but I couldn't.

Gunner examined my taped-up hands, making sure his knife would be able to have access to my fingers. He congratulated Harter on a nice preparation. My mouth went dry and I could feel my body trembling all over.

"First though, Duff, I'm going to get things going by letting some blood out. This wonderful little device pierces neatly through flesh and lets the blood spill out like a faucet. Then, as I cut off a finger, you'll be springing leaks all over the place." Gunner's face lost expression and he handled the arrow, examining where he would insert it in my side.

"You're a scumbag, Gunner. Fuck you," I said and spit whatever saliva I could muster at him.

"You'll pay for that," he said, and he reached for the knife. He stuck the tip just under my chin, piercing a hole in my flesh. Being tied up kept me from flinching, which somehow made the pain more intense.

Gunner took a step back to size me up, looking at me like a specimen.

"Now, the fun begins," he said and then stepped forward.

I felt my stomach start to turn and my chest heave like I was going to pass out. Gunner was workmanlike as he looked closely at my sides. He lifted up my T-shirt and I felt his hands prod the sides of me. He stood back up and looked me in the eye.

"You're about to pay for your sins," he said.

There was a whistling sound of movement past my right ear and then a dull *thwack* sound.

Gunner's feet were together and he stood straight up inches from my face. He gasped and reached for his eye, which was gushing blood. He had something stuck deep into his eye socket, which was now covered in scarlet and torn flesh.

There came another whistling past my ear and another *thwack*. Gunner grabbed his throat, which had a shiny hunk of metal stuck right in its center. His face was a distorted mess with his left eye gone and in its place a shiny hunk of metal. Blood gushed from his eye socket, and in a silent scream he coughed more out of his mouth.

"WASABIIII!!!!!" echoed through the forest. "WASABIIII!!!!"

I felt something slash through the duct tape, freeing my hands, and there in front of me, barely visible in his Nu-Breath Karateka Deep of Night ninja suit was the best karate student a sensei ever had.

Gunner's face was streaked in his own blood and he fell face down. I could hear him choke on the combination of his own blood and the mud.

"WASABIIII!!!!!"

My head was spinning and I couldn't control my breathing, but I looked up in time to see Billy heading toward Mitchell, who was still holding the gun. While he was distracted by Gunner's demise, Billy jumped into a flying spinning axe kick, but he misjudged Mitchell's distance and fell on his back. Mitchell had raised his arm in defense, and though Billy's kick landed him on his ass, the bell-bottoms of his ninja suit had caught Mitchell's hand and he lost the gun.

Now, it was me and Mitchell, just as I had spent the last month hoping for.

"C'mon, motherfucker. You're about to take a beating from one of life's big losers," I said.

Mitchell circled me with his hands in a karate pose. I had my guard up in a boxing stance and ready.

Mitchell skipped in to throw a front kick to my groin. I pivoted left and took it on the muscle of my thigh like I did every day when Al lunged at my nuts. I used the pivot for leverage and drilled a left hand straight down the pipe onto Mitchell's nose. I heard the familiar crackle of cartilage and he instinctively reached up to hold it. As the blood poured out him, I drilled him with a body combination.

He came back with an elbow to my temple that wobbled me a bit, and he stepped in with a chop aimed at my neck. I recovered in time and stopped him with a jab to his broken nose that I could tell hurt him. I finished with a straight left that he was able to block, and he countered me with his own hook.

This time my recoil was perfectly in place and I blocked it with my left and immediately drilled him on the point of the jaw with that same left. His head snapped around and he was out before he hit the ground.

Smitty would've been proud.

41

I told Billy to cut Howard loose and to tape Mitchell up to the tree, then we all got in the SUV and headed across the brush. Howard looked like he was in shock and he didn't say a word while Billy was talking nonstop. I didn't hear any of it because all I could think about was that pit bull's jaws tearing poor Al to death.

Harter's cell phone was fastened to the dashboard and I used it to call AJ's. Kelley wasn't going to be happy, but this went way beyond pissing him off. The SUV banged and bumped across the muddy field and it didn't handle the terrain anything like it did on the TV commercials. It was a fifteen-minute ride and my heart was racing faster than the engine was.

I skidded the SUV to a stop in time to hear the fit of barking. I instructed Billy to drive toward town and look for the police. Harter had the lights on and the meditation garden was all lit up. From the distance, I could see that Al was running around and around with Seagal chasing him, growling and showing his teeth the whole way. I ran to the fence and took a running leap onto it and scaled it as fast as I could. I got toward the top and saw the layers upon layers of razor wire that would shred my hands and arms if I went through it.

I heard myself yell "Shit!" and Al stopped to look up at me while the pit charged him with its jaws wide open. At the last split second Al started to run again and for whatever reason, maybe his own sense of flight or fight, he started running all crazy zigzagging around the stone garden. The pit bull was athletic and mean but it didn't have Al's ability to change direction and Al had him baffled with his open-field maneuvers. Unfortunately, this just fueled the pit's anger.

I knew there was no way Al could keep this pace up for long and I struggled to the razor wire, slicing my index finger pretty good in the process. Al was barking and his ears were flapping as he barely evaded the pit's charges. I looked close at Al as the razors got caught in my jeans, and it dawned on me that Al didn't look scared and he didn't look angry. The crazy-ass hound looked like he was playing a game.

Al stopped suddenly and skidded on the stones with the pit bull dead straight ahead of him at a distance of less than ten feet. Al barked, almost baiting him, and waited for his charge. I screamed to Al to run and he waited to the last second, taking off with the pit literally right behind him. Al was heaving for air as he switched directions, and the pit bit the very end of his tail. He was closing ground on Al and snapping his jaws when Al ran around the Buddha.

It appeared Al was losing his breath and starting to slow down on his third trip around the Buddha. I pulled hard to free a leg and the razors cut through one leg of my jeans. It cut me but I had one leg free. My heart felt like it was in the back of my throat as Al started another trip around the Buddha at a much slower speed. He was tiring out.

The pit bull wasn't and he got past Al's tail and jumped toward Al's shoulders to bring him down. There was no way Al could survive a dogfight with this animal. The pit bull jumped to tackle Al and Al leaped too, but as he did, he took a mid-air, ninety-degree turn like he would in the Moody Blue. The pit bull tried to follow but as Al ducked his low-flying frame under one of the stone benches in front of the Buddha, the pit bull came in high.

The pit bull's head cracked just like my shin on a coffee table, except he was flying from a distance of ten feet and the bench was made of solid granite.

The pit bull's head split open and the dog collapsed a few feet from the bench that Al was now safely tucked under. I pulled my second leg through the razor and I was now cut all up and down my legs and over my hands, but I pulled myself through and fell the fifteen feet down to the stones, landing on my back. I got up and charged the door to the steel building to find Harter. The door flew open before I could get there, and there stood Harter in front of what looked like some very sophisticated lab equipment.

He was holding a gun and had it pointed at my head.

42

"I HAVE TO ADMIT, Duffy, you impress me," Harter said. "Of course, now I'm going to kill you."

"The thing I want to know is how much you knew about Gunner," I said.

"Gunner?"

"Abadon. He went by the name Gunner when he was doing this in other places. Did you know he was the slayer and didn't care, or was he able to keep that from you?"

"That's not for you to know, Duffy—man you're an inquisitive pain in the ass."

"As long as you got your steroids."

"Shut up—I'm tired of listening to you. Move!" With his gun, he motioned me inside the steel building and shut the door. I could hear Al barking from outside.

"Your dog doesn't ever fucking shut up, does he? After I take care of you, I'll quiet him down forever," he said.

"Al's got more balls than you'd ever dream of having—you fucking pussy," I said.

Al kept barking and barking and barking.

Behind Harter there were blinking lights, heaters, refrigerators, and all sorts of equipment. This wasn't your average bathtub crank lab. Gunner had thrown some cash into his operation.

Harter moved over to a beaker filled with a cloudy liquid.

"You know, Duff, this is hydriodic acid, and it burns skin all the way down to the bone." He paused to smile. "It will give your face a distinctive look in the casket."

He carefully placed the gun down on the counter and picked up some long rubber gloves. He picked up the beaker of acid and smiled again. Then, with the gun in the other hand, he walked toward me.

I scanned the room and saw the door that led to the meditation garden and the single smoked window on the other side of the building. To get to the window I'd have to somehow get past Harter, the gun, and the acid. To make it to the door I'd have to outrun a bullet.

Through it all, Al kept barking outside and it kept annoying Harter.

"I hate that fucking dog. I'm going to enjoy pouring acid on him," he said.

Then a loud bang rocked the other side of the building. Harter's head snapped around and he put down the beaker but held on to his gun. A few seconds passed and another bang came on the same side of the building ... then another.

"Don't move," Harter said, and he headed to the window.

Another metallic bang slammed the side of the building.

Harter raised his gun in his right hand as he waited by the window.

Another bang.

Harter's attention was on the banging, and it gave me a second to think. He cocked his right arm and readied it to fire. He unlocked the window just as another bang slammed the building.

Harter threw open the window with his gun drawn but was startled by another face staring straight at him from a six-inch distance. The startle was all the delay the man needed, and he raised the steel spear and jammed it with all of his force through Harter's throat. The gun discharged over Harter's head and the bullet smashed through a series of lab bottles.

The spear went through one side of Harter's throat and came out the other end. He spun around, his face a horrible mask of pain as blood curdled out of his mouth and throat. In the window was the redheaded face of Howard Rheinhart.

A smell rose in the room and I didn't want to hang around for the chemistry lesson. I opened the door and scooped up Al, who was still barking himself hoarse, stepped over Harter, and stuffed Al through the window on the other side. I climbed through the window to see Howard and Billy waiting for me. Billy had a pile of rocks in front of him.

"Let's go! It's going to blow!" I screamed and the four of us ran as hard and as fast as we could to the marsh. In less than thirty seconds we had made it a couple of hundred yards when the series of cascading explosions started. There were four or five little ones that ripped into a final big one, and the whole steel compound blew up in a fiery greenish-yellow ball.

The night lit up with a series of fireworks and the air was filled with a putrid stench.

"Fellas, this is going to be one of the biggest understatements you'll ever hear," I said. "Thanks."

I took turns hugging the two of them while Al howled in song.

Howard smiled for the first time ever in my presence.

"It's nice to know I still got it," he said.

The three of us laughed so hard it hurt.

43

IT WASN'T LONG AFTER the fireworks that the police came...and the FBI...and the U.S. Marshals. Then, within seconds, it was the news and the media with satellite trucks and reporters and camera people. There was crime-scene tape, there were detectives with notepads, there were crime-scene investigators—you name it. If they had a badge, a pen, or a camera, they were there. Thank God, Kelley pulled up in his cruiser.

They got Mitchell off the tree Billy taped him to and took him away in a paddy wagon, and they interviewed the three of us, first separately and then together. We talked to federal guys, state guys, and the local guys. Kelley stayed with us during each of the interviews and helped with the questions. For a short period of time, they had Howard in cuffs and were reading him his rights, but after a lot of explaining and, I mean a *lot* of explaining, they uncuffed him and told him to stay in town and check in with parole later that day.

The blown-apart laboratory, the weapons, the dead pit bull, Mitchell's arrest, and the chemical and blood tracings left in Abadon's vehicles stacked the evidence, and it was pretty clear we were the heroes not the villains. When there was a break in all the interviewing and interrogating, there was a moment when it was just Kelley and the three of us.

"Fellas, you mind if I have a word alone with Duff?" Kelley said.

We walked about fifteen feet away and out of earshot, at least temporarily, from everyone else.

"You're fuckin' nuts, you know that?" he said.

"Yeah," I said.

"This shit's going to hit you hard eventually, you know."

"Yeah, I realize that."

"You going to be all right?"

"Nothing that a Schlitz and the love of a fine basset hound won't cure."

Kelley just shook his head and walked back to his cruiser.

———————

Late that afternoon they let us go. I had told everything I knew and how if it wasn't for Billy Cramer and Howard Rheinhart, I'd be dead. Billy's mom came and got him at the police station. She was crying and all disheveled and sick with worry. She looked at me, taking me for the lunatic that I am, and went to hurry Billy away. I broke away from whatever cop was processing my paperwork at that moment and ran to catch up with them.

"Whoa, whoa … just a second, Mrs. Cramer," I said.

"Please, let us go home," she said.

"Just a second." I stopped and looked Billy right in the eye. "Kid, you saved my life," I extended my hand and he shook it. It wasn't enough though, and I pulled him to me and hugged him.

"It was a pleasure, sir," Billy said.

"Oh God, we have to go—," Billy's mom said, and she ran down the corridor with him.

That left me and Howard and Al, and we left together with Kelley as an escort. The reporters were waiting for us outside and they crowded us and shouted questions, but we forced past them and got in Kelley's cruiser and headed home. The three of us were in the back seat with Al sitting on my lap, and I believe the complete exhaustion hit us. We were silent for most of the ride to Howard's halfway house and Kelley pulled into his driveway. Howard had his hand on the door to get out, but he stopped and put his head down.

"Duff," he said. "Why?"

"Why what?" I said.

"Why did you come for me? Even after Abadon made me confess, you still kept after me. With my history, why would you do that?"

"I guess everyone deserves a second chance, Howard."

Howard nodded, though I'm not sure he believed me. He got out and headed toward his front door. Kelley threw it in reverse and started to back down the driveway when I asked him to stop. I lowered the window.

"Hey, Howard," I said, and he turned.

"You saved my life, you know," I said. "Thanks."

"You're welcome," he said and then headed inside.

Kelley dropped Al and me off, and I grabbed a beer and filled Al's dish. The beer went down easy, as did the next four or five and maybe more. I'm not sure because I went to sleep and slept hard for I don't know how long.

The deadness of the sleep was overtaken by a vivid image of a huge Abadon head with rivers of blood pouring out of every hole in his head and all over me. I awoke and I felt cold, and when my head cleared I noticed I was trembling all over. The last mess I stuck my head into gave me nightmares for a long time. *Here we go again*, I thought to myself.

The idea of sleep didn't much appeal to me, though it didn't seem to lose its appeal at all with Al. He was on his back with all four legs pointing straight up and his head cocked to one side, both ears acting as an eye mask. Pain in the ass that he was, I couldn't imagine a better friend.

I made coffee and flipped on the TV, but stayed far away from any channel that could have possibly reported any news. I didn't read the paper but I sat down to watch a Classic SportsCentury feature on Greg Louganis. I was exhausted and found myself unable to think of anything.

An hour or so later Al stirred, shook the drool out of his mouth and onto my bedspread, and joined me on the couch. We sat for a while but I was really struggling with just sitting, so I threw Al in the car and headed for the park. It made sense to give Al a chance to unwind and for both of us to head someplace outside of the walls of the Blue.

We took a leisurely stroll through the park, and I noticed that the cuts and scratches all over my body stung as my body moved. We came up on the dog park and I wanted to sit and stop the stinging.

The snooty brunette and her Corgi were there though at first I didn't see them because she was on her back on her yoga mat with headphones. The Corgi was sitting alone in the fenced-in dog run.

Al took notice and started to pull hard on the leash. I struggled to keep him under control because I didn't really want to take shit from the blue-blooded, uppity yogi. Al looked up at me and it dawned on me that with what I'd been through and what Al had been through, who was I to worry about a snooty chick, especially one with headphones on with her eyes closed.

I put my hand over my lips to shush Al and it worked. It never had before, but to Al the stakes were probably never like this before either. I lifted Al, which made my whole body feel like it was ripping and plopped him over the side of the fence. I avoided the gate because it was too close to my meditating friend to chance it.

Al wasted no time and headed right over to his own cute brunette. He sniffed for a while and in turn let himself be sniffed. Then, without even a Barry White soundtrack to set the mood, Al let loose with the Allah-King love-tron.

I'm not sure if you've ever seen a basset hound make love to a Corgi, but if you haven't, don't rush to. Al was using muscles I've never seen him use before, and I swear his brown eyes rolled back just before he closed them for his final drives. Apparently, Al had it going on because Ms. Corgi started to bark in what I could only imagine was some sort of canine bliss. Good for Ms. Corgi, not good for her yogasizing mother and unfortunate for me.

"Oh my God, Matisse!" she screamed. "What has he done to you?"

Al, meanwhile, kind of slumped down in the middle of the park and looked at me like he wanted a Kool Menthol. Matisse ran toward her traumatized mother with what I thought was an extra little spring in her short step.

"You pig, you, you, you...keep that thing away from my Matisse!" she continued to yell, her face flushed and her hair coming out of place. I wondered what happened to her meditative state.

"C'mere, Al," I said, and Al slowly rose and stretched and then waddled to the fence where I lifted him over and put him back on his leash. I swear he looked up and winked at me. I decided not to try to say anything.

We walked back to the Eldorado, and I noticed the sun was starting to set and thought that it might be a good time to head to AJ's. Who was I kidding? It was almost always a good time to go to AJ's.

I wasn't sure if the Foursome had gotten wind of the news. Coverage was all over the place, but you never could tell what was hitting the brain trust's radar. My questions were answered the second I walked through the door.

"There he is, our favorite Mick/Polack superhero!" Jerry Number One said before I got a foot in the joint. The four of them gave me a standing ovation.

"Don't forget his kemosabe, Al, the frog dog," Rocco said.

"Actually, that would be his Tonto," Jerry Number Two said.

"Tonto? I know Al's short, but I don't think he looks like one of those toy trucks," TC said.

"No, no, no. Tonto was Dorothy's little dog in *The Wizard of Oz*," Rocco said.

"He wasn't a basket hound," TC said.

"That's bastard hound. Remember, because of the drool? They swim underwater to find explosives," Jerry Number One said.

"No, they don't. They're French, not underwater swimmers," Jerry Number Two said.

"What do you got against the French and what makes you think the French can't swim?" TC asked.

"I got plenty against the French," Rocco said.

"Like what?" Jerry Number Two said.

"First of all, making their bastard hounds swim underwater," Rocco said.

"Tonto wasn't French, he was Indian," Jerry Number One said.

"That's what I've been trying to tell you," Rocco said.

I decided to break in.

"Thanks fellas. AJ, set everybody up with a Jameson and get a cheeseburger going for Al. It's good to be here—shit, it's good to be anywhere," I said.

Kelley had his Coors Light in front of him and he took a sip after we all threw back the Jameson.

"How you feeling?" Kelley asked.

"Like I'm on Mars," I said.

"Yeah, I think I know what you mean."

"What happened to Mullings—what was that shit all about?"

"Turns out he was just overanxious to get Howard and was trying to break the case on his own. He was hiding evidence and investigating on his own free time."

"Is he in big trouble?"

"Probably not a good career move—there will be hearings and whatnot." We both paused to sip beer.

"Hey, here's some news. Al got laid this afternoon."

"That makes one of us."

"Yeah, the guy interrupts me every time I get close and yet I turn him loose on some hot Corgi in the park."

"Uh, Duff? Hot Corgi? I'm starting to worry about you," Kelley said, shaking his head and taking a long chug of beer.

"Starting?" I said.

"Yeah, who am I kidding?"

"Hey Duff, what was the story on the karate kid?"

"He was the kid whose mother's boyfriend was smacking them around. He's a goofy kid who I think took on all the karate shit as a persona to make up for the lack of a dad and a real sense of who he is," I said.

Kelley shook his head.

"Now you're getting deep on me," he said.

"Maybe, but you know what I mean. He's sixteen and a goofy, pizza-faced kid who gets picked on all the time. So he goes into this kind of fantasyland of karate and works hard at it. In his own way, he's a courageous and tough son of a bitch," I said.

"I think I got you. The kid becomes a karate guy as a protection and to find some structure in his life. It's kind of good but kind of sad at the same time—why should a kid like that have to try so hard?" Kelley said.

"Hey, maybe there's a future in social work for you after all."

"Yeah, not in this lifetime. That kid saved your ass, though."

"No doubt. I wish I could pay him back." I sat and looked at my Schlitz, as the Yanks' game went on in the background. If it wasn't for Billy, I'd be dead. Without a doubt, the kid was a hero's hero and it was important that he feel that somehow.

Then it came to me.

"Kell, I need a favor," I said.

"What else is new?" he said.

"Go get Billy and bring him here in about an hour."

"What? Why?"

"Trust me on this, will you?"

"Geez, you're nuts," Kelley said and then finished his beer before getting up to go get Billy.

44

I CALLED DR. PACQUOA and told him what I was thinking. He said he would round up Javier Sanchez for help. Their participation was a must because with the way Billy perceived the world, appearance was going to be important. I filled Rocco in and he was psyched to be part of it—after all he did some hand-to-hand shit in Okinawa when he was in the service and he could bullshit with the rest of them. Most importantly, I went back to the Moody Blue because I had something to find.

The Moody Blue doesn't come complete with walk-in closets, so when you go to look in your storage, there's really only a couple of places that you have to look. In the living room that was built as an addition, there's a small closet and there's a few boxes where I kept various things in absolutely no order at all. Some things like my first set of gloves really meant something, but I also had an eighth-grade report card that I held on to for no other reason than the fact that I held on to it for years.

It took a while but I found what I was looking for. It was next to an empty Schlitz Tall Boy that I kept from the night in high school I went bush drinking with Delores Boyajin and, well, special things happened that night. I threw Al back in the car and raced back to AJ's.

Billy and Kelley weren't back but Dr. Pacquoa and Sanchez were already there and they were standing mesmerized by the Four-some, who were kicking around an idea about what cloning would do to the pet industry. I peeled Rocco away from a point he was making about Pablo's dog and how he died from eating that an-noying little bell that Pablo kept ringing in his ear. I briefed Rocco, Sanchez, and Pacquoa and asked AJ for the key to the basement, which he gave me after rolling his eyes about my plan.

AJ's cellar smelled like eighty-five years of spilt beer. There was a bare lightbulb hanging off a cord and I lined up a few cases of beer for the guys to sit on. I went over everyone's lines again and they all seemed to be onboard and actually kind of happy about the plan.

I had run through everything a second time and it wasn't a half a minute after I finished that I heard the basement door creak open. I nodded everyone into place as Billy came down the stairs with the same look on his face that he would've had if he had landed on Mars. Kelley walked behind him, rolling his eyes.

"Sir, wha—," Billy said, his eyes checking out his company.

"Silence!" I led Billy to a spot directly under the lightbulb. "Come to attention!" Billy snapped into a formal attention stance and he look terrified.

The four guys followed their cue and stood in formal karate attention.

Sanchez called out his lines. "Student! Attention! Bow!"

Billy did as he was told and the group, with their best hard-ass faces, returned his bow.

"Mr. Dombrowski." Sanchez nodded. That was my cue and I couldn't remember a more important speech.

"Mr. Cramer, as your instructor I have given you very little information about my karate heritage. I am from an eclectic training background, but more importantly from an organization that keeps itself out of the public eye. You are here today because of a special caucus I have called on your behalf," I said.

I wasn't sure if "caucus" was the right word, but it sounded cooler than "meeting."

"Caucus, sir?" Billy said.

"Silence!" Sanchez barked. He was so good it was scary.

I continued.

"The IBOSK, the International Brotherhood of Silent Karateka, is headed by Tenth-Degree Grand Master Javier Sanchez." I motioned toward Sanchez.

Billy's eyes were saucers and he swallowed hard.

"Its officers include Dr. Manny Pacquoa, fifth degree, Mr. Kelley, fourth degree, and Rocco Manuccucci, third degree."

Billy was trembling.

"Unlike other karate organizations, the IBOSK sees training as a component of life and life as a component of training. One cannot be separated from another, yet, real life is where a man's real dojo reigns," I said.

This shit was coming off better than I expected.

Dr. Pacquoa took over.

"Mr. Cramer, I was informed by Mr. Dombrowski about your actions in the last few days and your dedication to training. I brought this to Grand Master Sanchez's attention." Pacquoa was flawless.

"You would be an asset to our organization," Rocco said, employing his best badass face.

"Mr. Dombrowski." Sanchez nodded in my direction.

"Mr. Cramer, if you choose to be recognized by the IBOSK, you must keep your training secret. You must not appear as a karateka to the outside world, except in the way you carry yourself. In that way you must be a karateka at all times, understand?" I said.

"I think so, sir." Billy looked as confused as Mike Tyson at a spelling bee.

"In that case, by virtue of your intense commitment to training but to a greater degree because of your character, selflessness, and bravery to help your fellow man ..." I paused for dramatic effect while I fished it out of my pocket.

"The IBOSK confers upon you the rank of first-degree black belt," I said, and I held the black belt I had gotten as a teenager.

I didn't think it was possible for Billy's eyes to get wider but they did. He was visibly shaking and his eyes welled up. He wasn't the only one with overactive tear ducts at the moment.

I approached Billy and tied the belt around his waist while tears streaked both our cheeks.

"Mr. Cramer, sir. Welcome to the rank of black belt!" I said then I turned to the group and yelled the command "Attention! Bow!"

"WASABIIIII!!!!!" the group yelled out in unison as they bowed to the IBOSK's newest black belt.

Billy came to attention and bowed with as much pride as I'd ever seen on a human being's face.

And he deserved every bit of it.

45

Rocco convened the IBOSK to their first-floor clubhouse where the group threw down the ceremonial shot of Jameson's. Grandmaster Sanchez pulled rank and made Rocco buy him three more, which because of the IBOSK's protocol, he had to do.

I put my arm around Billy and welcomed him to the club. He couldn't stop thanking me.

"Sir, I don't know—" I didn't let him finish.

"It's not 'sir' anymore. We're the same rank," I said, smiling.

"Sir?"

"Ahhh." I waved my finger at him.

"Duff?"

"Yeah, that works," I said.

Then, I told him how his new rank meant no more Bad-Breath Karateka Ninja suits and how in the IBOSK we wore our rank on the inside and carried it in our hearts. He got it and didn't seem at all upset about his wardrobe. I figured getting Billy out of those goofy outfits would go a long way toward him not getting picked on. That, and what he now genuinely carried inside.

Billy's black-belt reception went on for another hour. When it was time for him to leave, he told me he wanted to walk home and make the day last. We shook hands and then I hugged him as hard as I ever hugged anyone.

Billy tucked his folded belt in his pocket and headed home. He already had a different walk. I thanked all the guys and bought a round for everyone.

"How come I'm only a second degree?" Rocco said. "I want a promotion."

"You not ready, yet," Sanchez said. He was a full head shorter than Rocco. "Buy your master another Jameson," Sanchez said.

"Duff, you're an interesting fellow," Dr. Pacquoa said.

"Doc, thanks for helping out. Sorry about the stereotyping," I said.

"Not at all. I happen to carry a rank in Kendo anyway."

"Really?"

"Yes, but I think I'd rather be in the IBOSK." He laughed. "Don't forget, if I can do you a favor sometime."

"You just did," I said.

"This was something else. If I can do something for *you*, I'd like to." I thought for a second and figured, what the hell…

"Actually, Dr. Pacquoa, there is something…"

———————

As it turned out, September 2, the day my work suspension ended, fell the next day. The good news was the suspension was over and the bad news was the Michelin Woman was going to fire me. She'd had a month to get the approvals and to get her angry little ducks in a row, and I just knew she was drooling with anticipatory delight at the prospect of looking me straight in the eyes and letting me know I was canned.

"Hey, Duff." Just my luck that Sam would be the first guy to greet me when I came through the clinic's door. "Did you hear about the Polack who confronted the ventriloquist about making Polack jokes?"

"Good morning, Sam. It's good to be back," I said.

"He goes up to the ventriloquist and says 'I'm sick of you making fun of my people and now I'm going to kick the shit out of you.' And you know what the ventriloquist says, Duff?"

"No, Sam."

"He says, 'Hey Buddy, relax. It's just an act.' And you know what the Polack says, Duff?"

"No, Sam."

"He says, 'I wasn't talking to you. I'm talking to that little asshole on your knee.'" Sam laughed extra hard all the way back to his cubicle.

I went to see Trina while at the same time trying to avoid Claudia, which wasn't easy to do because Trina's desk was just outside Claudia's office.

"Hey, Duff, welcome back." Trina's smile was precious.

"Hey, Trina, thanks. Hey, I'm waiting for a fax. Did anything—" Claudia interrupted before I could finish.

"Duffy, I didn't know you were in. The instructions in your letter were clear about you meeting with me before talking to anyone else in the clinic," she said.

"Uh, yeah. Sorry, Claudia. I—" She interrupted me again.

"Please go to your desk and get your keys."

"Uh, doesn't all the shit that happened count for anything?"

"Duffy, the events that occur outside of this office have nothing to do with your performance and your behavior in this office. Get your keys and meet me in my office immediately." She finished it off with a glare and a smile.

I headed off to my desk without looking at Trina whose head was down, looking at her blotter. She sniffled as I walked away.

I got my keys out of my desk and headed into Claudia's den of power. Losing the job was one thing, but losing to Claudia was another. I could find another job, but I couldn't take letting her win. I sat in her office and she had a series of forms and statements for me to sign acknowledging that I was given several warnings for "inappropriate behavior" and that I full well knew the consequences. There were forms about insurance cancellation and about taking clinic property when I was leaving. She also had a form about a private security guard to come in to escort me out.

I looked at all the forms in front of me and took my time reading them and asking stupid questions to slow things down. Claudia sat with her hands folded, glaring the whole time with her Starsky-do seeming to expand by the second. Twenty, thirty minutes went by, and I decided not to prolong the inevitable; I picked up the termination notice to sign off on it.

"You know something, Claudia? You may not believe this, but I care about the people who come here. I may not follow the rules, but I care about the people," I said.

"Rules are important, Duffy, and you don't follow them," she said.

"What's the use," I said, mostly under my breath, and I picked up the pen.

"Claudia, you have a fax," Trina said from the doorway.

"I'm busy, Trina," she said.

"I think this is important," Trina said, and she walked in and handed the fax to Claudia. She flashed me a wink as she headed back to her desk.

I put the pen down and studied Claudia's face.

"Oh, I don't believe this," she said, continuing to read. "Are you kidding me? I won't allow this! Oh, the nerve!" she said. She placed the paper down on her desk.

"You must think you're pretty cute," she said.

"Well, I've been told—"

"Shut up and get out of my office, now!" The Michelin Woman's face went bright red.

"Uh—" was all that came out of my mouth.

Claudia handed, actually threw, the fax at me and snorted out her nose.

It was on Dr. Manny Pacquoa's stationery. It read:

Please be advised that Duffy Dombrowski has been under my care for the last six weeks with the diagnosis of posttraumatic stress disorder. His condition is such that he requires full temporary disability. This diagnosis was rendered six weeks ago, and it has come to my attention that Mr. Dombrowski was still attending work during that period. Because of his disability any disciplinary action taken against him cannot be enforced. He must be given full pay, and it is my recommendation that his leave be extended four weeks for him to deal with the stress he has been under. Please be advised that this diagnosis is on file with the New York State Labor Department and has been approved.

Sincerely,
Manuel Pacquoa, MD

"I don't care what this says. I'm firing you," Claudia said.

"Now Claudia, you know you can't do that. Have some sympathy for us PTSD sufferers," I said.

"Just watch me."

"You know, Claudia, rules are important and you must follow them," I said, and I couldn't help but feel a smile spread over my face.

"Get out and go home, now!" she said. Her bright red face clashed with her purple polyester blouse.

"What about—?"

"I said go home!"

I walked past Trina, who smiled, winked, and started whistling "Hound Dog."

———————

I left but I didn't go home. Instead, I headed to the Y and I let Elvis bring me there with "Follow That Dream." I wrapped my hands, threw my gear bag over my shoulder, and headed down to the gym.

Smitty had a young middleweight in the ring and he was working the recoil drill. There was no one else in the gym. The bell sounded and Smitty directed the middleweight to the ropes for three rounds of work.

"Duff, in the ring," Smitty said. I climbed through the second and third rope.

"You ready to work today?" Smitty said.

"Yeah, I'm ready to work," I said.

Smitty took me through the same workout he'd been taking me through all my life. It felt automatic, like it should, and it felt good to sweat and get the heart rate up again. Ten rounds of drills later, Smitty called it a day and asked me if I'd be in tomorrow.

"Yeah," I said.

"I got a phone call last week about a show in Rochester. Guy's 10 and 14 and he's from Erie," Smitty said.

"I'm in," I said.

"Good," Smitty said. "I'll make the call."

I headed up the stairs to the showers and coming down the stairs at the same time was Billy Cramer. He had on gray sweats and a white T-shirt.

"Hey, Billy. What's up, man?" I said.

"Just heading to the boxing gym for a workout," he said.

"Not going to the karate room?"

"Inside, Duff. I'm keeping it inside."

It dawned on me that Billy's face had cleared up—not a single zit, anywhere.

"Have a good workout," I said.

"Thanks, Duff," Billy said, and he went in for his workout with Smitty.

46

AL WAS HAPPY TO see me back at the Blue and even happier to get his dinner. I cracked open a Schlitz and noticed I was down to my last one. That wasn't going to get it done and I felt like a night away from AJ's. I sat on the couch and flipped through the cable deciding how I was going to address the impending Schlitz drought. Al joined me and we sat there watching an A&E special on John Wayne Gacy.

I was about to flip the channel when I heard a knock on the door. I looked through the window and it was Trina. She had a gift-wrapped box with a shiny bow.

"Hey, what're you doing here?" I said, holding the door open for her.

"I've heard that PTSD people need lots of social interaction," she said.

"How beautiful was that? I thought the Michelin Woman was going to have a shit hemorrhage," I said.

Al jumped off the couch and up Trina's legs to say hello. I opened the package and it was a cold twelver of Schlitz.

"Ahh … and just my size," I said.

She smiled at me and tilted her head in that way that made her hair gently rest on one shoulder. She had on her faded Levis that were tight without being slutty and a white men's button-down shirt that she left untucked. Her high-heeled boots made her legs seem even longer.

"You cut it pretty close this time, Duff," she said, taking the beer I handed her.

"Too close," I said.

Our eyes met and I pulled her close to me. She was tall enough to kiss me without going on tiptoes, but she did have to stretch and I loved the way the small of her back felt in my hands. She closed her eyes and kissed me hard.

I let my hands go under her shirt and I held the small of her back. Her back and abdomen had that wonderful combination of being hard and soft at the same time. Trina ran her hands over my shoulders and across my back as we kissed.

Al slumped off the couch and mumbled something that sounded like a stifled bark. I knew that sound and its prelude to a long barking fit. Unfortunately. Trina knew that sound too. She pulled back from our kiss.

"Duff, I can't do this if Al's going to be part of it," she said.

Al was sitting, quite comfortably, his eyes going back and forth between me and Trina like he was watching tennis. Then he kind of snorted and got up and turned away from us on his way toward the stereo.

Trina and I watched as Al waddled over to the eight-track and sat in front of it. He paused and then nosed in the tape that was sticking out. The tape played "Rock-a-Hula Baby" and Al nosed the program button. It played "Ku-U-I-Po" and he nosed it again. He got the tape to the fourth track and the King kicked in with "Can't Help Falling in Love."

Al turned and looked at me and then Trina and then me again. He barked loudly once and headed off to the kitchen.

I swear to God I saw him wink.

Not long after that, Trina and I got lost in the uninterrupted bliss, first on and then off my sofa. My attention was going in and out but at one brief interlude it focused on the lyrics Elvis was crooning. It was the second verse of Al's favorite.

It had something to do with the sin but more with letting yourself go for love.

THE END

ACKNOWLEDGMENTS

Since *On the Ropes* came out, Duffy and Al have made all sorts of friends, and I want to tell you about a few.

First of all, there's Wildwood Programs, which provides comprehensive services for people of all ages with developmental disabilities, learning disabilities, and autism. At their gala last year, they auctioned off a chance to have a character named in this book and a woman named Elaine Woroby won. She requested that her husband, Mark, who is the executive director at the Wildwood Foundation, get killed. I work my day job at Wildwood, and I am happy to report that Mark and I remain on good terms. Read more about Wildwood at www.wildwood.edu.

There are also our friends at the Albany Leukemia and Lymphoma Society. My friend Mike Noonan is on the board there and he owns a tavern called the Orchard, which bears a striking resemblance to AJ's (though the conversations at the Orchard aren't quite as sophisticated as those at AJ's). Jimmy Carter (not the former president) won the auction at their gala and promptly requested that I rub out Danielle Thomson, his wife. Read about that organization at www.leukemia.org.

The Catie Hoch Foundation is an organization named for a precious little girl who was taken from us much too soon. Gina Peca, her mom, turned the tragedy into something wonderful and started a foundation to help kids going through cancer. Last year, John Snow won an auction and immediately wanted his wife,

Terri, executed. Check out this great organization at www.catie hochfoundation.org.

You might know Teddy Atlas, the ESPN boxing analyst and former trainer to a bunch of world champions. His foundation named for his dad, Dr. Theodore Atlas, does unbelievable things in and around Staten Island. Teddy was nice enough to blurb *On the Ropes*, and even though he sometimes criticizes my judging when he's calling a fight, you'll never hear me complain. I'm proud to have helped out his foundation in whatever small way through Duffy. Read about Teddy's great work at www.dratlasfoundation .com.

We can't forget Connie Carter, who won a chance to get killed at Murder and Mayhem in Muskego, the world's absolute best library event run by Penny Halle with help from Ruth and Jon Jordan. All of these folks are about the best friends a mystery writer can have. Visit the library online at www.ci.muskego.wi.us/library/.

There's also the New England Basset Hound Rescue, which hosted my very first book signing. This organization rescues and helps out basset hounds just like Al who have been abandoned, abused, and neglected. Last summer I was proud to be among hundreds of Al's best friends and to give them the proceeds from the book sales. If you'd like a dog every bit as precious as Al, find a basset rescue group and give a hound a home. Aroooo!

Pick out your new best friend at www.newenglandbassethound rescue.org.